William Henry Giles Kingston

James Braithwaite

The Supercargo - The Story of his Adventures Ashore and Afloat

William Henry Giles Kingston

James Braithwaite
The Supercargo - The Story of his Adventures Ashore and Afloat

ISBN/EAN: 9783337060275

Printed in Europe, USA, Canada, Australia, Japan

Cover: Foto ©Raphael Reischuk / pixelio.de

More available books at **www.hansebooks.com**

JAMES BRAITHWAITE

THE SUPERCARGO.

The Story of His Adventures Ashore and Afloat.

BY

W. H. G. KINGSTON,

AUTHOR OF

"PETER TRAWL"; OR, THE ADVENTURES OF A WHALER,"
"HENDRICKS THE HUNTER," 'JOVINIAN,' ETC.

WITH EIGHT FULL-PAGE ILLUSTRATIONS.

New York:

A. C. ARMSTRONG & SON,

714 BROADWAY.

—

1884.

INTRODUCTION.

THE readers of this book may like to know something about the author, whose name is so well known as the writer of many stories for boys.

WILLIAM HENRY GILES KINGSTON was the eldest son of the late L. H. Kingston, Esq., and grandson of the Hon. Mr. Justice Rooke (Sir Giles Rooke). He was born in Harley Street, London, on February 24th, 1814. The family resided many years in Oporto, where his father was then in business as a merchant,

and he had many voyages in boyhood between his
home in Portugal and school in England. His education was carefully attended to, both at school and
with private tutors. What he was taught from books
was amply supplemented by what he learned in conversation and travel.

From his earliest boyhood young Kingston evinced
a strong liking for the sea. In consequence of family
connections, and his father's occupation, he had much
opportunity of being in the society of seafaring men,
and their tales of peril and adventure fostered his own
inclination for the life of a sailor. At one time he was
nearly joining the navy, but circumstances required
him to remain in his father's business house at Oporto
till he was beyond the age for entering the King's
service. He never, however, lost his first taste, and
he had opportunity for several voyages. To the end
of his days he cherished an ardent affection for seamen, and took deep interest in everything that tended
to their welfare. He was proud, also, of the history of
the British navy, as he has shown in many of his
spirit-stirring sea-stories. When the *Boy's Own
Paper* was started, in 1879, he led off with a
characteristic story of the navy in the time of the
great wars of the reign of George III., under the title
of " From Powder Monkey to Admiral."

Mr. Kingston's preference for literary over business
life early asserted itself. He published various books

of history and travel, but he soon found that his special calling was to write sea-stories for the young. His first boys' book was "Peter the Whaler," which was followed in rapid succession by a whole series of tales of travel and adventure by land and sea. The sea-stories were the most popular, many of which appeared first in magazines, to be afterwards reprinted as separate volumes. One of the best of these stories is now presented to the reader.

The sub-title requires a word of explanation. The name of supercargo has now almost disappeared from the nautical vocabulary. Changes in commerce and in navigation have made obsolete many persons, as well as things, once familiar. In the old days of mercantile venture and trade, ships sailed with great variety of cargo, to be disposed of in various ports, either by arrangement of the owners or at the discretion of the captain. There was an officer specially charged with the management and the sale of the goods shipped by the merchants, and he was called the Supercargo. It was a responsible and difficult post to fill, and gave scope for much knowledge and tact, as well as requiring good character, from the valuable goods entrusted to his charge. There was a partial revival of the name and the duty during the American civil war. The blockade-runners had sometimes a very miscellaneous cargo to dispose of, requiring the tact and knowledge of a special Supercargo. In ordinary times the more mechanical part of this duty is performed by a ship's clerk. An experienced and clever Supercargo in old times was not only a shrewd merchant and man of business, but he was sure to have seen many aspects of life in different parts of the globe. It was therefore a happy thought in Mr. Kingston to make a Supercargo the narrator of a voyage, and this at a time when the perils of war were added to the ordinary risks and adventures of the sea. The illustrations accompanying the story are, with permission, taken from the pages of the _Leisure Hour_ and the _Boy's Own Paper._

Having referred to the early life of Mr. Kingston, it may be well to speak also of his closing years. Till the last he retained his love of the sea, and his love of boys. He wrote recently, in addition to a book on the "Life and Voyages of Captain Cook," and a "Yacht Voyage round England," a capital story reprinted from the _Boy's Own Paper_, entitled, " Peter Trawl; or, The Adventures of a Whaler;" and at the time of his being seized with the fatal illness which removed him on the 5th of August, 1880, he was engaged in preparing a story of Arctic adventure. Only three days before his death he wrote a touching letter, which was sent by him for publication to the _Boy's Own Paper._ Although many have seen it there, this striking and affectionate farewell letter cannot be too widely known, and we have pleasure in quoting it :—

"STORMONT LODGE, WILLESDEN,

Aug. 2nd, 1880.

" MY DEAR BOYS,--I have been engaged, as you know, for a very large portion of my life in writing books for you. This occupation has been a source of the greatest pleasure and satisfaction to me, and, I am willing to believe, to you also.

" Our connection with each other in this world must, however, shortly cease.

" I have for some time been suffering from serious illness, and have been informed by the highest medical authorities that my days are numbered.

" Of the truth of this I am convinced by the rapid progress the disease is making. It is my desire, therefore, to wish you all a sincere and hearty farewell !

" I want you to know that I am leaving this life in unspeakable happiness, because I rest my soul on my Saviour, trusting only and entirely to the merits of the great Atonement, by which my sins have been put away for ever.

" Dear Boys, I ask you to give your hearts to Christ, and earnestly pray that all of you may meet me in Heaven."

CONTENTS.

CHAPTER I.

" WHAT'S the name of the craft you want to get aboard, sir ? " asked old Bob, the one-legged boatman, whose wherry I had hired to carry me out to Spithead.

" The *Barbara*," I answered, trying to look more at my ease than I felt; for the old fellow, besides having but one leg, had a black patch over the place where his right eye should have been, while his left arm was partially crippled; and his crew consisted of a mite of a boy whose activity and intelligence could scarcely make up for his want of size and strength. The ebb tide, too, was making strong out of Portsmouth Harbour, and a fresh breeze was blowing in, creating a tumbling, bubbling sea at the mouth ; and vessels and boats of all sizes and rigs were dashing here and there, madly and without purpose it seemed to me, but at all events very likely to run down the low narrow craft in which I had ventured to embark. Now and then a man-of-war's boat, with half-a-dozen reckless midshipmen in her, who looked as if they would not have the slightest scruple in sailing over us, would pass within a few inches of the wherry ; now a ship's

1

launch with a party of marines, pulling with uncertain strokes like a huge maimed centipede, would come right across our course and receive old Bob's no very complimentary remarks; next a boatful of men-of-war's men, liberty men returning from leave. There was no use saying anything to them, for there wasn't one, old Bob informed me, but what was " three sheets in the wind," or " half seas over,"—in other words, very drunk; still, they managed to find their way and not to upset themselves, in a manner which surprised me. Scarcely were we clear of them when several lumbering dockyard lighters would come dashing by, going out with stores or powder to the fleet at Spithead.

Those were indeed busy times. Numerous ships of war were fitting out alongside the quays, their huge yards being swayed up, and guns and stores hoisted on board, gruff shouts, and cries, and whistles, and other strange sounds proceeding from them as we passed near. Others lay in the middle of the harbour ready for sea, but waiting for their crews to be collected by the press-gangs on shore, and to be made up with captured smugglers, liberated gaol-birds, and broken-down persons from every grade of society. Altogether, what with transports, merchantmen, lighters, and other craft, it was no easy matter to beat out without getting athwart hawse of those at anchor, or being run down by the still greater number of small craft under way. Still it was an animated and exciting scene, and all told of active warfare.

On shore the bustle was yet more apparent. Every-

body was in movement. Yellow post-chaises convey-
ing young captains of dashing frigates, or admirals'
private secretaries, came whirling through the streets
as if the fate of the nation depended on their speed.
Officers of all grades, from post-captains with glittering
epaulets to midshipmen with white patches on their
collars and simple cockades in their hats, were hurrying,
with looks of importance, through the streets. Large
placards were everywhere posted up announcing the
names of the ships requiring men, and the advantages
to be obtained by joining them: plenty of prize money
and abundance of fighting, with consequent speedy
promotion; while first lieutenants, and a choice band
of old hands, were near by to win by persuasion those
who were protected from being pressed. Jack tars,
many with pig-tails, and earrings in their ears, were
rolling about the streets, their wives or sweethearts
hanging at their elbows, dressed in the brightest of
colours, huge bonnets decked with flaunting ribbons
on their heads, and glittering brass chains, and other
ornaments of glass, on their necks and arms. As I
drove down the High Street I had met a crowd surrounding a ship's gig on wheels. Some fifty seamen
or more were dragging it along at a rapid rate, leaping
and careering, laughing and cheering. In the stern
sheets sat a well-known eccentric post-captain with
the yoke lines in his hands, while he kept bending
forward to give the time to his crew, who were
arranged before him with oars outstretched, making
believe to row, and grinning all the time in high glee

from ear to ear. It was said that he was on his way
to the Admiralty in London, the Lords Commissioners
having for some irregularity prohibited him from leaving his ship except in his gig on duty. Whether he
ever got to London I do not know.

On arriving at Portsmouth, I had gone to the Blue
Posts, an inn of old renown, recommended by my
brother Harry, who was then a midshipman, and who
had lately sailed for the East India station. It was
an inn more patronised by midshipmen and young
lieutenants than by post-captains and admirals. I
had there expected to meet Captain Hassall, the
commander of the *Barbara*, but was told that, as he
was the master of a merchantman, he was more
likely to have gone to the Keppel's Head, at Portsea. Thither I repaired, and found a note from him
telling me to come off at once, and saying that he
had had to return on board in a hurry, as he found
that several of his men had no protection, and were
very likely to be pressed, one man having already
been taken by a press-gang, and that he was certain
to inform against the others. Thus it was that I
came to embark at the Common Hard at Portsea, and
had to beat down the harbour.

"Do you think as how you'd know your ship when
you sees her, sir?" asked old Bob, with a twinkle in
his one eye, for he had discovered my very limited
amount of nautical knowledge, I suspect. "It will
be a tough job to find her, you see, among so many."

Now I had been on board very often as she lay

alongside the quay in the Thames. I had seen all her cargo stowed, knew every bale and package and case ; I had attended to the fitting-up of my own cabin, and was indeed intimately acquainted with every part of her interior. But her outside—that was a very different matter, I began to suspect. I saw floating on the sea, far out in the distance, the misty outlines of a hundred or more big ships ; indeed, the whole space between Portsmouth and the little fishing village of Ryde seemed covered with shipping, and my heart sank within me at the thought of having to pick out the *Barbara* among them.

The evening was drawing on, and the weather did not look pleasant ; still I must make the attempt. The convoy was expected to sail immediately, and the interests of my employers, Garrard, Janrin and Company, would be sacrificed should the sailing of the ship be delayed by my neglect. These thoughts passed rapidly through my mind and made me reply boldly, " We must go on, at all events. Time enough to find her out when we get there."

We were at that time near the mouth of the harbour, with Haslar Hospital seen over a low sand-bank, and some odd-looking sea-marks on one side, and Southsea beach and the fortifications of Ports-mouth, with a church tower and the houses of the town beyond. A line of redoubts and Southsea Castle appeared, extending farther southward, while the smooth chalk-formed heights of Portsdown rose in the distance. As a person suddenly deprived of

sight recollects with especial clearness the last objects
he has beheld, so this scene was indelibly impressed
on my mind, as it was the last near view I was des-
tined to have of old England for many a long day.
For the same reason I took a greater interest in old
Bob and his boy Jerry than I might otherwise have
done. They formed the last human link of the chain
which connected me with my native land. Bob had
agreed to take my letters back, announcing my safe
arrival on board—that is to say, should I ever get there.
My firm reply, added to the promise of another five
shillings for the trouble he might have, raised me again
in his opinion, and he became very communicative.

We tacked close to a buoy off Southsea beach.
"Ay, sir, there was a pretty blaze just here not many
years ago," he remarked. "Now I mind it was in '95
—that's the year my poor girl Betty died—the mother
of Jerry there. You've heard talk of the *Boyne*—a fine
ship she was, of ninety-eight guns. While she, with
the rest of the fleet, was at anchor at Spithead, one
morning a fire broke out in the admiral's cabin, and
though officers and men did their best to extinguish it,
somehow or other it got the upper hand of them all;
but the boats from the other ships took most of them
off, though some ten poor fellows perished, they say.
One bad part of the business was, that the guns were
all loaded and shotted, and as the fire got to them they
went off, some of the shots reaching Stokes Bay, out
there beyond Haslar, and others falling among the
shipping. Two poor fellows aboard the *Queen Charlotte*

were killed, and another wounded, though she and the other ships got under way to escape mischief. At about half-past one she burnt from her cables, and came slowly drifting in here till she took the ground. She burnt on till near six in the morning, when the fire reached the magazine, and up she blew with an awful explosion. We knew well enough that the moment would come, and it was a curious feeling we had waiting for it. Up went the blazing masts and beams and planks, and came scattering down far and wide, hissing into the water; and when we looked again after all was over, not a timber was to be seen."

Bob also pointed out the spot where nearly a century before the *Edgar* had blown up, and every soul in her had perished, and also where the *Royal George* and the brave Admiral Kempenfeldt, with eight hundred men, had gone down several years before the destruction of the *Boyne*. "Ay, sir, to my mind it's sad to think that the sea should swallow up so many fine fellows as she does every year, and yet we couldn't very well do without her, so I suppose it's all right. Mind your head-sheets, Jerry, or she'll not come about in this bobble," he observed, as we were about to tack round the buoy.

Having kept well to the eastward, we were now laying up to windward of the fleet. There were line-of-battle ships, and frigates, and corvettes, and huge Indiamen as big-looking as many line-of-battle ships, and large transports, and numberless merchantmen—ships and barques, and brigs and schooners; but as to

what the *Barbara* was like I had not an idea. I fixed
on one of the largest of the Indiamen, but when I told
old Bob the tonnage of the *Barbara* he laughed, and
said she wasn't half the size of the ship I pointed out.

It was getting darkish and coming on to blow pretty
fresh, and how to find my ship among the hundred or
more at anchor I could not possibly tell.

"Well, I thought from your look and the way you
hailed me that you was a sea-faring gentleman, and
on course you'd ha' known your own ship," said old
Bob, with a wink of his one eye. "Howsomever, we
can beat about among the fleet till it's dark, and then
back to Portsmouth; and then, do ye see, sir, we can
come out to-morrow morning by daylight and try
again. Maybe we shall have better luck. The convoy
is sure not to sail in the night, and the tide won't serve
till ten o'clock at earliest."

"This comes of dressing in nautical style, and assuming airs foreign to me," I thought to myself, though I
could not help fancying that there was some quiet
irony in the old man's tone. His plan did not at all
suit my notions. I was already beginning to feel very
uncomfortable, bobbing and tossing about among the
ships; and I expected to be completely upset, unless
I could speedily put my foot on something more stable
than the cockle-shell, or rather bean-pod, of a boat
in which I sat. I began to be conscious, indeed, that
I must be looking like anything but "a seafaring
gentleman."

"But we *must* find her," I exclaimed, with some

little impetuosity; "it will never do to be going back, and I know she's here."

"So the old woman said as was looking for her needle in the bundle of hay," observed old Bob, with provoking placidity. "On course she is, and we is looking for her: but it's quite a different thing whether we finds her or not, 'specially when it gets dark; and if, as I suspects, it comes on to blow freshish there'll be a pretty bobble of a sea here at the turn of the tide. To be sure, we may stand over to Ryde and haul the boat up there for the night. There's a pretty decentish public on the beach, the Pilot's Home, where you may get a bed, and Jerry and I always sleeps under the wherry. That's the only other thing for you to do, sir, that I sees on."

Though very unwilling to forego the comforts of my cabin and the society of Captain Hassall, I agreed to old Bob's proposal, provided the *Barbara* was not soon to be found. We sailed about among the fleet for some time, hailing one ship after another, but mine could not be found. I began to suspect at last that old Bob did not wish to find her, but had his eye on another day's work, and pay in proportion, as he might certainly consider that he had me in his power, and could demand what he chose. I was on the point of giving up the search, when, as we were near one of the large Indiamen I have mentioned, a vessel running past compelled us to go close alongside. An officer was standing on the accommodation-ladder, assisting up some passengers. He hailed one of the people in the boat, about some luggage. I knew the voice, and, looking more narrowly, I recognised, I thought, my old schoolfellow, Jack Newall. I called him by name. "Who's that?" he exclaimed. "What, Braithwaite, my fine fellow, what brings you out here?"

When I told him, "It is ten chances to one that you pick her out to-night," he answered. "But come aboard; I can find you a berth, and to-morrow morning you can continue your search. Depend on it your ship forms one of our convoy, so that she will not sail without you."

I was too glad to accept Jack Newall's offer. Old Bob looked rather disappointed at finding me snatched from his grasp, and volunteered to come back early in the morning, and take me on board the *Barbara,* promising in the meantime to find her out.

The sudden change from the little boat tumbling about in the dark to the Indiaman's well-lighted cuddy, glittering with plate and glass, into which my friend introduced me—filled, moreover, as it was, with well-dressed ladies and gentlemen—was very startling. She was the well-known *Cuffnels,* a ship of twelve hundred tons, one of the finest of her class, and, curiously enough, was the very one which, two voyages before, had carried my brother Frederick out to India.

I had never before been on board an Indiaman. Everything about her seemed grand and ponderous, and gave me the idea of strength and stability. If she was to meet with any disaster, it would not be

for want of being well found. The captain remembered my brother, and was very civil to me; and
several other people knew my family, so that I spent
a most pleasant evening on board, in the society of
the nabobs and military officers, and the ladies who
had husbands and those who had not, but fully expected to get them at the end of the voyage, and the
young cadets and writers, and others who usually
formed the complement of an Indiaman's passengers
in those days. Everything seemed done in princely
style on board her. She had a crew of a hundred
men, a captain, and four officers, mates, a surgeon,
and purser; besides midshipmen, a boatswain, carpenter, and other petty officers. I was invited to
come on board whenever there was an opportunity
during the voyage.

" We are not cramped, you see," observed Newall,
casting his eye over the spacious decks, " so you will
not crowd us; and if you cannot bring us news, we
can exchange ideas."

True to his word, old Bob came alongside the next
morning, and told me that he had found out the
Barbara, and would put me on board in good time for
breakfast.

I found Captain Hassall very anxious at my non-
appearance, and on the point of sending the second
officer on shore to look for me, as it was expected
that the convoy would sail at noon; indeed, the *Active*
frigate, which was to convoy us, had Blue Peter
flying at her mast-head, as had all the merchantmen.

" You'd have time to take a cruise about the fleet, and I'll spin you no end of yarns if you like to come, sir," said old Bob, with a twinkle in his eye, as his wherry was see-sawing alongside in a manner most uncomfortable to a landsman.

" No, thank you, Bob; I must hear the end of your yarns when I come back again to old England; I'll not forget you, depend on it."

Captain Hassall had not recovered his equanimity of temper, which had been sorely ruffled at having had two of his best men taken off by a press-gang. He had arrived on board in time to save two more who would otherwise also have been taken. He inveighed strongly against the system, and declared that if it was continued he would give up England and go over to the United States. It certainly created a very bad feeling both among officers and men in the merchant service. While we were talking, the frigate which was to convoy us loosed her topsails and fired a gun, followed soon after by another, as a signal to way. The merchantmen at once began to make sail, not so quick an operation as on board the man-of-war. The pipe played cheerily, round went the capstan, and in short time we, with fully fifty other vessels, many of them first-class Indiamen, with a fair breeze, were standing down Channel; the sky bright, the sea blue, while their white sails, towering upwards to the heavens, shone in the sunbeams like pillars of snow.

The *Barbara* proved herself a fast sailer, and could

easily keep up with our *Active* protector, which kept
sailing round the majestic-looking but slow-moving
Indiamen, as if to urge them on, as the shepherd's dog
does his flock. We hove-to off Falmouth, that other
vessels might join company. Altogether, we formed
a numerous convoy—some bound to the Cape of
Good Hope, others to different parts of India—two
or three to our lately-established settlements in New
South Wales, and several more to China.

I will not dwell on my feelings as we took our
departure from the land, the Lizard lights bearing N.
half E. I had a good many friends to care for me,
and one for whom I had more than friendship. We
had magnificent weather and plenty of time to get
the ship into order; indeed I, with others who had
never been to sea, began to entertain the notion that
we were to glide on as smoothly as we were then
doing during the whole voyage. We were to be
disagreeably undeceived. A gale sprang up with
little warning about midnight, and hove us almost
on our beam ends; and though we righted with the
loss only of a spar or two, we were tumbled about in
a manner subversive of all comfort, to say the least
of it.

When morning broke, the hitherto trim and well-
behaved fleet were scattered in all directions, and
several within sight received some damage or other.
The wind fell as quickly as it had risen, and during
the day the vessels kept returning to their proper
stations in the convoy. When night came on several

were still absent, but were seen approaching in the distance. Our third mate had been aloft for some time, and when he came into the cabin he remarked that he had counted more sail in the horizon than there were missing vessels. Some of the party were inclined to laugh at him, and inquired what sort of craft he supposed they were, phantom ships or enemy's cruisers.

"I'll tell you what, gentlemen,—I think that they are very probably the latter," said the captain. "I have known strange things happen; vessels cut out at night from the midst of a large convoy, others pillaged and the crews and passengers murdered, thrown overboard, or carried off. We shall be on our guard, and have our guns loaded, and if any gentry of this sort attempt to play their tricks on us they will find that they have caught a tartar."

CHAPTER II.

I MAY as well here give an account of the *Barbara*, and how I came to be on board her. Deprived of my father, who was killed in battle just as I was going up to the University, and left with very limited means, I was offered a situation as clerk in the counting-house of a distant relative, Mr. Janrin. I had no disinclination to mercantile pursuits. I looked on them, if carried out in a proper spirit, as worthy of a man of intellect, and I therefore gladly accepted the offer. As my mother lived in the country, my kind cousin invited me to come and reside with him, an advantage I highly appreciated. Everything was conducted in his house with clock-work regularity. If the weather was rainy, his coach drew up to the door at the exact hour; if the weather was fine, the servant stood ready with his master's spencer, and hat, and gloves, and gold-headed cane, without which Mr. Janrin never went abroad. Not that he required it to support his steps, but it was the mark of a gentleman. It had superseded the sword which he had worn in his youth. I soon got to like these regular ways, and found them far pleasanter than the irregularity of some houses

where I had visited. I always accompanied Mr.
Janrin when he walked, and derived great benefit from
his conversation, and though he offered me a seat in
the coach in bad weather, I saw that he was better
pleased when I went on foot. "Young men require
exercise, and should not pamper themselves," he
observed; "but, James, I say, put a dry pair of shoes
in your pocket—therein is wisdom; and don't sit in
your wet ones all day."

Thus it will be seen that I was treated by my
worthy principal from the first as a relative, and a
true friend he was to me. But I was introduced into
the mysteries of mercantile affairs by Mr. Gregory
Thursby, the head clerk. He lived over the counting-
house, and on my first appearance in it, before any of
the other clerks had arrived, he was there to receive
me. He took me round to the different desks, and
explained the business transacted at each of them.
"And there, Mr. James, look there," he said, pointing
to a line of ponderous folios on a shelf within easy
distance of where he himself sat: "see, we have Swift's
works, a handsome edition too, eh!" and he chuckled
as he spoke.

"Why, I fancied that they were ledgers," said I.

"Ha! ha! ha! so they are, and yet Swift's works,
for all that, those of my worthy predecessor, Jeremiah
Swift, every line in them written by his own hand, in
his best style; so I call them Swift's works. You are
not the first person by a great many I have taken in.
Ha! ha! ha!"

This was one of the worthy man's harmless conceits. He never lost an opportunity of indulging in the joke to his own amusement; and I remarked that he laughed as heartily the last time he uttered it as the first.

I set to work diligently at once on the tasks given me, and was rewarded by the approving remarks of Mr. Janrin and Mr. Thursby. Mr. Garrard had long ago left, not only the business but this world; the " Co." was his nephew, Mr. Luttridge, who was absent on account of ill-health, and thus the whole weight of the business rested on the shoulders of Mr. Janrin. But, as Thursby remarked, " He can well support it, Mr. James. He's an Atlas. It's my belief that he would manage the financial affairs of this kingdom better than any Chancellor of the Exchequer, or other minister of State, past or present; and that had he been at the head of affairs we should not have lost our North American Colonies, or have got plunged over head and ears in debt as we are, alack! already; and now, with war raging and all the world in arms against us, getting deeper and deeper into the mire." Without holding my worthy principal in such deep admiration as our head clerk evidently did, I had a most sincere regard and respect for him.

Our dinner hour was at one o'clock, in a room over the office. Mr. Janrin himself presided, and all the clerks, from the highest to the lowest, sat at the board. Here, however, on certain occasions, handsome dinners were given at a more fashionable hour

2

to any friends or correspondents of the house who
might be in London. Mr. Thursby took the foot of
the table, and I was always expected to be present.
At length I completed two years of servitude in the
house, and by that time was thoroughly up to all the
details of business. I had been very diligent. I had
never taken a holiday, and never had cause to absent
myself from business on account of ill-health. On the
very day I speak of we had one of the dinners mentioned. The guests were chiefly merchants or planters
from the West Indies, with a foreign consul or two,
and generally a few masters of merchantmen. The
guests as they arrived were announced by Mr. Janrin's
own servant, Peter Klopps, who always waited on
these occasions. Peter was himself a character. He
was a Dutchman. Mr. Janrin had engaged his services
many years before during a visit to Holland. He had
picked Peter out of a canal, or Peter had picked him
out, on a dark night—I never could understand which
had rendered the service to the other; at all events, it
had united them ever afterwards, and Peter had afterwards nursed his master through a long illness, and
saved his life. The most important secrets of State
might have been discussed freely in Peter's presence.
First, he did not understand a word that was said,
and then he was far too honest and discreet to
have revealed it if he had.

Several people had been announced. Ten minutes
generally brought the whole together. I caught the
name of one—Captain Hassall. He was a stranger, a

strongly-built man with a sunburnt countenance and bushy whiskers; nothing remarkable about him, except, perhaps, the determined expression of his eye and mouth. His brow was good, and altogether I liked his looks, and was glad to find myself seated next to him. He had been to all parts of the world, and had spent some time in the India and China seas. He gave me graphic accounts of the strange people of those regions; and fights with Chinese and Malay pirates, battles of a more regular order with French and Spanish privateers, hurricanes or typhoons. Shipwrecks and exciting adventures of all sorts seemed matters of everyday occurrence. A scar on his cheek and another across his hand, showed that he had been, at close quarters, too, on some occasion, with the enemy.

Mr. Janrin and Mr. Thursby both paid him much attention during dinner. Allusions were made by him to a trading voyage he had performed in the service of the firm, and it struck me from some remarks he let drop that he was about to undertake another of a similar character. I was not mistaken. After dinner, when the rest of the guests were gone, he remained behind to discuss particulars, and Mr. Janrin desired me to join the conclave. I was much interested in all I heard. A large new ship, the *Barbara*, had been purchased, of which Captain Hassall had become part owner. She was now in dock fitting for sea. She mounted ten carriage guns and four swivels, and was to be supplied with a proportionate quantity of small arms, and to be well manned. A letter of marque was to be obtained for her, though she was not to fight except in case of necessity; while her cargo was to be assorted and suited to various localities. She was to visit several places to the East of the Cape of Good Hope, and to proceed on to the Indian Islands and China.

"And how do you like the enterprise, James?" asked Mr. Janrin, after the captain had gone.

"I have not considered the details sufficiently to give an opinion, sir," I answered. "If all turns out as the captain expects, it must be very profitable, but there are difficulties to be overcome, and dangers encountered, and much loss may be incurred."

I saw Mr. Janrin and the head clerk exchange glances, and nod to each other. I fancy that they were nods of approval at what I had said.

"Then, James, you would not wish to engage in it in any capacity?" said Mr. Janrin. "You would rather not encounter the dangers and difficulties of such a voyage?"

"That is a very different matter, sir," I answered. "I should very much like to visit the countries you speak of, and the difficulties I cannot help seeing would enhance the interest of the voyage."

Again the principal and clerk exchanged glances and nodded.

"What do you say, then, James, to taking charge of the venture as supercargo? My belief is that you will act with discretion and judgment as to its disposal, and that we shall have every reason to be satisfied with you. Mr. Thursby agrees with me, do you not, Thursby?"

"I feel sure that Mr. James will bring no discredit on the firm, sir," answered Mr. Thursby, smiling at me. "On the contrary, sir, no young man I am acquainted with is so likely to conduce to the success of the enterprise."

I was highly gratified by the kind remarks of my friends, and expressed my thanks accordingly, at the same time that I begged I might be allowed two days for consideration. I desired, of course, to consult my mother, and was anxious also to know what another would have to say to the subject. She, like a sensible girl, agreed with me that it would be wise to endure the separation for the sake of securing, as I hoped to do, ultimate comfort and independence. I knew from the way that she gave this advice that she did not love me less than I desired. I need say no more than that her confidence was a powerful stimulus to exertion and perseverance in the career I had chosen. My mother was far more doubtful about the matter. Not till the morning after I had mentioned it to her did she say, "Go, my son; may God protect you and bless your enterprise!"

I was from this time forward actively engaged in the preparations for the voyage. My personal outfit was speedily ready, but I considered it necessary to examine all the cases of merchandise put on board, that I might be properly acquainted with all the articles in which I was going to trade. "It's just what I expected of him," I heard Mr. Janrin remark to Mr. Thursby, when one evening I returned late from my daily duties. "Ay, sir, there is the ring of the true metal in the lad," observed the head clerk.

Captain Hassall was as active in his department as I was in mine, and we soon had the *Barbara* ready for sea with a tolerably good crew. In those stirring days of warfare it was no easy thing to man a merchantman well, but Captain Hassall had found several men who had sailed with him on previous voyages, and they without difficulty persuaded others to ship on board the *Barbara*.

Our first officer, Mr. Randolph, was a gentleman in the main, and a very pleasant companion, though he had at first sight, in his everyday working suit, that scarecrow look which tall gaunt men, who have been somewhat battered by wind and weather, are apt to get. Our second mate, Ben, or rather "Benjie" Stubbs, as he was usually called, was nearly as broad as he was long, with puffed-out brown cheeks wearing an invincible smile. He was a man of one idea : he was satisfied with being a thorough seaman, and was nothing else. As to history, or science, or the interior of countries, he was profoundly ignorant. As to the land, it was all very well in its way to grow trees and form harbours, but the sea was undoubtedly the proper element for people to live on ; and he seemed to look with supreme contempt on all those who had the misfortune to be occupied on shore. The third

mate, Henry Irby, had very little the appearance of a
sailor, though he was a very good one. He was slight
in figure, and refined in his manners, and seemed, I
fancied, born to a higher position than that which he
held. He had served for two years before the mast,
but his rough associates during that time had not been
able in any way to alter him. Our surgeon, David
Gwynne, was, I need scarcely say, a Welshman. He
had not had much professional experience, but he was
an intelligent young man, and had several of the
peculiarities which are considered characteristic of his
people; but I hoped, from what I saw of him when he
first came on board, that he would prove an agreeable
companion. Curious as it may seem, there were two
men among the crew who by birth were superior to
any of us. I may, perhaps, have to say more about
them by-and-bye. We mustered, officers and men,
forty hands all told.

I will pass over the leave-takings with all the dear
ones at home. I knew and felt that true prayers, as
well as kind wishes, would follow me wherever I
might go.

" James," said my kind employer as I parted from
him, " I trust you thoroughly as I would my own son
if I had one. I shall not blame you if the enterprise
does not succeed; so do not take it to heart, for I
know that you will do your best, and no man can do
more." Mr. Thursby considered that it was incum-
bent on him to take a dignified farewell of me, and to
impress on me all the duties and responsibilities of my

office ; but he broke down, and a tear stood in his eye
as he wrung my hand, and said in a husky voice,
"You know all about it, my dear boy; you'll do well,
and we shall have you back here, hearty and strong,
with information successfully to guide Garrard, Janrin
and Co. in many an important speculation; and,
moreover, I hope, to lay the foundation of your own
fortune. Good-bye, good-bye; heaven bless you, my
boy!"

I certainly could not have commenced my undertaking under better auspices. Having obtained the
necessary permission of the Honorable East India
Company to trade in their territories, the *Barbara*
proceeded to Spithead, and I ran down to pay a flying
visit to my friends, which was the cause of my joining
the ship at Spithead in the way I have described, and
where I left my readers to give these necessary ex-
planations.

The convoy was standing on under easy sail to
allow the scattered vessels to come up, and as long as
there was a ray of daylight they were seen taking up
their places. Now and then, after dark, I could see a
phantom form gliding by; some tall Indiaman, or
heavy store-ship, or perhaps some lighter craft, to part
with us after crossing the line, bound round Cape
Horn. The heat was considerable, and as I felt no
inclination to turn in, I continued pacing the deck till
it had struck six bells in the first watch.* Mr. Ran-

* This ordinary watch consists of four hours, and the bell is
struck every half-hour. As the first watch commences at eight,

dolph, the senior mate, had charge of the deck. He, I found, was not always inclined to agree with some of the opinions held by our captain.

"He's a fine fellow, our skipper, but full of fancies, as you'll find; but there isn't a better seaman out of the port of London," he observed, as he took a few turns alongside me. "I have a notion that he believes in the yarns of the *Flying Dutchman*, and of old Boody, the Portsmouth chandler, and in many other such bits of nonsense, but as I was saying——"

"What, don't you?" I asked, interrupting him; "I thought all sailors believed in those tales."

The captain had been narrating some of them to us a few evenings before.

"No, I do not," answered the first mate, somewhat sharply. "I believe that God made this water beneath our feet, and that He sends the wind which sometimes covers it over with sparkling ripples, and at others stirs it up into foaming seas, but I don't think He lets spirits or ghosts of any sort wander about doing no good to any one. That's my philosophy. I don't intend to belief in the stuff till I see one of the gentlemen; and then I shall look pretty sharply into his character before I take my hat off to him."

"You are right, Mr. Randolph, and I do not suppose that the captain differs much from you. He only wishes to guard against mortal enemies, and he has

it was then eleven. There are two dog-watches from four to six and from six to eight p.m., in order that the same men may not be on duty at the same hours each day.

shown that he is in earnest in thinking that there is some danger, by having come on deck every half-hour or oftener during the night. There he is again."

Captain Hassall stood before us: " Cast loose and load the guns, Mr. Randolph, and send a quarter-master to serve out the small arms to the watch," he said quietly ; " there has been a sail on our quarter for some minutes past, which may possibly be one of the convoy, but she may not. Though she carries but little canvas she is creeping up to us."

The mate and I while talking had not observed the vessel the captain pointed out. "The skipper has sharp eyes," said the first mate, as he parted from me to obey the orders he had received. Our crew had been frequently exercised at the guns. Having loaded and run them out, the watch came tumbling aft to the arm chest. Cutlasses were buckled on and pistols quickly loaded, and boarding pikes placed along the bulwarks ready for use. The men did not exactly understand what all this preparation was for, but that was nothing to them. It signified fighting, and most British seamen are ready for that at any time. The captain now joined me in my walk. "It is better to be prepared, though nothing come of it, than to be taken unawares," he observed. "It is the principle I have gone on, and as it is a sound one, I intend to continue it as long as I live." I agreed with him. We walked the deck together for twenty minutes or more, engaged in conversation. His eye was constantly during the time looking over our starboard quarter.

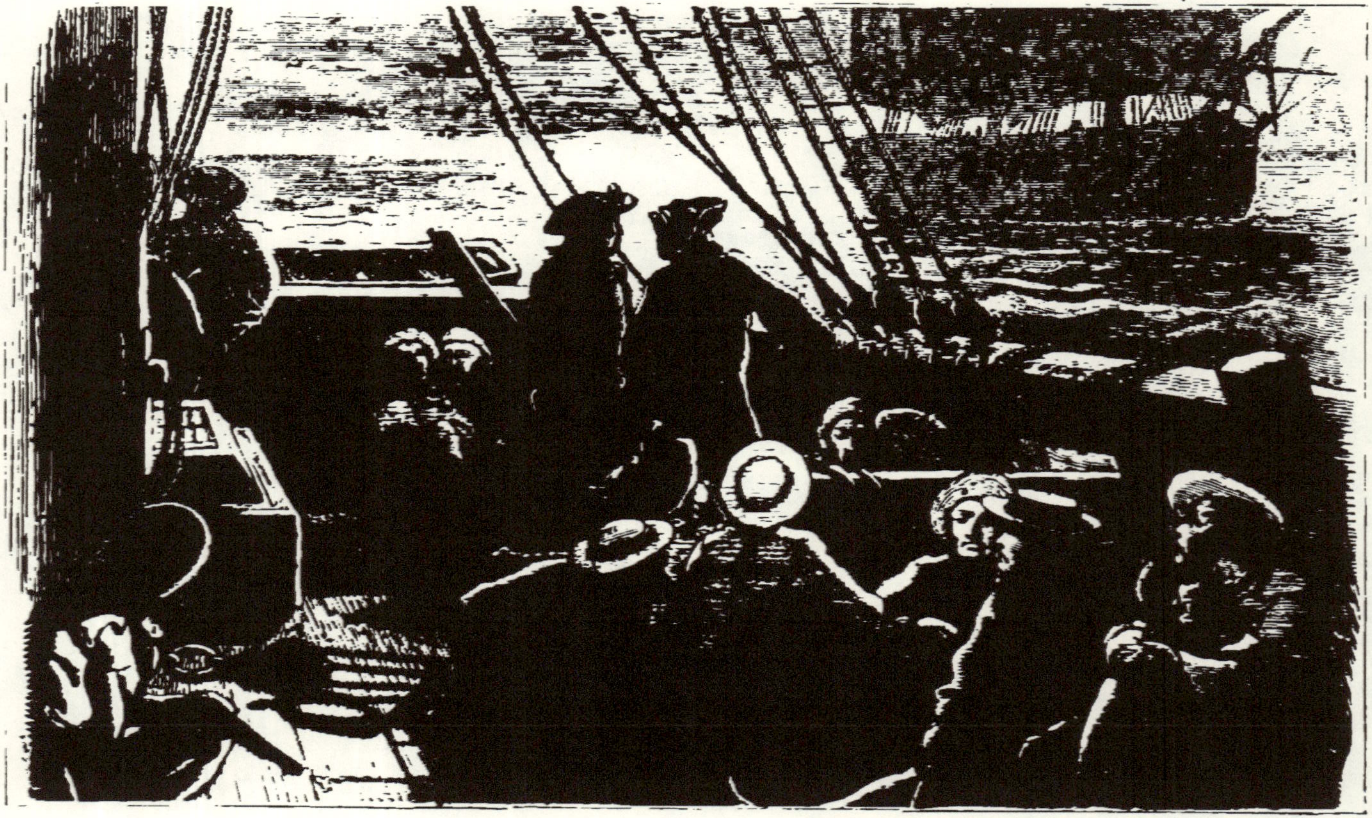

PREPARED FOR EMERGENCIES.—*Page* 27.

Even I could at length distinguish the dim outline of a vessel in that direction. Gradually the sails of a ship with taut raking masts became visible.

"That craft is not one of our convoy, and I doubt that she comes among us for any good purpose," exclaimed the captain. "I should like to bring the frigate down upon the fellow, but we should lose our share of the work, and I think that we can manage him ourselves. Call the starboard watch, Mr. Stubbs.

The men soon came tumbling up from below, rather astonished at being so soon called. The other officers were also soon on deck. Mr. Randolph agreed that the stranger, which hung on our quarter like some ill-omened bird of prey, had an exceedingly suspicious appearance, and that we were only acting with ordinary prudence in being prepared for him.

"The fellow won't fire, as he would bring the frigate down upon him if he did," observed the first mate; "he will therefore either run alongside in the hopes of surprising us, and taking us by boarding before we have time to fire a pistol, which would attract notice, or, should the wind fall light, he may hope to cut us out with his boats."

Eight bells struck. We could hear the sound borne faintly over the waters from two of the Indiamen to windward of us, but no echo came from the deck of the stranger. The men were ordered to lie down under the bulwarks till wanted. Had Captain Hassall thought fit, he might, by making sail, have got out of danger, but he had hopes that instead of being taken by the stranger he might take him. It struck me that we might be running an unwarrantable risk of getting the vessel or cargo injured by allowing ourselves to be attacked.

"Not in the least," answered the captain; " we serve as a bait to the fellow, and shall benefit directly by catching him. If we were to give the alarm he would be off like a shot, and depend on it he has a fast pair of heels, or he would not venture in among us, so that the frigate would have little chance of catching him."

The truth is, Captain Hassall had made up his mind to do something to boast of. Orders were now given to the men to remain perfectly silent; the stranger was drawing closer and closer; grapnels had been got ready to heave on board him, and to hold him fast should it be found advisable. It was, however, possible that his crew might so greatly outnumber ours that this would prove a dangerous proceeding. As to our men, they knew when they shipped that they might have to fight, and they all now seemed in good heart, so that we had no fear on the score of their failing us. Our officers were one and all full of fight, though each exhibited his feelings in a different way. The surgeon's only fear seemed to be that the stranger would prove a friend instead of a foe, and that there would be no skirmish after all.

" She's some craft one of the other vessels has fallen in with, and she has just joined company for protection," he observed. "For my part I shall turn in, as

I am not likely to be wanted, either to fight or to dress wounds."

The wind, which had much fallen, had just freshened up again. "Whatever he is, friend or foe, here he comes," exclaimed Mr. Randolph. "Steady, lads!" cried the captain, "don't move till I give the word."

As he spoke the stranger glided up, her dark sails appearing to tower high above ours. We kept on our course as if she was not perceived. With one sheer she was alongside, there was a crash as her yards locked with ours, and at the same moment numerous dark forms appeared in her rigging and nettings about to leap on to our deck. "Now give it them!" cried our captain. Our men sprang to their feet and fired a broadside through the bulwarks of the enemy. The cries and shrieks which were echoed back showed the havoc which had been caused. Shouts and blows, the clash of cutlasses, the flash of pistols, immediately followed. I felt a stinging sensation in my shoulder, but was too excited to think anything of it as I stood, cutlass in hand, ready to repel our assailants. Many of those who were about to board us must have sprung back, or fallen into the water; a few only reached our deck, who were at once cut down by our people. One man sprang close to where I stood. I was about to fire my pistol at him, when I saw that he was unarmed, so I dragged him across the deck out of harm's way. The next instant the vessels parted.

"Give it them, my lads! Load and fire as fast as

you can, or they will escape us," cried the captain in an excited tone.

" Wing them! wing them! knock away their spars, lads!" He next ordered the helm to be put down, the tacks hauled aboard, and chase to be made after our flying foe, while a blue light was burned to show our locality, and to prevent the frigate from firing into us when she followed, as we hoped she would.

We had no doubt that the enemy, when he met with the warm reception we had given him, took us for a man-of-war corvette, and on this came to the conclusion that prudence was the best part of valour. There could be little doubt, however, that he would soon discover that our guns were of no great size ; and then possibly he might turn on us, and give us more of his quality than would be desirable. Still we kept on peppering away at him as fast as we could, in the hopes of bringing down one of his masts, and enabling the frigate to come up. The lights of the convoy were, however, by this time almost lost sight of. In vain we looked out for a signal of the approach of the frigate. No gun was heard, no light was seen. We were afraid of losing the convoy altogether, and certainly it would have been against the spirit of our instructions to have attempted to deal single-handed with our opponent. Giving the enemy a parting shot most reluctantly, Captain Hassall therefore ordered the helm to be put up, and we ran back in the direction in which we expected to find the convoy.

CHAPTER III.

"HILLO ! who have we here ? " I heard one of the mates exclaim, as I was taking a last look of our receding antagonist. " Is this a dead man ? "

" No, not entirely, as yet," said a voice which proceeded, I found, from a person lying on the deck.

I remembered my prisoner, and ran to lift him up. He recognised my voice. " If it hadn't been for you I should have been dead enough by this time," he said, getting on his feet.

" Who are you ? " I asked, "a friend or a foe ? "

" A friend; or I wouldn't be here at all," he answered, in a tone which made me feel certain that he spoke the truth.

" Well, come into the cabin, and tell me all about the matter," I said; for though he spoke broad Irish, I saw by his manner that he was above the rank of a common seaman. His appearance when he came into the light justified me in my opinion.

" It's just this; I was first mate of a fine brig, the *Kathleen.* We had been down in the eastern seas, and away into the Pacific, over to America, trading for some time with the natives, and bringing hides, seal-skins, and sandal-wood to the Chinamen; and at last, having made a successful voyage, we were on our homeward passage, when yonder piratical craft fell in with us. Each man had been promised a share of the profits, so that we had something to fight for. Fight our poor fellows did, till there was scarcely one of them left unhurt. We none of us thought of striking, though; but at last the rascally pirates ran us aboard, and as they swarmed along our decks cut down every man who still stood on his legs. How I escaped without a hurt I don't know. I soon had other troubles; for, being uninjured, I was at once carried aboard our captor, but before the Frenchmen could secure their prize, she blew up, with every soul on board, and there was I left a prisoner alone. I almost envied the fate of our crew. The loss of the prize, which had cost them so many lives and so much trouble, made the Frenchmen very savage, especially their captain, who is about as daring a villain as ever ploughed salt water. This determined him, when he fell in with your convoy, to try and cut one of them out. He fixed on you because you were of a size which he thought he could tackle easily, and he hoped to take you by surprise. Why he did not kill me outright I do not know, for he treated me like a brute from the moment he got me in his power; and when we ran you alongside he made me get into the rigging that I might be shot at; and I thought to myself, The safest plan is to jump aboard, and if I escape a knock on

the head I may stow myself away before any one sees
me. Such is the end of my history at present."

The name of the vessel which had attacked us was
the *Mignonne*, privateer, of twenty guns and eighty
men, Captain Jules La Roche, of the port of Brest, we
learned from the stranger. "And your own name, my
friend?" I asked, not feeling very sure that the truth
had been told us. "Dennis O'Carroll. My name will
tell you where I hail from, and you may look at me
as a specimen of one of the most unfortunate men in
the world," he answered. If O'Carroll's account of the
size of our antagonist was correct, we had good reason
to be thankful that we had escaped so easily. Our
chief anxiety was now about finding the fleet. We
had no business to have separated from them; for
though we might easily have run out to the East
without encountering an enemy, yet, should any
accident have happened to us, our insurers might
have considered our charter invalidated, and Garrard,
Janrin and Co. would have been the sufferers.

We were much relieved by seeing a blue light
suddenly burst forth in the darkness. It came from
the deck of the frigate, which had stood after us to
ascertain the cause of the firing. Our adventure had
the effect of keeping the convoy much closer together;
for no one could tell when Captain La Roche would
take it into his head to pounce down upon us and
pick up a stray bird, should the frigate be at a distance.
He would have had no chance, however, with the
Indiamen, whose officers were in a very combative

3

mood. Not long before a very gallant action had been performed by a squadron of them in the Eastern seas —indeed, no country ever possessed a body of officers in her mercantile marine equal to those of the Honorable East India Company.

I heard all about the action on board the *Cuffnells.* One morning, when I went on deck, I found that there was what might well be called a calm; the sails of the ships hung up and down the masts without moving, except every now and then, as they slowly rolled from side to side to give a loud thundering clap, and once more to subside into sullen silence. The sea, smooth as a mirror, shone like burnished silver, its surface ever and anon broken by the fin of some monster of the deep, or by a covey of flying fish, which would dart through the air till, their wings dried by the sun, they fell helpless again into their native element.

Looking round I recognised the *Cuffnells* not far off, and, remembering my promise, asked for a boat to go on board. I was received in the most friendly manner, and was asked to stop to tiffin and to dinner, if I could remain as long.

"Yes, sir, he richly deserved it; every rupee he got —that's my opinion," observed a yellow-faced gentleman in nankeens and white waistcoat, sitting at the other end of the table. "I was on board the *Earl Camden* on my way home, and I know that, including public and private investments, the cargoes of our ships could not have been of less value than eight millions of pounds sterling. We had fifteen Indiamen

and a dozen country ships, with a Portuguese craft
and a brig, the *Ganges;* Captain Dance, our captain,
was commodore. This fleet sailed from Canton on the
31st January, 1804. After sighting Pulo Auro, near
the Straits of Malacca, the *Royal George,* one of the
Indiamen, made the signal for four strange sail in the
south-west. On this the commodore directed four of
the Indiamen to go down and examine them. Lieutenant Fowler, of the navy, who was a passenger on
board the *Earl Camden,* offered to go also in the
Ganges to inspect the strangers more nearly. It was
a time of no small anxiety, you may be sure. The
Ganges was a fast sailer, and before long Lieutenant
Fowler came back, with the information that the
squadron in sight was French, and consisted of a
line-of-battle ship, three frigates, and a brig. The
question was now, Should we fight or not? If we
attempted to make our escape the enemy would pursue
us, and very likely pick us off in detail. Our safest
plan was to put a bold face on the matter, and show
that we were prepared for fighting. This was our
gallant commodore's opinion, and all the other captains
agreed with him, especially Captain Timins, of the
Royal George, who acted as his second in command.
The look-out ships were now recalled by signal, and
the line of battle formed in close order. As soon as
the enemy could fetch in our wake they put about,
and we kept on our course under easy sail. At near
sunset they were close up with our rear, which it
seemed as if they were about to attack. On seeing

this Captain Dance prepared with other ships to hasten to the assistance of that part of our line. Just as the day was closing, however, the French, not liking our looks, and unwilling to risk a night engagement, hauled their wind. Lieutenant Fowler was now sent in the *Ganges* to station the country ships on our lee-bow, by which means we were between them and the enemy. He brought back some volunteers, whose assistance was acceptable. We lay to all night—our men at their quarters. At daybreak of the 15th we saw the enemy also lying to, and so, hoisting our colours, we offered them battle if they chose to come down. At nine, finding that they would not accept our challenge, we formed the order of sailing, and steered our course under easy sail. The enemy on this filled their sails and edged down towards us. Now was the time that the mettle of our merchant skippers was to be tried. Did they flinch?—Not a bit of it! The commodore, finding that the enemy proposed to attack and cut off our rear, made the signal for the fleet to tack and bear down on him, and engage in succession—the *Royal George* being the leading ship, the *Ganges* next, and then the *Earl Camden*. This manœuvre was beautifully performed, and we stood towards the Frenchmen under a press of sail. The enemy then formed in a very close line and opened fire on the headmost ships, which was not returned till they got much closer. What do you think of it? Two merchantmen and a brig engaging a line-of-battle ship, two frigates, and two other ships of war—for the rest of the fleet had not yet got up. The *Royal George* bore the brunt of the action, for Captain Timins took his ship as close to the enemy as they would let him, and the *Ganges* and *Earl Camden* opened their fire as soon as their guns could take effect. Before, however, any of the other ships could get into action the Frenchmen hauled their wind and stood away to the eastward, under all the sail they could set. On this, at about two p.m., the signal was made for a general chase, and away went the fleet of merchantmen after the men-of-war. We pursued them for two hours, when the commodore, fearing that we might be led too far from the mouth of the straits, made the signal to tack, and in the evening we anchored ready to pass through the straits in the morning. We afterwards found that the squadron we had engaged was that of Admiral Linois, consisting of the *Marengo*, 84 guns, the *Belle Poule* and *Semillante*, heavy frigates, a corvette of 28 guns, and a Batavian brig of 18 guns. That the Frenchmen either took some of our big ships for men-of-war, or fancied that some men-of-war were near at hand and ready to come to our assistance, is very probable, but that does not detract from the gallantry of the action. The Patriotic Fund voted swords and plate to Captain Dance and other officers, and the East India Company presented him with 2,000 guineas and a piece of plate worth 500, and Captain Timins 1,000 guineas and a piece of plate, and all the other captains and officers and men rewards in plate or money, the whole amounting to not less than 50,000. But they deserved it, sir—they deserved it; and I suspect that Admiral Linois and his officers must have pulled out the best part of their hair when they discovered the prize they had lost. Besides the reward I have mentioned, Commodore Dance was very properly knighted. In its result," continued the speaker, "the action was most important."

"But it was scarcely so annoying to the enemy as another in which some Indiamen were engaged in 1800," observed a military officer, laying down his knife and fork, and wiping his moustache. "I was on my passage out on board the *Exeter*, one of the Indiamen of 1,200 tons, commanded by Captain Meriton. We had in company the *Bombay Castle*, *Coutts*, and *Neptune*, of the same tonnage, besides other ships under the convoy of the *Belligeux*, of 64 guns, Captain Bulteel. A French squadron of three large frigates, it appeared, after committing a good deal of mischief on the coast of Africa, had crossed over to Rio de la Plata to refit, and had just again put to sea, when, early in the morning, they made out a part, and some of the lighter ships, probably, of our convoy. Hoping to pick up some prizes, the Frenchmen stood towards us, and we, quite ready for the encounter, bore down towards them. No sooner, however, did the Frenchmen see our big China ships, with their two tiers of ports and warlike look, than they bore up under a press of sail, and by signal separated. While the *Belligeux* steered for the largest of the French ships, she signalled to the India-

men I have mentioned to proceed in chase of the
others, we and the *Bombay Castle* of one of them, the
Médée, and the other two of the *Franchise*. We, at
the time, were nearer the *Médée* than was the *Bombay
Castle*, and we also sailed better. The chase was a
long one, but we kept the enemy in sight, and it was
near midnight before we came up with her. The
Bombay Castle was a long way astern, and the frigate
might have handled us very severely, if not knocked
us to pieces, before she could have come up to our
assistance. Captain Meriton was not a man to be
daunted. With the decks lighted and all our ports
up, he ran alongside the Frenchman—'Strike, monsieur, to a superior force, to his Britannic Majesty's
ship *Thunderaboo*,' he shouted out. 'Strike, I say,
or——' We did not know whether the Frenchman
would reply with a broadside, which would have
greatly staggered us. Instead of that the Frenchman
politely replied that he yielded to the fortune of war.
'Come aboard immediately,' was the order our bold
captain next gave. Not to be surpassed by the
Frenchman, we had a guard ready to assist the captain
up our high side. With the profoundest of bows he
delivered his sword, and he was then asked into the
cabin. Immediately we had him safe, keeping the
frigate under our guns, we sent armed boats on board,
and brought away part of her people. When the
Bombay Castle came up she received the remainder,
and we then placed a prize crew on board. Meantime
the suspicions of the French captain had been aroused.

He had observed the small size of our guns. The appearance of the Indiaman's cuddy and the gentlemen and lady passengers—not that there were many of the latter—must have raised curious doubts in his mind. Suddenly he jumped up and asked to what ship he had struck.

"'To the Honorable East India Company's ship *Exeter,*' answered Captain Meriton, with a bow which beat the Frenchman's.

"'What, to a merchantman?' exclaimed the Frenchman, with a look of dismay.

"'Yes, monsieur, to a merchantman,' said Captain Meriton, with a gentle smile, which it would have been difficult to repress.

"'It is not fair; it is vile! it is a cheat!' exclaimed the Frenchman, beginning to stalk up and down the cabin, to grind his teeth, and to pull out his hair. 'I say it is a cheat; give me back my ship, send on board my men, and I will fight you bravely. You will soon see if you take me again.'

"'I am ready to acknowledge that you would very likely take me, as I should certainly deserve to be taken for my folly in agreeing to your proposal. You will excuse me if I therefore decline it,' was the answer. Though we pitied the feelings of the poor man, it was very difficult to keep our countenance as he uttered his expressions of indignation and anger. He did not recover his spirits till his frigate was out of sight."

This anecdote was followed by several others.

Those were pleasant hours I spent on board the old Indiaman. My visits to her were indeed an agreeable change from the sea-life routine of my own ship. I was amused by the progress in intimacy made among themselves by the younger portion of the passengers since I first went aboard at Spithead. The captain confided to me the fact that it cost him much more trouble to maintain discipline in the cuddy than among his crew. "What with my young ladies and my chronometers, it is as much as an elderly gentleman can well accomplish to keep all things straight," he observed, glancing at several young couples who were pacing the deck, the gentlemen being cadets or writers. "The friends of those girls now—nice young creatures they are too,—have sent them out fully expecting that they would marry nabobs or colonels at least, and in spite of all my precautions, they have gone and engaged themselves to those young fellows who have only just got their feet on the ratlines. Small blame to the gentlemen, however, for a more charming consignment I never had, only the more charming the more difficult to manage."

While the calms lasted, I paid daily visits to my friends, but at length a breeze springing up we proceeded on our voyage, as I must with my narrative, or I may chance not to get to the end of it. We called off the beautiful island of Madeira, with its picturesque town of Funchal—more attractive on the outside than within; we procured, however, a welcome supply of fresh meat, vegetables, and fruits. On our crossing the line, Neptune and his Tritons came on board and played their usual pranks. Jack little thinks that on such occasions he is performing a very ancient ceremony, practised by those bold voyagers, the Carthaginians; to them there is little doubt that the secret of the mariner's compass was known. On sailing between the Pillars of Hercules into the wide Atlantic they were visited, not by Hercules himself, but by his representative priests, to whom they were wont to deliver certain votive offerings that the propitiated divinity might protect them on their perilous voyage. The custom of performing ceremonies of a like description was continued to later times by the mariners of the Levant, Greece, and Italy, long after the temple of Hercules was in ruins. When they, and those northern seamen who had learned the scientific parts of navigation from them, extended their voyages across the line, they continued the practices, substituting Neptune for Hercules, and adding a few caricatures to suit their own more barbarous taste.

Having crossed the line, and there being no longer much risk of our meeting the cruisers of the enemy, Captain Hassall, who had long fumed at being kept back by the slow sailing of our companions, determined to part company. We accordingly hoisted our colours, gave a salute of nine guns in acknowledgment of the civilities we had received, and under all sail soon ran the dignified moving convoy out of sight. Light and contrary winds and calms kept us so long under the sun of the tropics that the seams of our decks began to open, and, to get them caulked and other repairs executed, we bore up for St. Salvador on the coast of Brazil, belonging to Portugal. We saluted the fort on entering, and paid every necessary respect to the authorities; but we soon found that they either suspected our character, or were not inclined, for some other reason, to treat us in a friendly spirit. A guard was put on board, and we were told that neither officers nor crew must leave the ship.

We were still ignorant of the cause of this treatment, when the master of an English whaler came alongside with his men armed to the teeth. He told us that he had a letter of marque, and that on the strength of it, having fallen in with a Spanish merchantman some way to the south-west, he had chased and captured her, and found a large number of dollars on board. Having come into St. Salvador he found there no less than seven other Spanish vessels, the masters and crews of which were favoured by the Portuguese, and he heard that they threatened to follow him out and capture him and his prize. Our arrival had turned the scales in his favour, and he offered to remain if we would accompany him out when we were ready. This Captain Hassall readily promised to do. As the whaler was strongly manned, a good-sized crew had been put on board the prize, and thus our three vessels were somewhat of a match for the Spaniards, we hoped. At length the Governor of the place ordered the officers of the ship to appear before him. Accordingly Captain Hassall, the first mate, and I, accompanied by Dennis O'Carroll, who seemed to be able to speak every language under the sun except pure English, as interpreter, went on shore under an escort. The Governor, a fat, swarthy personage in the full dress uniform of a general, received us in a haughty manner, and cross-questioned us in the most minute and tedious manner. Dennis somewhat puzzled him by the style of his answers, which were anything but literal translations of what Captain Hassall said. The result, however, was favourable, and we were allowed to go wherever we chose about the city, and to get the necessary repairs of our ships executed, and to obtain all the stores and provisions we required.

Much relieved, we made our bows, and then took a turn through the place before going on board. I was much struck with the number of churches, of priests and monks, and black slaves, the latter habited in the most scanty garments, and the former perambulating the streets in parties, dressed up in the richest attire of coloured silks and gold, with banners and crosses, and statues of saints, or representations of events mentioned in the Scriptures, the figures as large as life. A large number of friars in black, or brown, or grey gowns of coarse cloth, with ropes round their waists, were going about two and two, with small figures of saints on money boxes. The figures they literally thrust into the faces of the passers-by to be kissed. We saw no one refuse to drop a coin into the box.

"'These must be a very religiously disposed people,' I observed to Dennis.

"If you knew what I do you wouldn't say that," he answered. "They're fond of sinning, and they are ready to pay for it. The reason that all these priests and monks flourish is this—they have succeeded in teaching the people that they can buy pardon for all the sins they commit. The only scrap of real religion the poor people are allowed to possess is the knowledge that sin must be punished if not forgiven. Instead, however, of showing them how forgiveness can alone be obtained, they make them believe that money can buy it through the prayers of the saints; but when they've got the money in their own pockets, it's very little trouble they give the saints about the matter at all."

"How did you learn all this, Mr. O'Carroll?" I asked.

"Just because I believed it all myself," he answered quickly. "I'll tell you some day how I came to find out that I had been sailing on a wrong tack; but you think me now a harum-scarum Irishman, and I'm afraid to talk about the matter."

On our way we passed through the dock-yard, where a fifty-gun ship was building, and several smaller vessels of war. We were looking at one repairing alongside the quay, when I saw O'Carroll start, and look eagerly at the people on board.

"That's her, I'm certain of it!" he exclaimed. "She has got into trouble since she parted from you, or you may have done her more harm than you thought for, and she has put in here with false papers and under false colours to repair damages."

"What vessel do you mean?" I asked.

"Why, the *Mignonne* to be sure, or by what other name she may go," he answered. "Probably she is now the *San Domingo*, or some other saint under Spanish colours, and hailing from some port on the other side of the Horn. Our friend, Captain Brown, of the whaler, had better make haste, or she will be after him and his prize."

"Why not after us then?" I asked.

"Because Captain La Roche has had enough of your quality, I suspect," he replied. "He is a fellow who only fights when he is sure of booty, and though I daresay that he would like to send you to the bottom, he would not go out of his way either for revenge or glory."

To satisfy ourselves we examined the stranger as narrowly as we could, and O'Carroll was thoroughly convinced that he was right in his suspicions. While thus employed a man appeared at the companion watch.

"Why, there is La Roche himself!" he cried out. Scarcely had he spoken than a bullet whizzed by his head. "That settles the matter," he said, quite coolly. "Let us be out of this, or he will be following up this compliment." We hurried out of the dockyard. I proposed making a complaint to the authorities.

"And be detained here several weeks and gain

nothing in the end," he answered, shaking his head. " My advice is, get ready for sea as fast as you can, and if you wish to serve Captain Brown see him safe out of sight of land before the *Mignonne* can follow. We'll keep a watch on him in the meantime, or he'll play us some trick or other. Above all things, don't be on shore after dark. La Roche has plenty of friends here, depend on that, and he will find means to pick us off if he thinks that we are likely to inconvenience him."

Following O'Carroll's suggestions I immediately returned on board. Captain Hassall at first scarcely credited the account we gave him—indeed, he did not, I saw, put thorough confidence in O'Carroll. However, he agreed that we ought to warn Captain Brown, and that it would be well for us also to sail before the supposed privateer was ready for sea.

CHAPTER IV

WE had got our decks caulked, our rigging set up, and other repairs finished, when, one forenoon, O'Carroll, who had at length ventured on shore, returned in a great hurry with the information that there was much bustle on board the *Mignonne*, and that her people were evidently hurrying to the utmost to get ready for sea. Had Captain Hassall followed his own inclinations, he would have given the piratical Frenchman the opportunity of trying his strength with the *Barbara;* but as that would have been decidedly objected to by Garrard, Janrin and Co., we, with the whaler and her prize, and another English vessel, cleared out as secretly as we could, and, with a fair breeze, put to sea. We had to lay to for the other vessels, and after they had joined us Captain Brown hailed us, to say that the look-out from his maintopgallant masthead had seen a large ship coming out of the harbour under all sail, and that he thought it possible she might be the *Mignonne*. As, however, a mist had soon afterwards arisen, she was concealed from sight. We promised, however, to stand to the northward with Captain Brown during the night, and

in the morning, should no enemy be in sight, let him
and his consorts proceed on their voyage homewards,
while we kept on our course for the Cape of Good
Hope. Nothing could have given our people greater
satisfaction than to have found the Frenchman close
to us at daybreak. I spent most of the night in
writing letters home, to send by the whaler. When
morning dawned, not a sail, except our own little
squadron, was to be seen. We kept company till
noon, and then, with mutual good wishes, stood away
on our respective courses. We hoped that the *Mignonne* would follow the *Barbara* rather than our
friends, should she really have sailed in chase of any
of us. The possibility of our being pursued created
much excitement on board. At early dawn, till the
evening threw its mantle over the ocean, we had
volunteers at the mastheads looking out for a strange
sail. At the end of four or five days all expectation
of again meeting with the *Mignonne* ceased, somewhat
to the disappointment of most of the crew, who were
wonderfully full of fight. Having beaten the Frenchman once, they were very sure that they could beat
him again. We had other good reasons for having
our eyes about us—first, to avoid in time any foe too
big to tackle; and then, as we had the right to capture
any Spanish vessels we might fall in with, to keep a
look-out for them. However, the ocean is very broad,
and though we chased several vessels, they all proved
to be Portuguese. After sighting the little rocky and
then uninhabited island of Tristan D'Acunha, we made

4

the Cape of Good Hope, and, entering Table Bay, dropped our anchor off Capetown.

The colony had lately been recaptured from the Dutch by Sir David Baird and Sir Home Popham, with a well-appointed force of 5,000 men. The two armies met on the plain at the foot of Table Mountain ; but scarcely had the action been commenced by General Ferguson, at the head of the Highland brigade, than the wise Hollanders, considering that the English were likely to prove as good masters as the French, retreated, and soon after offered to capitulate, which they were allowed to do with all the honours of war. The Dutch, French, and English were now living on very friendly terms with each other. The Cape colony, with its clean, well-laid-out English capital, its Table Mountain and Table Cloth, its vineyards, its industrious and sturdy Boers, its Hottentot slaves, and its warlike Kaffirs, is too well known to require a description. I did a good deal of trading—a matter of private interest to Garrard, Janrin and Co., so I will not speak of it. The ship was put to rights, we enjoyed ourselves very much on shore, and were once more at sea. Strong easterly winds drove us again into the Atlantic, and when we had succeeded in beating back to the latitude of Capetown, the weather, instead of improving, looked more threatening than ever. I had heard of the peculiar swell off the Cape, but I had formed no conception of the immense undulations I now beheld. They came rolling on slow and majestically, solid-looking, like mountains of malachite, heaving up our stout ship as if she were a mere chip of deal cast on the face of the ocean. We were alone on the waste of waters, no other objects in sight besides these huge green masses, which, as the clouds gathered, were every instant becoming of a darker and more leaden hue.

"We shall get a breeze soon, and I hope that it will be from the right quarter for us," I remarked to Benjie Stubbs, the second mate, who had charge of the deck.

"We shall have a breeze, and more than we want, Pusser" (intended for Purser, a name Benjie always persisted in giving me), he answered, glancing round the horizon. "You've not seen anything like this before, eh ? A man must come to sea to know what's what. There are strange sights on the ocean."

"So I have always heard," I remarked.

"Yes, you'd have said so if you had been on deck last night in the middle watch," he observed, in a low tone.

"How so! what happened ?" I asked.

"Why, just this," he answered. "There was not more wind than there is now, and the sky was clear, with a slice of a moon shining brightly, when, just as I was looking along its wake, what did I see but a full-rigged, old-fashioned ship, under all sail, bearing down towards us at a tremendous rate. When she got within a couple of hundred fathoms of us she hove-to and lowered a boat. I guessed well enough what she was, so, running forward, I cast loose one of the guns and pointed at the boat. They aboard the stranger knew what I was after; the boat was hoisted in again, and away she went right in the teeth of the wind."

"Did you see this last night?" I asked, looking the mate in the face. "I should like to speak to some of the men who saw it at the same time."

"I don't say all saw it. You may ask those who did, and you won't get a different story from what I've told you," he replied.

"And what think you was the ship you saw?" I asked.

"The *Flying Dutchman*,* of course, and no manner of doubt about the matter," he answered promptly. "If you had been on the look-out you would have seen him as clearly as I did. Remember, Pusser, if you ever fall in with him, don't let him come aboard, that's all. He'll send you to the bottom as surely as if a red-hot shot was to be dropped into the hold."

"Who is this *Flying Dutchman*?" I asked, wishing to humour Benjie by pretending to believe his story.

"Why, as to that, there are two opinions," he answered, as if he was speaking of authenticated facts. "Some say that he was an honest trader, that he was bound in for Table Bay, when he was ordered off by the authorities, and that, putting to sea, he was lost; others say that he was a piratical gentleman, and that

---

* We never hear of the *Flying Dutchman* now-a-days. The fact is that he had the monopoly of sailing or going along rather in the teeth of the wind. Now steamers have cut him out, and he is fain to hide his diminished head.

on one occasion, when short of provisions, being driven off the land by contrary winds, he swore a great oath that he would beat about till the day of doom, but that get in he would. He and all his crew died of starvation, but the oath has been kept ; and when gales are threatening, or mischief of any kind brewing, he is to be met with, trying in vain to accomplish his vow."

I smiled at Benjie's account, whereat he pretended to look very indignant, as if I had doubted his veracity. I afterwards made inquiries among the seamen. Two or three asserted that they had witnessed an extraordinary sight during the night, but they all differed considerably in their accounts. It may be supposed that they were trying to practise on the credulity of a greenhorn. My belief is that they really fancied that they had seen what they described.

The clouds grew thicker and thicker till they got as black as ink. The sea became of a dark leaden hue, and the swell increased in height, so that when we sank down into the intermediate valley, we could not see from the deck beyond the watery heights on either side of us.

" Ah, the skipper is right; we shall have it before long, hot and furious."

This remark, made by Benjie Stubbs, followed the captain's order to send down all our lighter spars, and to make everything secure on deck, as well as below. The ship was scarcely made snug before the tempest broke on us. The high, smooth rollers were now torn and wrenched asunder as it were, their summits wreathed with masses of foam, which curled over as they advanced against the wind, and breaking into fragments, blew off in masses of snowy whiteness to leeward. I scarcely thought that a fabric formed by human hands could have sustained the rude shocks we encountered till the ship was got on her course, and we were able to scud before the gale. Often the sea rose up like a dead wall, and seemed as if it must fall over our deck and send us to the bottom. The scene was trying in the daytime, but still more so when darkness covered the face of the deep, and it needed confidence in the qualities of our ship, and yet greater in God's protecting power, not to feel overcome with dread. There was a grandeur in the spectacle which kept me on deck, and it was not till after the steward had frequently summoned me to supper that I could tear myself from it. Curious was the change to the well-lighted, handsome cabin, with the supper things securely placed between fiddles and puddings * on the swing table. The first mate had charge of the deck. Stubbs was busily employed fortifying his nerves. "You now know, Pusser, what a gale off the Cape is," he observed, looking up with his mouth half full of beef and biscuit.

"Yes, indeed," said I. "Fine weather, too, for your friend the *Dutchman* to be cruising."

"Ay, and likely enough we shall see him, too," he answered. "It was just such a night as this, some

* Contrivances to prevent articles falling off a table at sea.

five years back, that we fell in with him off here; and
our consort, as sound a ship as ever left the Thames,
with all hands, was lost. It's my belief that he put a
boat aboard her by one of his tricks." I saw Captain
Hassall and Irby exchange glances. Stubbs was getting
on his favourite subject.

" Well, now, I've doubled this Cape a dozen times or
more, and have never yet once set eyes on this Dutch
friend of yours, Benjie," exclaimed O'Carroll. " Mind
you call me if we sight his craft; I should like to ' ya,
ya' a little with him, and just ask him where he comes
from, and what he's about, and maybe if I put the
question in a civil way I'll get a civil answer." By-
the-bye, Captain Hassall and I had been so well pleased
with O'Carroll, and so satisfied as to his thorough
knowledge of the regions we were about to visit and
the language of the people, that we had retained him
on board as supernumerary mate.

" Don't you go and speak to him now, if you value
the safety of the ship, or our lives," exclaimed Stubbs,
in a tone of alarm. " You don't know what trick
he'll play you if you do. Let such gentry alone,
say I."

We all laughed at the second mate's earnestness,
though I cannot say that all the rest of those present
disbelieved in the existence of the condemned *Dutchman.* The state of the atmosphere, the strange, wild,
awful look of the ocean, prepared our minds for the
appearance of anything supernatural. The captain
told me that I looked ill and tired from having been

on deck so many hours, and insisted on my turning in, which I at length unwillingly did.

In spite of the upheaving motion of the ship, and the peculiar sensation as she rushed down the watery declivity into the deep valley between the seas, I fell asleep. The creaking of the bulkheads, the whistling of the wind in the rigging, the roaring of the seas, and their constant dash against the sides, were never out of my ears, and oftentimes I fancied that I was on deck witnessing the tumult of the ocean—now that the *Flying Dutchman* was in sight, now that our own good ship was sinking down overwhelmed by the raging seas.

" Mr. Stubbs wants you on deck, sir; she's in sight, sir, he says, she's in sight," I heard a voice say, while I felt my elbow shaken. The speaker was Jerry Nott, our cabin-boy. I slipped on my clothes, scarcely knowing what I was about.

" What o'clock is it ? " I asked. " Gone two bells in the morning watch," he answered. I sprang on deck. The dawn had broke. The wind blew as hard as ever. The sky and sea were of a leaden grey hue, the only spots of white were the foaming crests of the seas and our closely-reefed foretop sails. " There, there! Do you see her now ? " asked Stubbs, pointing ahead. As we rose to the top of a giant sea I could just discover in the far distance, dimly seen amid the driving spray, the masts of a ship, with more canvas set than I should have supposed would have been shown to such a gale. While I was looking I saw another ship not far beyond the first. We were clearly nearing them.

" What do you think of that ? " asked Stubbs.

"That there are two ships making very bad weather of it, Mr. Stubbs," answered the captain, who at that moment had come on deck.　He took a look through his glass.

" She is a large ship—a line-of-battle ship, I suspect," he observed.

" Looks like one," said Stubbs.　" She'll look like something else by-and-by."

The rest of the officers had now joined us except Mr. Randolph, who had the middle watch.　We were all watching the strangers together.　Now, as we sank down into the hollow, the masses of spray which blew off from the huge sea uprising between us and them, hid them from our sight.　Some differed with the captain as to the size of the largest ship.　One or two thought that she was an Indiaman.　However, she was still so distant, and in the grey dawn so misty-looking and indistinct, that it was difficult to decide the question.　The captain himself was not certain. " However, we shall soon be able to settle the matter," he observed, as the *Barbara*, now on the summit of a. mountain billow, was about to glide down the steep incline.　Down, down, we went—it seemed that we should never be able to climb the opposite height. We were all looking out for the strangers, expecting to settle the disputed point.　" Where are they ? " burst from the lips of all of us.　" Where, where ? " We looked, we rubbed our eyes—no sail was in sight. "I knew it would be so," said Stubbs, in a tone in which I perceived a thrill of horror. O'Carroll asserted that he had caught sight of the masts of a ship as if sinking beneath the waves.

"Very likely," observed Stubbs, "that was of the ship he was sending to the bottom,—the other was the *Dutchman*, and you don't see her now."

"No, no, they were craft carrying human beings, and they have foundered without a chance of one man out of the many hundreds on board being saved!" exclaimed the captain.

Stubbs shook his head as if he doubted it. We careered on towards the spot where the ships had gone down, for that real ships had been there no doubt could be entertained. A strict look-out was kept for anything that might still be floating to prove that we had not been deceived by some phantom forms. Those on the look-out forward reported an object ahead. "A boat! a boat!" shouted one of them. "No boat could live in such a sea," observed the captain. He was right. As we approached, we saw a grating, to which a human being was clinging. It was, when first seen, on the starboard bow, and it was, alas! evident that we should leave him at too great a distance even to heave a rope to which he might clutch. By his dress he appeared to be a seaman. He must have observed our approach; but he knew well enough that we could make no attempt to save him. He gazed at us steadily as we glided by—his countenance seemed calm—he uttered no cry—still he clung to his frail raft. He could not make up his mind to yield to death. It was truly a painful sight. We anxiously watched him till we left the raft to which he still clung far astern. No other person was seen, but other objects were seen—floating spars, planks, gratings—to prove that we were near a spot where a tall ship had gone down. " It is better so," observed the captain; " unless the sea had cast them on our deck we could not have saved one of them." We rushed on up and down the watery heights, Stubbs as firmly convinced as ever that the *Flying Dutchman* had produced the fearful catastrophe we had witnessed.

On we went—the gale in no way abating. I watched the mountain seas till I grew weary of looking at them; still I learned to feel perfectly secure—a sensation I was at first very far from experiencing. Yet much, if not everything, depended on the soundness of our spars and rigging : a.flaw in the wood or rope might be the cause of our destruction. I went below at meal-time, but I hurried again on deck, fascinated by the scene, though I would gladly have shut it out from my sight. At length, towards night, literally wearied with the exertion of keeping my feet and watching those giant seas, I went below and turned in. I slept, but the huge white-crested waves were still rolling before me, and big ships were foundering, and phantom vessels were sailing in the wind's eye, and I heard the bulkheads creaking, the wind whistling, and the waves roaring, as loudly as if I was awake; only I often assigned a wrong sign to the uproar. Hour after hour this continued, when, as I had

at last gone off more soundly, a crash echoed in my
ears, followed by shrieks and cries. It did not, however, awake me. It seemed a part of the strange
dreams in which I was indulging. I thought that the
ship had struck on a rock, that I escaped to the shore,
had climbed up a lofty cliff, on the summit of which
I found a wood fire surrounded by savages. They
dragged me to it—I had the most fearful forebodings
of what they were about to do. Then I heard the
cry, "Fire! fire!" That was a reality—the smell of
fire was in my nostrils—I started up—I was alone in
the cabin. The ship was plunging about in an awful
manner. I hurried on my clothes and rushed on
deck. Daylight had broke. The ship lately so trim
seemed a perfect wreck. The foremast had been
carried away, shivered to the deck, and hung over the
bows, from which part of the crew were endeavouring
to clear it. The main and mizen topmasts had likewise been carried away. Smoke was coming up the
fore hatchway, down which the rest of the people
were pouring buckets of water. I went forward to
render assistance. The foremast had been struck by
lightning, and the electric fluid, after shattering it, had
descended into the hold and set the ship on fire. We
worked with the desperation of despair. Should the
fire once gain the mastery, no human power could
save us. The sea was running as high as ever; it was
with difficulty that the ship could be kept before it.
I exchanged but a few words with my companions; a
bucket was put into my hands, and I at once saw

what I had to do. The smoke after a time had decreased, for as yet no flames had burst forth. " Now, lads, follow me," cried Randolph, the first officer, leaping below with his bucket and an axe in his hand. Irby and four men sprang after him. With his axe the mate cut a way to get at the heart of the fire. We handed down buckets to his companions, who kept emptying them round where he was working. The smoke was still stifling. Those below could scarcely be seen as they worked amidst it. The bulkhead was cut through. The seat of the mischief was discovered. Flames were bursting forth, but wet blankets were thrown on them. The buckets were passed rapidly down. The smoke was decreasing. " Hurrah, lads! we shall have it under!" cried the first mate, in an encouraging tone. We breathed more freely. The fire was subdued. The peril had indeed been great. We had now to clear the wreck of the mast, which threatened to stave in the bows. " The gale is breaking," cried the captain, after looking round the horizon; " cheer up, my lads, and we shall do well!" Encouraged by the captain the men laboured on, though from the violent working of the ship it was not without great difficulty and danger that the mass of spars, ropes, and canvas could be hauled on board or cast adrift. As a landsman my assistance was not of much value, though I stood by clinging to the bulwarks, to lend a hand in case I should be required.

While glancing to windward, as I did every now

and then, in hopes of seeing signs of the abatement of the gale, I caught sight of what seemed the wing of an albatross, skimming the summit of a tossing sea. I looked again and again. There it still was as at first. I pointed it out to the captain. "A sail running down towards us," he observed; "it is to be hoped that she is a friend, for we are in a sorry plight to meet with a foe." The captain's remark made me feel not a little anxious as to the character of the approaching stranger. After a time it became evident that the wind was really falling. The wreck of the mast was at last cleared away, but a calm sea would be required before we could attempt to get up a jurymast. We had watched the approach of the stranger: she was steering directly for us. As she drew nearer I saw O'Carroll examining her narrowly through the glass. "Here comes the *Flying Dutchman* again," I observed to Stubbs.

"Not at all certain that she isn't," he answered, quite in a serious tone.

"No, she's not that, but she's ten times worse," exclaimed O'Carroll; "she is the *Mignonne*, as I am a seaman, and will be bothering us pretty considerably, depend on that."

We heartily hoped that he was mistaken, but certainly she was very like the craft we had seen at St. Salvador. She passed us as near as the heavy sea still running would allow her to do without danger to herself. A man was standing in the mizen rigging. I caught sight of his face through my telescope. I thought that I distinguished a look of satisfaction in his countenance as he gazed at us. "That's La Roche; I know the villain!" cried O' Carroll; "I thought from what I heard that he was bound out here. He'll work us ill, depend on that." We now wished that the sea had continued to run as high as it had hitherto been doing, when it would have been impossible for the privateer to have boarded us. It was now, however, rapidly going down, though as yet it was too rough to allow her to attempt to run alongside. It was possible that she might pass us. No! After running on a short distance her yards were braced sharp up, and she stood back, with the evident intention of attacking our helpless craft.

CHAPTER V.

A DESPERATE ENCOUNTER.

O'CARROLL'S alarm increased as he saw the privateer approaching. "We shall all have our throats cut to a certainty," he cried out. "They will not leave one of us alive to go home to our disconsolate widows to tell them all that has happened. I know them too well, the villains! Arrah! it was an unfortunate moment that ever I was brought to tumble twice into the hands of such gentry."

"We are not in their hands yet, and if we make a good fight of it, maybe we never shall," exclaimed Captain Hassall. "My lads, if you'll stand by me, I'll hold out as long as the craft can float. We beat off this same fellow once before—let's try if we can't beat him off again."

This brief address inspirited our crew, and, almost worn out with fatigue as they were, they promised to defend themselves to the last. My sensations, as we saw the enemy approach, were not altogether pleasant. We might beat him off in the end; but even that, in our present condition, was not likely; and how many of our number might not be struck down in the struggle! In the meantime, the men armed them-

selves with pistols and cutlasses, powder and shot
were got up, and every preparation made for the fight.
The enemy approached, but as he had run to leeward,
it was some time before he could work up to pass us
to windward. We had carried a stay from the mainmast to the bowsprit, and on this we managed to set
a sail, so that the ship was tolerably under control.
When the enemy, therefore, at last passed under our
stern, we were able to luff up and avoid the raking
fire he poured in. No damage was done to any of our
people, but a shot struck the mainmast, and wounded
it so badly that it was evident that, with any addi-
tional strain, it would be carried away altogether.
Putting up the helm, we again ran off before the wind.
The enemy was soon after us, but though he came up
abeam in the heavy sea still running, his aim was of
necessity uncertain, and for some time not a shot struck
us, while several of ours struck him. This encouraged
our men, who gave vent to their satisfaction whenever
he was hulled, or a shot went through his sails. Our
hopes of success were, however, soon brought to an
end, for, as we were compelled to luff up suddenly, to
avoid being raked, as he was about to cross our bows,
the heavy strain on our wounded mast carried it away,
and with it the mizen topmast, and there we lay a
helpless wreck in the trough of the sea, at the mercy
of the enemy. Still, as we could work our guns we
would not give in, but hoisting our flag on the mizen-
mast we continued firing as long as we could bring
our guns to bear. A loud cheer burst from the throats

5

of our crew; the Frenchman was standing away. This
exultation was rather too precipitate. As soon as he
got out of range of our guns, he hove-to and began
firing away from a long gun, the shot from which
occasionally hit us. One poor fellow was killed and
two wounded. It was clear that the privateer was
merely waiting till the sea should go down, when he
would run alongside and capture us without difficulty.

Captain Hassall at last, seeing what must inevitably
occur, called the officers round him, and proposed sur-
rendering. "The villains will cut all our throats if we
do, that's all," observed O'Carroll. "I would rather
hold out to the last and sell our lives dearly." Most
of us were of O'Carroll's opinion.

"Very well, gentlemen, so let it be," said the captain.
"I have done my duty in offering to surrender, when
I consider that successful resistance is hopeless; still
I agree with you that it would be better to die fight-
ing than to be murdered in cold blood."

When our guns became useless, the crew had been
set to work to clear the wreck of the mainmast, and
to prepare sheers for a jury foremast. "And this is to
be the termination of our enterprise," I thought. I
must own I gave way to some bitter reflection. While
all hands were busily employed, I turned my eyes
westward, and there, in the very place where the
Mignonne had appeared, I saw another white sail.
I pointed her out to the captain. "She may be a
friend, and turn the tables," he observed. "If a foe
we shall not be worse off than at present."

It soon became known that a sail was in sight. The crew came to the conclusion that she was a friend. The Frenchmen at last saw her. Whatever opinion they formed, they judged that it would be wise to finish the fight and take possession of us. Once more the enemy drew near. The firing became hotter than ever. I turned many an anxious glance at the approaching sail. I felt sure that, in spite of the staunchness of our men, we must inevitably be overpowered. The stranger was getting closer and closer.

"She is a frigate!" cried the captain. "She shows English colours! hurrah! hurrah!" The enemy saw that the chance of capturing us was gone. Sweeping round us, with diabolical malice he gave a parting broadside, which killed one man and wounded another, and then under all the sail he could set ran off before the wind. The frigate had now also made more sail and closed as rapidly. She came close to us. "Are you in a sinking state?" asked a voice from the frigate. "I hope not," answered Captain Hassall. "Then hold on and we'll come back to you," said the voice, which we took to be that of the captain. As I was watching the frigate through my glass, as she rushed by us, who should I see standing in the main rigging but my own midshipman brother William! I waved heartily to him, but he did not make me out. From my usual sedate manners, my shipmates seeing my gestures thought that I had gone mad, and was waving to be taken on board the frigate. "She is the *Phœbe* frigate," I exclaimed, jumping out of the rigging on deck. "No fear that we shall be deserted now!" I then explained how I came to know the name of the frigate. All hands were now set to work to get the ship to rights.

The chase, meantime, became very exciting. "The captain does not know what a fast pair of heels that privateering scoundrel possesses, or he would not have much hopes of catching him," observed Captain Hassall, as he watched the two vessels. The topsails of the Frenchman soon disappeared beneath the horizon, and the shades of evening at length closing down, we were left alone on the world of waters, into which the heavy swell made us roll our sides till we almost dipped our bulwarks under—each time showers of spray being sent dripping off them. The enemy had made several shot holes in our sides, and those were now, we found, taking in the water faster than was altogether agreeable. The carpenter and his mates had indeed hard work to stop them. I have heard of people's hair turning white in a single night. I felt as if mine would, for it became doubtful if after all the ship would swim, from the quantity of water she was taking in. We, indeed, had reason to regret that we had allowed the frigate to leave us. At last the morning broke. We eagerly looked round the horizon. No sail was in sight. Would the ship float another day? The shot holes had been stopped, but should bad weather again come on it would be impossible to say what would be the effect on the vessel. Noon came, but no sail was in sight. We were afraid that the cunning privateer had led the frigate a long chase, perhaps among shoals and reefs, and that she had got on shore, and that we might not see the frigate again.

"More likely that she was only the *Flying Dutchman*, taking a longer cruise than usual," muttered Stubbs. "There's no saying what tricks that fellow is not up to."

"What, not got the *Dutchman* out of your head yet, Stubbs?" said Randolph. "Why, Biddulph saw his brother on board, and two or three of our people know the *Phœbe*, and recognised her."

"Yes, I know that's what often happens. The *Dutchman* can make his ship look like any vessel he chooses," persisted Stubbs; "naturally—that is to say as she generally appears—she is a curious old-fashioned rigged craft—you may depend on that."

While we were speaking—taking a breath between our labours, for all hands had been working hard—"A sail, a sail!" was shouted by one of the seamen. We all looked in the direction in which he pointed, and there appeared the upper sails of a ship. Our hopes made us believe that it was the frigate. "As likely the Frenchman come to finish us off, or maybe only the *Flying Dutchman* again," said Stubbs. I thought that I detected a gleam of humour in his eye, as if he was not quite so credulous as he pretended to be. As the stranger approached, the belief that she was the *Phœbe* gained ground. At length those who knew her best said that there was no doubt about the matter. They were right. Before dark she hove-to close to us, and a boat with a midshipman in her boarded us.

The midshipman was my brother William. He almost tumbled back with surprise at seeing me, for he did not even know that I was coming out.

"Why, James, where have you sprung from?" he exclaimed. "I am thankful to see you unhurt, for we have been anxious about you all day. Couldn't tell how much damage the rascal might have done you. Well, he escaped after all. He has a fast pair of heels, indeed, and he led us a pretty chase, till he got in among some reefs, on which we were nearly leaving our bones. We saw our danger, however, and by the time we were clear he was out of sight."

The boat's crew were directed to remain on board to put the ship to rights. When, however, Captain Young found that this would occupy some time, he offered to take us in tow. A hawser was accordingly passed on board, and away we went in the wake of the frigate. Our course was for the Isle of Bourbon, lately captured from the French. At the end of a week we anchored in the Bay of St. Paul in that island. On our way there we had done our best to get the ship in order. Our crew were now set to work in earnest, aided by some of the men of the *Phœbe*, who were kindly spared to us by her captain. I took the opportunity of seeing something of the island. My brother William and some of the other midshipmen of the *Phœbe* got leave to accompany me, and merry parties we had.

Bourbon is about one hundred and fifty miles in circumference, and rises rapidly from the sea, forming one huge blunt-topped mountain in the centre; indeed, the whole island is not unlike a big tea-cup in the middle of the ocean, with some rather large cracks, however, in it. It is generally fertile, coffee and cotton being grown on it. On the south side, a few miles from the sea, there is a volcano, which grumbled and growled, but seldom did more than send forth a little smoke. The inhabitants did not appear to be at all soured at having been placed under British rule.

Probably, indeed, it was a matter of indifference to them, for they have themselves sprung from a mixture of half the races under the sun. Many of the inhabitants are descended from some of those English pirates whose headquarters were, for nearly a hundred years, on the island of Madagascar, but who, about the middle of the seventeenth century, growing weary of their lawless calling, settled here. As their wives were mostly from Madagascar, they are somewhat darkish, but not bad-looking. They are a lively, merry race, fond of dancing, and their climate is delightful. The names of some of the families belonging to the island are derived from the English, as are those of several places. I remember a bay in Madagascar, Antongil Bay, which clearly takes its name from the well-known pirate-leader, Antony Gill, who robbed and murdered on the high seas early in the seventeenth century.

A squadron and troops were collecting here, the latter under General Abercrombie, for an expedition to the Mauritius. We were greatly disappointed, I

must own, that our ship was not in a condition to
proceed to sea, or we should have been chartered to
convey troops and been witnesses of the triumphs we
hoped they would achieve. My object is, however,
to describe my own adventures in the pursuit of
pacific commerce. I will thus only briefly say that
the expedition arrived speedily off the Mauritius, the
troops were landed, and that after some sharp fighting,
by which we lost one hundred and fifty men killed
and wounded, the French General, De Caen, capitulated.
We had several sepoy regiments, and the French general,
in order to inspire the colonial troops with contempt for
them, publicly promised that whoever should capture
a sepoy should have him for a slave; but the militia
appear to have thought that by so doing they might
possibly catch a Tartar, for not a sepoy was made
prisoner.

I made some satisfactory sales at Bourbon, and as
soon as the ship was repaired she followed the men-of-
war to the Isle of France. The island is about thirty-
five miles long, and one hundred and fifteen in
circumference, with a surface greatly diversified by
hill and plain, wood and plantation, with several considerable mountains, the chief of which, Le Pouce and
Pieter Botte, in the neighbourhood of Port Louis, are
well known. The harbour was a complete forest of
masts, filled with vessels of all sorts and sizes, from the
huge line-of-battle ship to the humble canoe, not unlike
a butcher's tray, scooped out of a single log. The British
flag waved triumphantly on all the batteries; and India-

men, transport prizes, merchant craft of all descriptions,
displayed English colours, in most cases flying over
the French. Numerous boats, too, were plying to and
fro filled with naval and military officers, captains of
Indiamen, sailors, lascars, negroes, and Frenchmen,
some on business, some on pleasure, but all seeming to
be in a hurry. I looked out with no little curiosity
for any craft which might answer the description of
our late antagonist, the *Mignonne.* If she had entered
the harbour, she had again escaped before the capture
of the place, for she was nowhere to be seen. It would
have been satisfactory to have seen our friend caged,
but it was too probable that he was still roving over
the ocean, on the watch to plunder any English craft
he could venture to attack.

The scene on shore was even more animated than
on the water. The streets were crowded with people
of many nations: naval and military officers, English
and French Government civilians, merchants and
other traders, Asiatics and negroes, almost naked
slaves dragging along horse-loads in carts, with
mongrels of every shade of colour. The town, though
in a bustle, was perfectly orderly ; the shops were all
open, and their owners seemed to be driving a thriving
trade, as were also the keepers of taverns, which were
full of visitors from fleet and camp. We fortunately
had several articles among the cargo of the *Barbara*,
of which our countrymen were much in want, not to
be found in the stores of the place. They were, however, quickly disposed of, and I was then at leisure to

amuse myself as I thought fit. I made several excursions on shore with my brother when he could get leave, and I had thus an opportunity of learning the productions of the island. The chief food of the lower orders and slaves is yams and the *jatropha*, or cassada, of which there are two species commonly known, the *jatropha janipha*, and the *jatropha manihot*. The former contains a strong vegetable poison, which is destroyed by boiling; the latter is merely slightly narcotic in its effects, and both are easily converted into wholesome food. The root, after being well washed and dried in the sun, is usually scraped into a coarse powder, from which the juice is expressed: it is then dried a second time and formed into thin cakes, very similar in appearance to Scotch barley-cakes. The bread thus made is called manioc. Tapioca is also a preparation of the root. Plantains, bananas, melons, and mangoes abound, and the last are especially fine. The climate is healthy, but the Mauritius is occasionally visited by terrific hurricanes, which commit great damage both afloat and on shore.

We soon made friends among the French residents, and one of them, with whom I had had some transactions, invited William and me, and a military acquaintance, Captain Mason, to his house in the country. We were most hospitably entertained by our worthy host. The house was large and airy, with a verandah running round it on one side sufficiently broad to enable us to sit out and enjoy the cool breeze, while we sipped our coffee. We had proposed returning that evening, but the wind got up, it rained heavily, and became very dark. Our host pressed us to stay, and as William's leave extended to the next morning we accepted his invitation, he undertaking to put my brother on board in time. Our companion, Captain Mason, was a quiet, amiable man. He was married, and as he expected to remain on the island, he had, he told us, sent for his wife from the Cape of Good Hope, where he had left her. I cannot now describe the incidents of our visit.

The next morning, soon after daybreak, having taken an early breakfast of a lighter character than suited our English appetites, we drove back to Port Louis. The weather had grown worse instead of improving, and as we drew near the town we saw in the distance two vessels with English colours approaching the harbour. William had to hurry on board his ship, but Mason and I drove on to a spot where we could see them enter. One gained an anchorage in safety, but the other still continued outside, steering wildly, as if uncertain what course to take. It was soon evident that she was in great danger. While we were looking on, Captain Hassall joined us. There were a number of naval officers, masters of merchantmen, and others collected on the shore. " She is said to have a pilot on board, and an ignorant fellow he must be, or he would have anchored outside ere this if he could not get in," observed Captain Hassall. While he was speaking, the vessel got into the swell of the sea which was dashing on the rocks close at hand. Rapidly she came drifting towards them. Probably the master then asserted his authority, for two anchors were let go.

The fate of the ship, and probably of all on board, depended on the anchors holding. With deep anxiety we watched her as the huge swells came rolling in. towards the rocks. A cry arose from the collected crowd—"The cables have parted—the cables have parted!" The hapless craft was lifted by the next surge, and hurried on amid the foaming breakers towards the rocks. At that instant the foresail was set, in the hopes of its helping to force her over them. It was useless; down she came with a tremendous .crash on the black rocks. For a few minutes she continued beating on them, rocking to and fro in the wildest agitation; then a huge surge, which appeared to have been for some time collecting its strength, struck her on the side, and rolled her over, as if she had been merely a child's plaything, towards the shore, to all appearance overwhelmed, so as never to rise again. The wild breakers dashed triumphantly over her, but she was not conquered, though it seemed a wonder that wood and iron should hold together under the tremendous shocks she was receiving. Once more she rose to an erect position, and it was seen that her dauntless crew were endeavouring to cut away her masts. "It is the only thing they can do to save their lives," observed Hassall, watching them through his glass. "And see,—yes—there is a woman on board—a lady by her dress. She is clinging to the windlass—probably secured to it." As he was speaking, the mizenmast

came down, followed quickly by the mainmast, which happily fell towards the shore. Again a surge covered the vessel. We feared that all on board would be swept from the decks; but when again the surge receded, the people were seen clinging fast as before. A boat from one of the men-of-war now approached the wreck, but the officer in command soon saw that he should only throw away his own life and the lives of those with him if he should attempt to go near enough to receive any one on board. The foremast now fell, and still the stout ship hung together. Other boats came up and got as near as it was possible to go. That those on board thought she would not hold together much longer was evident by the efforts they began to make to escape.

First we observed a man descend the foremast as if with the intention of swimming ashore. His courage, however, forsook him; he paused and returned. Again he climbed along the mast, but hesitated—it was indeed a desperate undertaking. At length he cast himself into the water: immediately he was overwhelmed. Would he ever again reach the surface? "Yes! yes! there he is," cried out several. For a moment he was seen struggling bravely. A groan escaped from the spectators: "He's gone! he's gone ". No, no, he is still floating," many shouted out. So he was; but whirled here and there, blinded and confused, he was unable to guide himself. He was seen, happily, from one of the boats: she dashed forward, and he was hauled on board without apparently having struck a rock. All this time the people on the wreck had been watching him with intense anxiety, especially the poor lady: "If a strong and bold swimmer could scarcely be saved, what chance had she?" Hassall made the remark. "Not one would have a prospect of being saved if trusting only to his own strength; but there is a Ruler above," said Captain Mason, who had hitherto been watching the wreck without speaking; "He may save that poor woman on the wreck as easily as the strongest seaman." I have often since thought of my friend's remark. It is not our own right arm, but God in heaven, without whose knowledge not a sparrow falls to the ground, who preserves us in many dangers. Captain Mason begged for the use of Hassall's glass, and looked steadfastly through it at the wreck. "It is impossible, yet the figure is like—I cannot make it out," I heard him say. The success of the first man induced another to attempt reaching the shore. He hurried along to the end of the mast and threw himself into the water. The boiling surges whirled him round and round—now he was concealed by the foam—now he appeared struggling onward—still it seemed scarcely possible that he could escape from the boiling cauldron—just then a broken spar floated near him. Had the end struck him he must have been lost, but it came on so that he could clutch the middle. Tightly he grasped it till like his shipmate he was floated near one of the boats and taken on board. Two other men, encouraged by the success of the first,

attempted to reach the boats by the same means, but
scarcely had they committed themselves to the water
when a huge roller came roaring on, dashing over the
ship, and as it receded swept them off far away to
sea; for a moment their forms were seen struggling
amidst the foam, and then they were hid for ever
from human eye. The lives of the remainder on board
seemed more than ever in danger. Should the storm
increase, of which there seemed every probability, the
ship must go to pieces, even if they were not first
washed off the deck, and then what effort could save
them? I was more than ever interested in their fate,
when suddenly the idea occurred to me that the lady
on board might be the wife of my friend Mason. I
thought that he had the same idea, though he would
not allow himself to entertain it, by the agitation he
exhibited, and which he in vain tried to control. As
yet the men who had been saved had not been brought
on shore. More boats were coming down the harbour.
At length a fine whale-boat was brought down not far
from where we were standing. A naval officer, whose
name I regret that I did not note, volunteered to take
the command, and to go alongside the wreck, if
volunteers could be found to man her. Hassall at
once offered his services, as did several other masters
of merchantmen standing by, and they were accepted.
Mason and I also volunteered. "Not unless you are
seamen," was the answer. "This work requires firm
nerves and skilful hands."

I must observe here that I have ever found the

officers of the mercantile marine ready to go forth, in spite of all dangers, to save the lives of their fellow-creatures. Though there are exceptions, the greater number are as gallant fellows as any of those who have fought the battles of our country.

The boat was manned and ready to go off, but it became a question whether it would be wise to wait on the prospect of the sea going down, or to risk all and to go off at once on the possibility of the gale increasing. The men who had been rescued were brought on shore. Mason hurried to them, and eagerly inquired who was the woman on board. They were common seamen, and did not know her name. She was a lady, and had come on board at Cape Town just as the ship was sailing. That was all they knew. The naval officer had earnestly been watching the huge rollers as they came tumbling on towards the shore. Suddenly he cried out, "Now, gentlemen, we'll be off." Away went the boat amid the foaming seas towards the hapless wreck.

CHAPTER VI

HASSALL had left me his telescope. I could see the people on board the wreck stretching out their hands towards the boat as she left the shore on her errand of mercy. Mason every now and then asked for the glass and looked towards the wreck. He seemed more and more convinced that the lady on board was his wife. Yet could he do nothing? Yes, he could. Though he could not exert his body I saw that he was doing all that man in his utmost extremity can do. His lips were moving, his head was bent forward, his eyes glancing at times at the boat and the ship, his hands were clasped tightly in prayer, forgetful of the crowds surrounding him. The boat, impelled by lusty strokes, darted on. She reached the wreck. The lady was lifted in. No one seemed inclined to follow. The danger was fearful. Not before, since she struck, had one of the huge rollers failed at much shorter intervals to dash over and over the ship. Should one of them overtake the boat her fate would be sealed. On came the boat towards the beach. A number of seamen rushed down into the surf to receive her and haul·her up as soon as she

6

should touch the sand. The excitement among the crowd was tremendous. Far off I saw one of these huge billows rushing onwards. If it broke before the boat could reach the beach it would overwhelm her. The least excited of the crowd, to all appearance, was my friend Captain Mason. He advanced slowly towards the spot which it seemed probable the boat would reach, then he stopped for a moment. On she came, her keel grated on the sand, sturdy shoulders bore her along upwards, and ere the coming roller burst she was safe beyond its reach. The lady lay almost overcome in the stern sheets. Mason uttered. his wife's name, she looked up, and in another moment she was placed in his arms. A communication was afterwards established between the wreck and the shore, and most of the crew landed before the gale again came down with redoubled fury. By the morning scarce a vestige of the ship remained. I had the pleasure of seeing Mrs. Mason completely recovered two days afterwards, and thankful for her providential escape.

My brother William got leave of absence for three or four days, and he was anxious to spend the time in a cruise along the coast, and to get me to accompany him. I had wound up my mercantile business at the place, but as the *Barbara* would be detained a few days longer to complete her repairs, in a weak moment I consented to his proposal, as if we had not enough knocking about on salt water in the pursuit of our professional duties. It is difficult to put old heads on young shoulders. We did not remember that it was still the stormy season, and that the natives might not be so inclined to be civil to us, their late conquerors, coming in a half-decked boat with fowling-pieces, as they would had we appeared under the protection of he frigate's guns.

We agreed that it would be as well to have companions. I asked O'Carroll, who was very ready to come, and William brought a friend, whom he introduced as " My messmate, Toby Trundle." His name was a curious one—at first I did not suppose that it was anything but a nickname—and he himself was one of the oddest little fellows I ever met. From the first glance I had of him, I fancied that he was rather a young companion for my brother, but a second look showed me that he was fully his age. We had hired a craft, a schooner-rigged, half-decked boat, about five-and-twenty feet long, with a well aft, in which we could sit comfortably enough. She was not a bad boat for smooth water, but if caught in a heavy sea, very likely to drown all on board.

Our crew consisted of a Frenchman, Paul Jacotot, the owner of the *Dore*, as our craft was called, his son Auguste, a boy of thirteen, and Jack Nobs, a boy I brought from the *Barbara*. The Frenchman was to act as pilot and cook. The boys were to scrape the potatoes—or rather prepare the yams, for we had none of the former root—and tend the head-sheets. A boatswain's mate, Sam Kelson, who had been in hospital, had been allowed to accompany the midship-

men before returning on board. The two midshipmen
were to act as officers. O'Carroll, whom they did not
know was a sailor, and I, were to be passengers, and
the rest of the party were rated as crew. We had laid
in all sorts of provisions, an ample supply for the few
days we were to be away. Port Louis, it must be
remembered, is on the north side of the island, and we
had agreed to make our cruise to the eastward, where
there are some small islands—Gunners Coin and Flat
Island. If the wind should prove favourable we hoped
to circumnavigate the island. With a fair breeze off
the land, and Le Pouce seen standing up astern beyond
the town, we sailed out of the harbour, the weather
being as fine as heart could desire. William and Toby
Trundle took it by turns to steer, Jacotot pointing out
the dangers to be avoided, for we kept close in shore
for the sake of the scenery. Toby Trundle sat aft
steering, looking, in a broad-brimmed straw hat, a
white jacket and trowsers, contrasting with his sunburnt complexion, more like a monkey than a midshipman. Jacotot, when not engaged in any culinary
matter below, was jabbering away at a rapid rate to
us, if we would listen; if not, he was addressing his
son, whom he kept constantly on the move, now
scolding, now praising with terms of tender endear-
ment.

We enjoyed ourselves, and lunched and dined with
great contentment, voting Jacotot a first-rate *chef*,
which he undoubtedly was. He was, however, a
better cook than seaman we before long discovered.

"The next prize we take I hope that we shall find some cooks on board; we must secure one for our mess," observed Toby, helping himself to one of the dishes Jacotot had sent aft. I had not been long on board before I found out, what seemed to have escaped the midshipmen's observation when they hired the boat, that the rigging was sadly rotten, and that she herself was in a somewhat leaky condition. They, however, only laughed at the leaking. "It will keep the boat sweet, and give Jack Nobs and Auguste something to do," observed Master Trundle, cocking his 'eye at me. Notwithstanding this, we stood on, the breeze shifting conveniently in our favour till nightfall, when we put into a small harbour, the entrance to which our pilot for a wonder knew. The next day we continued our course, landing in a bay, up which we ran to have a look at the country, and to get some goat's milk and fruit. We found a small farm, the only white people being an old-fashioned Frenchman, with a somewhat dingy wife, and two grown-up daughters. All the rest of the people were either brown Orientals or black Africans. The old Frenchman was very civil, merely shrugged his shoulders when he saw our flag, and observed that it was the fortune of war, and that, as we were the most numerous, France had 'lost no honour, though she lost the dependency. He supplied us for a trifle with a bottle of goat's milk, and as many melons, pines, and mangoes as we could manage to eat. He politely assisted in taking them down to the boat. As he did so he looked round the horizon seaward, and up at the sky. "Messieurs will do well to remain at anchor for a few hours longer," he observed. "We are going to have a change of weather. It may be slight, or it may be very great, and you will be more content on shore than at sea." We thanked him for his advice, but the midshipmen asserting that if we stopped they might not be able to rejoin their ship at the right time, it was disregarded. On standing out again, however, we saw that the hope of getting round the island was vain, and that our surest course would be to return by the way we had come. The weather soon changed; ugly clouds collected and came sweeping up from the west and south, though as yet but little wind filled our sails.

"I am afraid that we are going to have a storm," I observed.

"Oh, no fear; I don't think that there will be anything in it," answered Toby Trundle.

"I think that there'll be a great deal in it, and I would advise you gentlemen to make the best of your way back to the bay we have just left," said O'Carroll.

The midshipmen looked at him as much as to say, What do you know about the matter? Jacotot was too busy cooking an omelette to attend to the weather, or he should have warned us. The question was settled by a sudden gust which came off the land, and laid the boat on her beam-ends. I thought we were going to capsize, and so we should, but crack away went both our masts, and the boat righted, one-third full of water. We all looked at each other for a moment aghast. It was a mercy that no one was washed overboard. A second and stronger gust followed the first, and on drove the boat helplessly before it. "You'll pump and bale out the water, and get on board the wreck of the masts," said O'Carroll, quietly.

We followed his advice as best we could. Jacotot, who was attending to his little stove below when the squall struck us, popped up his head with his white nightcap on, and his countenance so ludicrously expressive of dismay that, in spite of the danger we were in, Trundle burst into a fit of laughter. The Frenchman had not time to get out before the vessel righted. He now emerged completely, and frantically seizing his cap, tore it off his head and threw it into the boiling water. He then joined in hauling on board the wreck of the rigging.

"If we are to save our lives we must forthwith rig a jurymast, so as to keep the boat before the gale," observed O'Carroll.

With the aid of a wood-axe we knocked out the stump of the foremast, and making a fresh heel to the broken spar, managed, in spite of the rolling of the boat, to slip it into its place. This was done not a moment too soon. The wind increased so rapidly, and blew with such fearful violence, that we should have been unable to accomplish the task, though as yet there was not much sea.

O'Carroll showed that he was a man for an emer-

gency. " This will be more than a gale," he observed;
" it will be a regular hurricane! we may expect that.
But still, if we manage properly, we may save our
lives."

Close-reefing the foresail, we got it ready to hoist
as a square sail; the rest of the spars we lashed fore
and aft on either side, while we cut up the mainsail
and raised the gunwale a foot or more all round to
help keep out the water. We also, as far as we could.
covered in the after-part of the little craft. While we
were thus engaged the boys were pumping and baling,
This task was scarcely accomplished before the wind'
had blown us helplessly so far off the land that we
became exposed to the full violence of the sea, which
had rapidly risen. The water was leaping on every
side tumultuously—the foam flying in thick masses
off it—each sea, as it rose high above our heads,
threatening to overwhelm us.

We gazed wistfully at the land which we had so
unwisely left, but we had no power of returning
there. Our only prospect of passing amidst the heavy
seas now rolling around us was to hoist our sail and
scud before the wind.

O'Carroll now took the helm. " I have had more
experience in these seas than you, young gentlemen,
and the slightest want of care may send such a craft
as this to the bottom!" he observed.

Without a word, they set to work to pump and
bale. Even Trundle grew serious. Jacotot every
now and then stopped pumping or baling, or what-

ever he was about, and pulled his hair, and made a hideous face, scolded Auguste, telling him to *depechez vites*, and then set to work himself harder than ever. The English seamen worked away without saying a word beyond what was absolutely necessary. Jack Nobs behaved very well, but cried in sympathy when Auguste was scolded. The latter always blubbered on till his father ceased speaking. I could not help remarking what I have described, notwithstanding the fearful danger we were running. The sky was of an almost inky hue, while the sea was of the colour of lead, frosted over with the driving spray torn off from the summits of the tossing seas by the fury of the wind. Our stump of a mast, as well as our sail, had been well secured, though I dreaded every instant to see the ring-bolts, to which the ropes had been made fast, dragged out of the sides, and the rotten boat torn to pieces.

Thus on we flew, right into the Indian Ocean, though in what direction we could only guess, for our compass, like everything belonging to the craft, was defective. Intending only to make a coasting trip, we had no chart, except one of the island from which we were now being driven rapidly away. To be in a gale of wind on board a stout ship in the open sea, is a fine thing once in one's life, but to have to sit in a rotten boat, with a hurricane driving her, one knows not where, across the ocean, is a very different matter. Our only prospect of saving our lives, humanly speaking, was to keep the boat dead

before the wind; a moment's careless steering might
have caused our destruction.

We were all so busy in pumping or baling that we
had no time to watch each other's countenances, or
we might have seen alarm and anxiety depicted on
them as the rising seas came following up astern,
threatening to engulf us. I felt for the young brother
who was with me, so lighthearted and merry, and yet
so little perpared for the eternity into which any
moment we might be plunged. After fervent inward
prayer, my own mind was comforted, so much so that
I was able to speak earnest words, not only to my
young brother, but to the others. Trundle and Jack
looked very serious, but rather bewildered, as if they
could not comprehend what was said.

Such is, I fear, too often the case under such circumstances. I remembered how, a few days before, I had
seen Mason praying at a time of the utmost extremity,
and I urged my companions to pray for themselves.
Jacotot was the only person who seemed averse to
listen to the word of truth. Though he had raged
and pulled his hair with grief at the injury done to
his vessel, he could not bring himself to care for anything beyond the passing moment. But while the
rest grew calm and resigned, he became more and more
agitated and alarmed. In each sea which rolled up
after us in the distance he saw the messenger which
was to summon him to destruction. Poor little
Auguste could only cry with fear of the undefined.
He had never been taught to believe in anything,

and thus he could not even believe in the reality of death till he was in its grasp.

Under the circumstances in which we were placed, people can talk but little, though the thoughts crowd through the mind with frightful rapidity. Unless when occupied, we for most of the time sat silent, watching the ocean. Night was coming on, and the fury of the tempest had in no way decreased. It was difficult to steer in the daytime—it was doubly difficult and dangerous at night. After O'Carroll had been steering for some time, Trundle begged that he might again take the helm.

" Trust me," he said, " I have been in a gale of wind in an open boat before now, and know how to steer carefully."

" But you've not steered in a hurricane in the Indian seas, Mr. Trundle," answered O'Carroll. " Any moment the wind may shift round, and if we were to be taken aback, it would be all over with us. As long as I can keep my eyes open I'll stay where I am, if you please." And O'Carroll was as good as his word ; hour after hour he sat there, as we rushed on up and down the watery hills through the pitchy darkness—it was indeed a long, long night. Though we had eaten nothing since the hurricane came on, we were all of us rather weary than hungry. As for sleepiness, that was very far from any one. When compelled to rest, we could employ our thoughts in little else than wishing for daylight, and hoping that the storm would soon cease. It was a relief to be

called on to pump or bale, for the increasing leaks
required three of us at a time to be actively engaged
in both operations. But I am wrong in saying that
I could think of nothing except my own fearful peril.
Frequently I thought of my dear mother and other
loved ones at home. The thought gave me comfort
and courage, and cheered me up through the horrors
of the night. Daylight came at last, and revealed the
tumultuous ocean on every side, but not a speck of
land was visible. Trundle was the first to exclaim
that he was hungry; but to light a fire was almost
impossible, and even Jacotot could not have cooked
by it had it been lighted. We managed, however,
to serve out some bread and the old Frenchman's fruit
to all hands, and then we had to turn to and clear
the craft of water, which was finding its way in
through every seam. It seemed scarcely possible that
she could float much longer, should the hurricane
continue, with the violent working to which we were
exposed. Had we been stationary, the tempest would
have passed over us; but driven along with it, we had
for a much longer time to endure its fury. It seemed,
indeed, surprising that the boat should have floated so
long. As far as we depended, indeed, on our own
exertions, the most careful steering could alone have
saved us. We had been longing for daylight; now
that it had come, the dangers of our condition appeared more evident, and we almost wished again
for night. We could not calculate, either, in what
direction we were being driven, but we feared it

might be where rocks and coral banks and islets abound, and that at any moment we might be hurled on one of them. O'Carroll still sat at his post. I asked if he did not feel tired. "Maybe, but till the gale is over, here I'll stick!" he answered. "And sure it's as pretty a sample of a hurricane as any of you'll be after wishing to see for many a day to come."

At length, towards noon, the wind began to fall, and in a very short time, though it still blew hard, and the sea ran almost as high as before, and was consequently as dangerous, it was evident that the hurricane was over. Our hopes revived. Still, we were obliged to run on before the wind; and to avoid the danger of being pooped by the quickly-following sea, we had to hoist more of our sail: indeed, we now dreaded not having wind enough to avoid the sea. Thus passed the day, and before nightfall we were rolling on a tolerably smooth swell with a moderate breeze. Still we had to exert ourselves as before to keep the boat afloat. The moment, however, that one of us was relieved at the pump or baling bucket, he dropped off to sleep. I was even afraid, at first, that we should all go to sleep together. Nothing, indeed, for some hours could rouse up the two boys. My young brother and Trundle were, however, after a short snooze, as lively as ever, and as merry too. Midshipmen-like, they did not seem to trouble themselves about the future. I, however, still felt very anxious about it. The Southern Cross and many another bright constellation not long familiar to my eyes were shining forth in the clear sky. Had we known our position, even though we had no compass, we might have shaped a course for the Mauritius. We calculated that we had been driven two hundred miles away from it in the direction of the equator. Should we steer south we were as likely to miss as to find it. We proposed, therefore, to steer to the west, knowing that we must thus reach some part of the coast of Madagascar, where the English had at that time a fort and a garrison. "But we must have our craft rigged before we talk of the course we'll steer," observed O'Carroll, who at that moment awoke from a long sleep. With the morning light we set to work to fit a mainmast, and to rig the boat as best we could. There was a light breeze, but as it was from the west we lay without any canvas set.

While all hands were busily employed fitting the rigging, I looked up and saw a brig under all sail approaching us at no great distance. Beyond her was another vessel, a ship—I pointed her out. O'Carroll took the telescope.

"She's an English vessel chased by an enemy," he observed. "She'll not stop to help us, so the closer we lie the better." He kept after this continually taking up the glass for some time, when suddenly he exclaimed, "As I'm an Irishman, it's that villain La Roche again!"

His countenance fell as he spoke. He handed me the glass—I took a steady look at the ship, and had little doubt that it was our old antagonist the *Mignonne* in sight.

CHAPTER VII.

"BREAKERS AHEAD!"

OUR chief hope of escaping an unpleasant examination by the pirate existed in the possibility that we had not been observed from her deck. Had we had any sail set we could not fail to have been so. Not, we knew, that so small a craft as ours would be considered worth overhauling; but in case we might give information of the pirate's whereabouts, it might be thought expedient to put us out of the way. So we feared. We therefore watched the progress of the *Mignonne* and the brig with intense interest, earnestly hoping that the latter would lead the pirate a long chase before she was captured, if she could not escape altogether, which of course we hoped she would. La Roche had certainly managed to inspire O'Carroll with an extraordinary dread and hatred of him, for brave and calm in danger as our friend had lately shown himself to be, he was now completely unnerved, and I saw him crouching down in the boat as if, even had she been seen, he could have been distinguished. On sailed the brig; gradually her sails began to disappear below the horizon. The pirate still continued the chase. For some time no one in the boat thought of working. We were roused up by finding that the water was rapidly gaining on us, and we all had to turn to and pump and bale harder than ever. We were in hopes that after all the brig might escape, when the boom of a gun came over the water, followed by another and another. It was too probable that the pirate had got her within range. Both vessels had now disappeared below the horizon, at the same time the wind where we were had completely died away. As far as the pirate was concerned, we began to breathe more freely; it was not likely that he would again pass near us. But the sun shone forth from the clear sky with intense heat, roasting our heads and the brains within them, and making whatever pitch remained between the planks of our deck bubble up as if it had been boiling. There we lay, our boat rolling from side to side, without a particle of shade to shelter us. Our little cabin was like an oven. When we were to rest it became simply a question whether in making the attempt we should be roasted on deck or baked below. We had not much time for idleness yet: though we worked very hard, it was not till nightfall that our rigging was set up sufficiently to enable us to make sail.

When the sun set there was not a breath of air, while the surface of the ocean was as smooth as a sheet of glass, though every now and then a swell rose under the boat's keel, making her roll for ten minutes afterwards, while it glided slowly away in the distance. The only sounds were the clank of the pump and the dash of water from the scuppers or buckets, and an occasional snort of some huge fish, or the splash it made when plunging down into its liquid home. Thus the hours of the night passed away. We were so weary and sleepy that the instant we were relieved from the pump we lay down and were lost in forgetfulness. The day broke, the sun rose higher and higher, and beat hotter and hotter, and all around us was the same smooth, glassy ocean. Now and then the surface was broken by a flight of flying fish as they rose out of it and darted along through the air, glittering bright in the sunbeams, like a covey of silver birds.

"Ah, now! if some of you would just have the goodness to come aboard here, you would serve us nicely for breakfast," exclaimed Trundle, as he observed them.

He had scarcely spoken when upwards of a dozen out of a large shoal leaped, or flew rather, right in among us, while as many more passed clean over the boat. It was a curious coincidence, and at all events afforded us not only a substantial, but a very delicious meal, cooked by the skilful hands of Monsieur Jacotot. It put us all in good spirits, and we began to look at the future in a tolerably hopeful spirit, till my midshipman brother exclaimed,—

"I say, if this sun lasts much longer, what shall we do for grub? The sea-pie we have brought has gone bad, and I am afraid that the beef and pork won't keep good many hours out of the brine."

"You may put them in the past instead of the future tense, my boy," observed Trundle, who had been examining the lockers; "I doubt if any stomach with less powers than a shark's could swallow a bit of the meat we have got on board."

"Then on what have we got to exist till we can reach the shore?" I asked, with a feeling of serious anxiety.

"Why," answered William, "we have biscuits and half a cheese—at least we had half when we sailed, but it is rather gone—and a few mangoes, and bananas, and plantains, and a melon or two, and some tea and coffee, and sugar. I am afraid we haven't much else, except a cask of water, and that was rather leaky, like this craft."

"Then let us look to the cask, gentlemen," said O'Carroll. "And don't throw the meat away, putrid though it may be. The Frenchman may cook it so as to make it go down, and we don't know how hard we may be pressed for food."

The water-cask was examined, happily not altogether too late, but a third of the precious liquid had run out. I said nothing, but sad forebodings filled my mind. Even with a compass to steer by and a good breeze to carry us along, we might be several days reaching Port Louis, or, indeed, any habitable coast we could make. We might be kept out much longer, and then how could we exist? We could scarcely hope that another covey of flying fish would come on board, though we might catch some others if we could

manufacture hooks, for I was afraid we had none on
board. This calm might continue for a week, and
then we might have another gale, for we were in the
hurricane season. I advised that we should at once
go on an allowance of food and water, a suggestion
which was, of course, adopted. We had no fishing
lines or hooks on board ; a bit of an old file was, however, discovered, and with it and a hammer Jacotot
undertook to make some hooks, while Kelson spun
some fine yarn for lines.

" I shall have plenty of time," observed the Frenchman, with a wan smile and a shrug of the shoulders,
"for without the fish I shall have nothing to cook."

Two days passed, and though the hooks were in use
we caught nothing, and some of the party began to
wish that the pirate had picked us up. Two days
more passed : matters had become very serious.
Hunger was gnawing at our insides, and what seemed
even worse, thirst was parching our lips and throats.
With the intense heat we were enduring, gallons of
water would scarcely have satisfied us, and we each
had but a small wineglass full three times a day.
When that was gone, as long as our fuel lasted we
could get a little water by condensing the steam from
our kettle. Our thirst became intolerable; yet the
few drops we did get kept us, I believe, alive. I do
not wish to dwell on that time. My own sufferings
were great, but they were increased by seeing those of
my young brother and his lighthearted companion,
both of them about, as I feared, to pass away from the

world they had found so enjoyable. The sun rose, and set, and rose again, and each day it appeared to send down its heat with an increased intensity of strength as we grew weaker and weaker. A new danger threatened us: we could even now scarcely keep the boat clear of water; should our strength fail altogether, as seemed but too probable, she would sink below us. Our lot was that which many poor seamen have endured, but that did not make it more supportable to us.

Our last particle of food had been eaten, the last drop of water nearly exhausted. The strongest might endure for a day or two, the weakest ones must sink within a few hours. Even O'Carroll, strong as he seemed, was giving way. He sat dull and unconscious, his eyes meaningless, only arousing himself by a great effort. My brother's head rested on my arm, and I was moistening his lips with the few drops obtained from the cask. Suddenly Kelson, who had been gazing round the horizon, started up, crying out, "A breeze! a breeze! I see it coming over the water!"

I turned my eyes to the west, the direction to which he pointed. There I saw a dark-blue line quickly advancing towards us. Even already, on either side, cat's-paws were to be seen just touching the surface, then vanishing again, once more to appear in a different direction as the light currents of air, precursors of the main body of the wind, touched the surface. The effect on our fainting party was magical; even the poor boys tried to lift up their languid eyes to look around. Another shout from Kelson a few minutes afterwards roused us all still more. "A sail! a sail! She's standing this way too!"

Even Jacotot, who had completely given way to despair, started to his feet at the sound, and, weak though he was, performed such strange antics expressive of his joy on the little deck that I thought he would have gone overboard.

"If you've got all that life in you, Mounseer, just turn to at the pump again and make some use of it, instead of jigging away like an overgrown jackanapes!" growled out Kelson, who held the poor Frenchman in great contempt for having knocked under, as he called it, so soon.

Jacotot gave another skip or two, and then, seizing the pump-handle, or break, as it is called, burst into tears. The two midshipmen and boys soon relapsed into their former state, while O'Carroll seemed to forget that relief was approaching, till on a sudden the idea seized him that the stranger which was now rapidly nearing us was no other than the *Mignonne*, though she had been last seen in an opposite direction, and there had been a dead calm ever since. "Arrah! we'll all be murdered entirely by that thief of the world, La Roche, bad luck to him!" he cried out, wringing his hands. "It was an unlucky day that I ever cast eyes on his ugly face for the first time, and now he's after coming back again to pick me up in the middle of the Indian Ocean, just as a big black crow does a worm out of a turnip-field!"

In vain I tried to argue him out of the absurdity of his notion. He turned sharply round on me.

"It's desaving me now ye are, and that isn't the part of a true friend, Mr. James Braithwaite!" he exclaimed. "Just try how he'll treat you, and then tell me how you like his company."

I saw that there was not the slightest use reasoning with him, but that it would be necessary to watch him, lest in his frenzy he should jump overboard. As the dreadful idea came on me that he might do so, I saw the black fin of the seaman's sworn foe, a shark, gliding toward us, and a pair of sharp eyes looking wistfully up towards me, so I fancied, as if the creature considered the leaky boat and its contents a dainty dish prepared for his benefit. It made me set to work to bale with all the strength I could muster. Seeing me so employed, O'Carroll for a moment forgot his mad idea, and followed my example. Often and often I turned my gaze towards the approaching ship. It seemed even still open to doubt whether she would pass near enough to observe us.

At length the breeze reached us, and hoisting our sails as well as our strength would allow, we stood in a direction to come across the course the stranger was steering. I told Kelson, in a whisper, to assist me in keeping a watch on O'Carroll, for as we drew nearer the stranger, so did his uneasiness increase, and he was evidently still under the impression that she was the dreaded *Mignonne*. William and Trundle looked at her with lack-lustre eyes. I asked Kelson what he

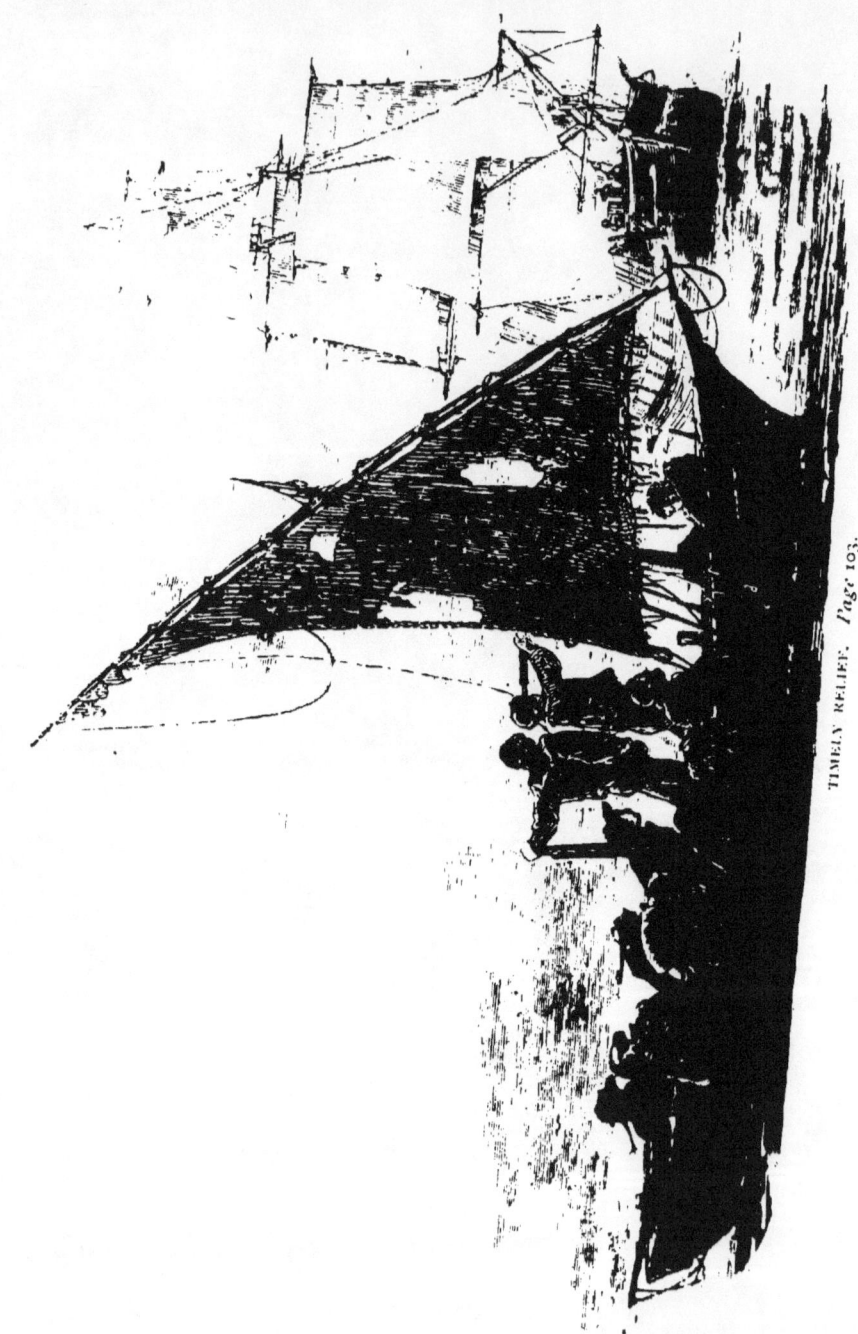

TIMELY RELIEF. *Page* 103.

thought she was. " A small Chinaman, or a store-ship, maybe, sir," he answered. "She's English, certainly, by the cut of her sails."

"You hear what he says," I observed to O'Carroll. "I think the same myself. We shall be treated as friends when we get on board."

"Ye are after desaving me, I know ye are," cried the poor fellow, turning round and giving a reproachful glance at me. "Don't ye see the ugly villain La Roche himself standing on the cathead ready to order his crew of imps to fire as soon as we get within range of their guns ? "

This notion so tickled Kelson's fancy that he fairly burst into a fit of laughter, in which I and the rest of the party faintly joined, from very weakness, for most of them had not heard what was said. Even O'Carroll himself imitated us. Suddenly he stopped. " It's no laughing matter, though, let me tell you," he observed gravely, after some time had elapsed, and the stranger had neared us so that we could see the people on deck. "But where's La Roche ? Oh, I see, he's aft there, grinning at us as usual." He pointed to a most respectable-looking old gentleman, who was, I supposed, the master of the ship.

" You are mistaken in that," said I, feeling the importance of keeping him quiet till he could be got on board. "If that is the *Mignonne*, she has been captured, and is in possession of a British crew. You'll see that I am right directly."

The ship was shortening sail as I spoke. We were

soon alongside. Even at a distance our pitiable condition had been observed. We were one after the other hoisted on deck, for even Kelson could scarcely get up without help. I gave a hint to the doctor to look after O'Carroll. "I am right," I remarked to my friend. "If La Roche is on board, he is safe under hatches; so the best thing you can do is to turn in, and go to sleep. You want rest more than any of us."

Led by the surgeon, he went quietly below, and I hoped with soothing medicine and sleep would be soon all to rights again.

The ship proved to be, not what Kelson had supposed, but a vessel with free emigrants bound out to the rising town of Sydney, in New South Wales—a colony generally called Botany Bay, established some few years before, by Captain Phillips of the navy, chiefly with convicts and the necessary soldiers to look after them. We had just told our tale, and the passengers had expressed their sympathy for us, when I heard Jacotot give a loud cry of dismay. On looking over the side the cause was explained—the masts of our unhappy little craft were just disappearing under the surface. This was the natural consequence of our neglecting to pump her out, and the ship, which was going ahead, dragging her through the water, when of course it rushed in through her open seams with redoubled speed. Poor Jacotot tore his hair and wrung his hands, and wept tears of grief for his wretched craft; but he did not gain as much sympathy as would have been shown him had he been more quiet, though

our new friends congratulated us the more warmly in
having got out of her before she met her fate. Food
and rest quickly set most of us to rights, and the following day William and Trundle and I were able to
take our places at the cabin table with the rest of the
passengers. O'Carroll was kept in bed with fever,
though he had got over his idea that La Roche was on
board. The old gentleman he had mistaken for him
proved to be a minister of the gospel, who had been
invited to accompany a party of the emigrants.

We found that things were not going on in at all
a satisfactory way on board. The master had died
before the ship reached the Cape : the first officer, Mr.
Gregson, who had now charge, was obstinate and self-
opinionated when sober, and he was very frequently
intoxicated ; the second was a stupid fellow and no
navigator ; and both were jealous of the third, who
was a superior, intelligent young man, and in numerous
ways they did their utmost to annoy him. This ac-
counted for the good ship, the *Kangaroo*, being very
much out of her proper course, which was far to the
southward of where she picked us up. Most disastrous
consequences were to occur. William and Trundle
told me that they had been making their observations;
that they wondered how the ship had got thus far,
and that they should be much surprised if she got
much farther. A very large proportion of the ships
cast away and lives sacrificed are so in consequence
of the habitual intoxication of the masters and their
officers. I venture to make this distinct assertion from

the very numerous instances I have known and heard
of. We did not wish to alarm the passengers, none of
whom had been at sea before, and were not aware of
the danger they were running. Had our schooner still
floated, I should have proposed taking her to the first
island we could make and there repairing her. We
asked Mr. Gregson if he would undertake to land us
at Port Louis, offering him at the same time payment
if he would do so; but he positively refused, declaring
that nothing should induce him to go out of his course,
and that we must stick to the ship and work our passage till she reached her destination.

Believing that, as he was short-handed, his object in
detaining us was to get more hands to work the ship,
this we positively refused to do. "Very well, then,
we'll see who is master on board the *Kangaroo*," he
replied, with an oath. "You tell me that three of you
belong to a man-of-war; but I find you in a French
boat, and how do I know that you are not deserters or
convicts? and I'll treat you as such if you don't look
out." This conduct was so unexpected, and so different
from the kind way in which we had been treated by
the passengers, that we did not know what to say.
We agreed to wait till we could consult O'Carroll; and
Trundle undertook to get a look at the chart the captain was using, and to try and find out where he had
placed the ship. The wind had hitherto continued
very light, so that we had made but little way since
we came on board. The day following the unpleasant
conversation I have described, O'Carroll was so much

recovered that he was able to come on deck. Though Irishmen have not the character in general of being good seamen, I considered from what I had seen of him that he was an exception to the general rule. I told him what we had remarked.

"When the time comes I'll see what I can do," he answered; "but it is ticklish work interfering with such fellows as the present master of this ship, unless one advises the very thing one does not want done."

"We may soon require the exercise of your skill," I remarked. "It appears to me that there will speedily be a change in the weather."

"Little doubt about that, and we shall have it hot and strong again soon," he answered, looking round the horizon.

"Not another hurricane, I hope," said I.

"Not quite sure about that," he answered. "Were I master of this ship I should make all snug for it; but if I were to advise Gregson to do so, he'd only crack on more sail to show his superior seamanship. I've had a talk with the surgeon, M'Dow, a very decent sort of young fellow, and so I know the man we have to deal with."

An hour or two after this, the wind had increased to half a gale, and the *Kangaroo* was tearing away through the sea with a great deal more sail than a prudent seaman would have carried. Unfortunately William or Trundle had remarked that it was much more important to shorten sail on the appearance of bad weather on board a short-handed merchantman,

than on board a man-of-war with a strong crew. I
saw O'Carroll looking anxiously aloft, and then again
to windward. At last he could stand it no longer.

" You'll let the wind take the topmasts out of the
ship if you don't look out, Captain Gregson," he remarked.

"What business have you to come aboard this ship
and to pretend to teach me?" answered the master,
who was more than half drunk. "If you do, take care.
I'll turn you out of her, and let you find your own
way ashore."

While he was speaking a loud crack was heard, and
the mizen-topmast was carried over the side. This
made him order the crew aloft to shorten sail. " You
go too, you lazy youngsters!" he exclaimed, seeing
William and Trundle on deck.

They sprung up the rigging without a word of
reply. I watched them with great anxiety, for the
masts bent like whips, and I was afraid every moment
to see the main share the fate of the mizen-mast, to
the destruction of all on the yards. Still the master,
as if indifferent to what might happen, was not even
looking aloft. The two midshipmen had just reached
the top, and were about to lie along the yard, when
O'Carroll shouted: "Down, all of you; down, for your
lives!"

His voice arrested their progress, and two of the
men already on the yards sprang back into the top;
but the warning came too late for the rest. A tremendous squall struck the ship. Over she heeled, till

the lee bulwarks were under water. A loud crash followed. Away went the main-topmast, and yard, and struggling sail, carrying six human beings with it. Five were hurled off into the now foaming sea. We saw them for an instant stretching out their arms, as if imploring that help which it was beyond our power to give. The ship dashed onward, leaving them far astern. One still clung to the rigging towing with the spar alongside. The ship still lay almost on her beam-ends.

O'Carroll saw the possibility of saving the poor fellow. Calling out to me to lay hold of a rope, one end of which he fastened round his waist, he plunged overboard. I could scarcely have held it, had not William and Trundle with Kelson come to my assistance. O'Carroll grasped the man. "Haul away!" he shouted. In another instant he was on board again, with the man in his arms. The helm was put up, the ship righted, the man had got off the foreyard, and away the ship flew, with the foretop-sail wildly bulging out right before the wind. In a few minutes it was blown from the bolt-ropes in strips, twisted and knotted together. The main-sail, not without difficulty, was handed, and we continued to run on under the foresail, the only other sail which remained entire, and it seemed very probable that that would soon be blown away.

All this time the terror of the unfortunate passengers was very great—the more so that it was undefined. They saw the captain, however, every now and then come into the cabin and toss off a tumbler of strong rum-and-water, and then return on deck, and shout out with oaths often contradictory orders. The gale all this time was increasing, until it threatened to become as violent as the hurricane from which we had escaped. I could not help wishing that we had not left our leaky little schooner. We might have reached some land in her. Now we did not know where we were going, except towards a region of rocks and sandbanks on which any moment the ship might be hurled. For ourselves it would be bad enough; but hard indeed for the poor women and children, of whom there were a dozen or more on board, several of them helpless infants.

As I looked on the man who was thus perilling the lives of his fellow-creatures by his senseless brutality, I could not help thinking what a load of guilt rested on his head. His face was flushed, his features distorted, his eyes rolling wildly, as he walked with irregular steps up and down the deck, or ever and anon descended to the cabin to gaze stupidly at his chart, which was utterly useless, and to take a fresh draught of the liquor which had brought him to that state. Yet he was a fine, good-looking fellow, and pleasant-mannered enough when sober and not opposed. I have known several such, who have for years deceived their owners and others on shore, led by outward appearance, till some fearful catastrophe has been the result of their pernicious habits.

Night came. The ship continued her mad career

through the darkness; the wind howling and whistling, the loose ropes lashing furiously against the masts,
and the sea roaring around. Below all was confusion.
Numerous articles had broken adrift and were rolling
about, the passengers crouched huddled together in
the cabin endeavouring to avoid them. Mothers
pressed their children to their bosoms; the men were
asking each other what was next to happen. The
answer came with fearful import. " Breakers ahead '
Breakers ahead!" There was a tremendous crash,
every timber in the ship shook. She was on the
rocks.

CHAPTER VIII

A COMPLETE WRECK.

"CUT away the masts—the shrouds first! Be smart, my men!" cried a voice.

"Who dares give that order?" shrieked out the captain; "she'll be over this in no time."

"I dare obey it!" exclaimed one of the seamen. "Come, lads, it's the best chance of saving our lives."

The men listened to the advice of their messmate, and, knowing where to find the axes, quickly severed the shrouds of the mizenmast, and some attacked it, while others went to the mainmast, in spite of the mad cries of the captain to "hold fast." Their object was thus to force the ship over the reef—if it was a reef we were on—head first, or closer to the shore if we were on an island. The seas came thundering against our sides, often dashing over the decks, so that with difficulty any of us could save ourselves from being carried away by them. Several poor people were thus swept away soon after the ship struck, and their despairing shrieks rang in our ears as they were borne away or hurled on the rocks amid the foaming breakers. We could see nothing beyond the ship except the troubled waters. Our chief hope rested on her not being wedged in the rocks. Now she lifted and drove on her bottom, grinding over the coral; now down she came again, and rocked to and fro in the surges. Directly the after masts were cleared away, her head paid off, and we drove on stern first. It was pitiable to hear the cries which rose from the terror-stricken passengers, but as we could as yet give them no comfort, I refrained from going below. William and Trundle, O'Carroll and I, stood together holding on to the stump of the mainmast; the Frenchman and his son had gone below at the commencement of the gale. I hoped that they were still there. The ship continued alternately grinding and bumping along, but still evidently progressing over the reef. She must have been new and well built, or she would have gone to pieces with the treatment she was receiving. Our anxiety was thus prolonged, for it was impossible to say, supposing the ship should drive over the reef, whether we should find land, and if not whether she would float. It seemed as if each blow she received must be knocking a hole through her planks. Oh! how we longed for daylight, at all events to see and face the dangers which beset us! In the dark we could do nothing but hold on for our lives and pray to be preserved from destruction.

At length the ship was lifted by a huge wave. On she drove. It seemed that the next time she came down on the hard rocks it must be to her destruction. On, on she went; the waters roared and hissed around her. Instead of the expected catastrophe, suddenly

R

she appeared to be floating with comparative calmness; she had been forced over the reef, but the furious wind was still driving her before it.

"We should anchor this instant!" said O'Carroll; but neither the master nor his mates were on deck to give the necessary orders. "Stand by to anchor!" cried O'Carroll.

The two midshipmen, with Kelson and several of the crew, hurried to carry out the order. Some delay occurred in consequence of the darkness. At length the anchor was let go, but as the ship's stern swung round it struck heavily on a rock. Again cries of terror came up from the passengers in the cabins; I therefore, as I could be of no use on deck, went below in the hopes of tranquillising their minds. They clung round me as I appeared, entreating to be told the truth. I assured them that there was no immediate danger, and that, though the ship had again struck on the rocks, there was so much less sea inside the reef than what she had already gone through, I hoped she might continue to hold together. In all probability we were not far off land. Some, on hearing this, especially those who had been most overcome with terror, expressed their joy in all sorts of extravagant ways, and seemed to consider that there was no longer any danger to be apprehended; others, again, would scarcely credit what I told them, and inquired what the captain thought on the subject.

"The captain! What does he know about anything?" exclaimed a young man, who appeared to be superior in education to most of the passengers. "If the ship is lost, and our lives sacrificed, on him will rest the blame. Look there!"

He threw open the door of the captain's cabin, where he and the first mate sat, both far too tipsy to move, yet still trying to pour spirits down their throats.

"What's that you say?" growled out the captain, with an indistinct utterance; "I'll have no mutiny aboard this ship."

He endeavoured to rise, but fell forward across the table, upsetting the bottle and tumblers. The mate was too far gone even to attempt to rise. He gazed at us with an idiotic glance for a minute or two, then his head dropped down on the little table at which he was sitting. It must be understood that all this time the ship was far from quiet; she was still grinding and striking heavily against the rocks, though the sea had not sufficient force to lift her over them. I hurried again on deck; my fear was that the ship would fill with water and drop off the rocks and sink. After hunting about we found the carpenter, and with his help sounded the well; already there were six feet of water in the hold. After waiting a short time we found that the water was increasing, the pumps must be set to work. Some of the crew said it was of no use, and refused; others came to our summons; and to help us we called up all the men passengers, while we set the example by labouring as hard as we could. Thus the night passed. It was indeed better for everybody that we had something to do. Dawn came at last. We eagerly looked out for the prospect which daylight was to reveal, whether we were to find ourselves amidst reefs just rising from the water, or near a mere sandbank, or on an inhabited shore. At first we could only see, as before, the white foam dancing up, then dark rocks and yellow sand, and beyond it brown hills and a few trees. As the light still further increased we discovered that the country was in a state of nature; in vain we looked for traces of inhabitants.

The passengers, hearing that we were close to land, came crowding on deck, all eager to get on shore. It was, however, no easy matter to do so. The sea came rushing round the ship, between which and the dry rocks the distance was considerable, so that anybody attempting to swim to them would have been swept away. One small boat alone remained, the rest had been knocked to pieces. In this only two rowers could sit, and a couple of passengers at the most. As far, however, as we could see on either side the surf broke too furiously to allow her to land, so that she could, we feared, be of no use.

At length my brother cried out, "We'll go in her; there is one place just inside the ship where we can jump on shore with a line. If we can do that we'll carry a hawser to the rocks, and all the people may land."

The two mids and Kelson agreed to go in the boat, towing a light line. We watched them anxiously. The water tossed and foamed around them, and they had hard work to contend with the reflux of the sea.

THEY WERE PLACED ONE AFTER THE OTHER, IN THE CRADLE."—*Page* 117

Earnestly I prayed that they might be protected and succeed, both for their sakes and ours. A shout of joy and thankfulness burst from the lookers-on as Kelson leaped on the rock, followed by the two midshipmen, who instantly hauled the boat up out of harm's way. A hawser had been prepared, which they at once hauled on shore and secured. A cradle was next fitted to it by the seamen, under O'Carroll's directions. It was a question who was to go forth to prove it. At that moment Jacotot made his appearance on deck. He was told that he must go on shore. He was secured forthwith to the cradle. In vain he struggled and protested : he was quickly drawn across. His son and Jack followed. Two men then went to assist in hauling the passengers across. They were placed, one after the other, in the cradle and landed in safety. I was thankful when they were all on shore. There they stood, grouped together, gazing helplessly at the ship, not knowing what to do. There was no one to guide them. Those wretches, the master and his mate, still remained utterly helpless in the cabin. Half the crew of the ship had been lost, and the young mate, who might have exercised some authority. From what I saw of the remainder of the crew I was afraid that they were mostly a very bad set. I dreaded their breaking into the spirit-room—which seamen often do under such circumstances. To prevent this it was necessary to keep them amply employed ; we urged them, therefore, to land all the provisions that could be got out of the hold.

To expedite this proceeding we got another hawser carried on shore. Our lives might depend on the amount of provisions we could save. All day we worked on, till towards evening the water had risen so much in the hold that nothing more could be got out. The heat was intense, but so important was the work that we scarcely stopped even to take food. No one had thought all this time of the captain and mate, the real cause of their misfortunes. Suddenly I recollected that they had been left in a side-cabin asleep. I hurried down. I was but just in time; the water was up to their heads, and in another minute would have washed over their faces and drowned them as they lay sleeping off their debauch. I shouted out their names, and called them to come on deck. They started up, their countenances exhibiting their horror and alarm, as they believed that the ship was sinking beneath them. Out into the water they tumbled. The mate slipped, and caught hold of the captain to save himself. Over they went, struggling together. I fancy that they thought themselves overboard; right under the water they dragged each other, once more to get their heads out, spluttering and shouting, and swearing most fearfully. At last, fearing that they might after all be drowned, I seized the mate, who was the smaller man of the two, and dragged him on deck, calling out to O'Carroll to assist in getting up the captain. He came to my assistance, and we hauled both the men on deck. Their sea bath and the struggle had brought them to their senses; but when, after staring around for some time, they saw that the ship was a hopeless wreck, cast away on an apparently barren island, they very nearly lost them again. To find fault with them at such a moment would have been folly. "Come, I advise you to go on shore, for very likely the ship will go to pieces during the night, if the wind rise again," I said quietly. They were far from disposed to thank me for my advice, though, after looking about for a few minutes, they took it, and were hauled on shore. After collecting everything of value to be found in the cabin, compass, charts, and some nautical books, I followed. O'Carroll was 'the last man to leave the ship. William and his messmate had been very active on shore, and got a tent rigged for the poor women and children, and some food cooked for them by Jacotot.

No sooner was a fire lighted than the Frenchman was himself again, hurrying about in search of the utensils necessary for his calling. He had cooked a capital supper for them, and he now offered to cook one for us. On collecting all the sails we had landed, we were able to form a shelter for ourselves, as well as for the seamen; and at length, weary with our exertions, we lay down to rest. The captain and mate were very silent, and I hoped ashamed of themselves. During the night there was a good deal of wind and sea. I was thankful that we were on shore, and when I looked out I almost expected to find that the ship had gone to pieces. There, however, she was, still holding fast together. Seeing this, the captain declared that he would get her off, and that if trees could be found in the island suitable for new spars, he could proceed on his voyage.

"If he knew of the bumping she got he wouldn't say so," observed O'Carroll. "That ship will never float again, and, strong as she is, another gale such as we had last night will break her to pieces."

As there was nothing more to be done, we started to explore the island. It seemed to be the chief of a group of rocky islets, being about six miles long and half as broad. Though we made diligent search as we walked on, we could find no water. A few small casks of the precious liquid had been landed, but sufficient only for another day or two.

"And what shall we do when that is gone?" asked William. It was a serious question.

"We must trust in God, for vain is the help of man in such a case," I answered; "at all events, we must use what we have got with the greatest economy."

On returning to the camp and reporting our want of success in finding water, what was our dismay to find that every drop in the casks had been consumed! All the poor people could say was that they were so thirsty, and the children were so constantly crying out for water, that they could not help giving it to them. We were ourselves already suffering greatly from thirst after our ramble, yet not a drop of water did we obtain. Our lips were parched, our tongues dry: without water we could not eat, we loathed food, supperless we lay down to sleep. All night long I was dreaming of sparkling fountains and running brooks. As soon as it was daylight we again set out with a spade and pickaxe, prepared, if we could find no running stream, to dig wherever verdure showed that moisture was at hand. We walked on and on, searching in every direction round the shore, but no sign of a stream emptying itself into the sea could we discover, and when we dug we soon met the hard rock. Faint and weary we turned to the camp. We found a fire blazing, and Jacotot with several men standing round it: two were working a rough pair of bellows, others hammers and tongs. All were employed under his directions, while he was engaged in riveting a pipe into a large copper vessel.

"Why you trouble to look for water?" he asked. "There is salt water, there is wood to make fire, then we have plenty of fresh water. We make steam, steam come out and leave the salt in de kettle, and then find a cold piece of iron and drop, drop, down into this tub all fresh and good for drink." He told us that he had seen a French doctor obtain fresh water from salt in that manner.

"Most men have their merits, if we could but discover them and put them in their right places," I thought to myself. "We were inclined to laugh at Jacotot, but if he can produce fresh water out of salt, he may be the means of saving all our lives."

We watched him anxiously, all eager to help him, but he would not be hurried. At length the machine was finished, and we hastened to fill it with salt water. It was placed on the fire, and slowly the drops of fresh water were distilled from it. How eagerly were they sought for by the poor creatures who stood round with lack-lustre eyes and parched lips. Jacotot insisted that the youngest should be served first. I think he was influenced by the wish to get his boy Auguste an early draught. That was but natural. Some of the crew grumbled, and so did the captain and mate, who were, in consequence of their late debauch, suffering fearfully from thirst; but O'Carroll, William, Trundle, Kelson, and two or three of the passengers formed a body-guard round the Frenchman, to enable him to do as he thought right. Only half a little liqueur glass of the precious fluid was served out to each person. It was pleasant to see the eyes of the poor children brighten as the pure water touched their lips. The younger ones, however, directly their allowance was gone, cried out for more. Several times we had to stop till more water was distilled.

While we were thus engaged, the wind had again got up, and the sea, dashing over the reef, began to burst with violence against the shore. The effect produced on the wreck was soon apparent. The remaining upper works began to give way. As the sea rolled in with increasing violence, plank after plank was torn off, then larger portions were wrenched from the hull, the deck burst up, and was soon dashed into pieces against the rocks. As soon as we had swallowed enough water somewhat to slake our burning thirst, we hastened to the beach to save what we could from the wreck. We hauled on shore all the planks and timber we could get hold of, with the vague idea that we might be able to build a raft of some sort, in which to make our escape. At all events the wood would be useful to construct huts for the women, or to burn. As darkness set in, a large portion of the wreck had disappeared, and even the captain was convinced that her keel would never leave its present position, except to be cast up in fragments on the rocks. He and the mate had been very quiet and lowspirited. They were craving for their accustomed stimulants, and several times I heard them grumbling at us for not having landed any liquor for them. Neither they nor the larger portion of their crew had exerted themselves in the slightest degree to assist us in our labours. Most of them sauntered along the beach with their hands in their pockets, or sat coolly watching us. Fatigued with our exertions, we at last returned to the camp, where Jacotot was able to give us a glass of water, and we then, thankful even for that small supply, lay down to rest.

It was not till late that any of us awoke; we then found that the captain and mate, and several of their men, had withdrawn themselves to a distance from the camp. We were glad to be rid of their company, though why they had gone away so suddenly we could not tell. We could not help suspecting, however, that they had done so with the intention of hatching mischief. When I speak of *we*, I mean our party from the *Dorè*, for we of necessity kept very much together. I have not particularly described the emigrants, for there was nothing very remarkable about them. Two or three were intelligent, enterprising men, who had made themselves acquainted with the character of the country to which they were going, and had tolerably definite plans for the employment of their capitals. The rest had mostly failed in England, and were rather driven by want into exile than attracted by the advantages the new colony had to offer. They were all married men with families, and this made them associate with each other for mutual assistance. The steerage passengers were generally small tradesmen, and had emigrated for much the same reason as the others. Three gentlemen of the first class, who were bachelors, had begged leave to join our mess. One of them had already been in New South Wales, and was able to give us much interesting information about it. So much taken was I, indeed, with what I heard, that I resolved, should I be unable to find the *Barbara*, to visit the colony before returning home. We thus, as I have explained, formed three chief messes. We were not as yet either very badly off. We had saved provisions from the wreck sufficient, with economy, to last us a couple of months or more; and now that we could obtain fresh water, though but in small quantities, we were not afraid of dying of thirst. We were in hopes, too, of finding turtles and turtles' eggs, and perhaps wild fowl, and we might also catch fish to add to our stock of provisions. Could we only find water, and some sort of vegetables, we might be able, we thought, to support existence for any length of time; and as far, indeed, as we could judge we might not have an opportunity of escaping from the island for months, or it might be for years. This was not, however, a subject pleasant to contemplate. I thought of my merchandise, William of his promotion, and of the opportunities he might lose of distinguishing himself, while Jacotot, though not idle, was unable to make money where he was. Toby Trundle, however, took things very easily. He laughed and joked as much as ever, and declared that he never was more jolly in his life. He used to say the same thing in the midshipmen's berth; he had said it on board the boat, and I believe he would have said it under nearly any circumstances in which he could have been placed. The poor emigrants, on the contrary, were very far from content. Most of them had lost all they possessed in the world, and knew that, should they even ultimately arrive at their destination, they must land as beggars, dependent on the bounty of others. They were therefore naturally very loud in their complaints of the captain and his mate, while they were continually bewailing their own hard lot. Those persons had, as I observed, removed themselves to a distance from the rest of our shipwrecked band.

We had retired to tents for the night, and had lain down to sleep, when after some time I was awoke by sounds of shouting and laughter, followed by shrieks and cries, which seemed to come up from the beach where the captain and his associates had taken up their quarters. The noises increased, and O'Carroll awoke. He got up, and we went together to the entrance of our tent. The night was very calm. The stars shone forth from the dark sky with a brilliancy I have never seen surpassed; even the restless sea was quiet, and met the shore with an almost noiseless kiss; all nature seemed tranquil and at rest. A shot was heard, and then another, and another, followed by shouts and execrations. "There will be bloodshed among those madmen," exclaimed O'Carroll. "They have got hold of some liquor unknown to us, and are fighting with each other: we must try and separate them." Calling my brother and the rest of the party to come to our assistance, we hurried off in the direction whence the sounds proceeded.

CHAPTER IX.

LIFE ON THE ISLAND.

WHEN we got sufficiently near the beach to distinguish objects, we saw the captain standing with a pistol in his hand, which was pointed at the mate, who held a long knife in his hand, with which he was about, it seemed, to make a rush at his opponent, while three or four men had arranged themselves on either side, and were flourishing various weapons. The shots we heard told us that they had already fired at each other several times, but were too tipsy to take a steady aim. One man, however, lay wounded on the ground, and from the gestures of the mate, he would in another instant plunge his knife in the bosom of the captain, unless stopped by the latter's bullet.

"You knock up the skipper's arm, while I seize the other fellow," exclaimed O'Carroll to me, springing forward.

I did as he bid me; he ran a great risk of being shot. The mate turned on O'Carroll with an oath, and the captain snapped his pistol at me, but fortunately he had already discharged it, and in another instant I brought him, as he attempted to grapple with me, to the ground. O'Carroll had mastered the mate, and the other men stood staring at us, but offering no opposition. "Is this the way for men to behave who have just been saved from death, to make yourselves worse than the brute beasts? This—this is the cause of it!" exclaimed O'Carroll, kicking a cask from which a stream of spirit was even then running out. "It would have been no loss to us if you had killed each other, but we could not see our fellow-creatures perish without trying to save them."

The bold and determined tone in which O'Carroll spoke, aided by the arrival of the rest of our friends, had such an effect on the seamen, that those who were still able to move slunk away to a distance, while the captain and his mate, when we let them go, sat down helplessly on the sand, forgetting entirely their quarrel and its cause. There they sat, laughing stupidly at each other, as if the affair had been a good joke. While O'Carroll was emptying the rum cask, which it appeared had been washed on shore and secreted by the captain, his men went to the wounded man. He did not speak: he seemed scarcely to breathe. I took his hand: it was already cold. All this time he had been bleeding to death: an artery had been shot through. We did our best in the dark to bind up the wound and stop the bleeding; the spirit which might have kept his heart beating till nature, in her laboratory, had formed more blood, was gone; indeed, probably in his then condition it would not have had its due effect. The wretched man's

breath came fainter and fainter. There was no re-
storative that we could think of to be procured. We
lifted him up to carry him to the camp, but before we
had gone many paces, we found that we were bearing
a corpse.

"That man has been murdered," exclaimed O'Carroll, turning to the captain. "By whose hand the shot
was fired which killed him I know not, but I do know
that his blood is on the head of the man who ought
to have set a good example to his inferiors, and prevented them from broaching the cask they had found."

Whether this address had any good effect we could
not tell, but hoping that the men would remain quiet
and sleep off the effect of their debauch, we returned
to our tent, leaving the body on the ground. The
next morning we returned to the beach. The captain
and his drunken companions still lay on the sand
asleep. They were out of the reach of the sea, but
the hot rays of the rapidly rising sun, which were
striking down on their unprotected heads, would, I
saw, soon give them brain fever or kill them outright,
if they were to be left long exposed to their influence.
I therefore proposed that we should rouse them up,
and advise them to go and lie down in the shade of
some shrubs and rocks at a little distance.

"Before we do so, we'll take away their weapons,
and at all events make it more difficult for them to
do mischief to us or to themselves," said O'Carroll.
Some of the men grumbled on being disturbed, as we
turned them round to take away their knives. We

left the unloaded pistols, which, as they had no powder, could do little harm. Having taken their arms to our tents, we returned and awoke them, not without difficulty, by shaking them and shouting in their ears. One after the other they got up, lazily rubbing their eyes and stretching themselves, and staring stupidly about them. The captain was one of the last to come to his senses. He started when he saw the dead body of his companion.

"Who killed that man?" he exclaimed, in an anxious tone.

"You did, most probably," answered O'Carroll. "We heard shots fired and found the man dead."

The captain felt in his pocket, and drew out a pistol with the hammer down: it had been discharged. "Then I am a murderer!" he exclaimed, in a tone of horror, his countenance expressing his feelings. "It wanted but that to make up the measure of my crimes."

"It is but too true, I fear," said O'Carroll.

"Yes, too true, too true!" cried the captain, rushing off towards the sea, into which he would have thrown himself, had not O'Carroll, William, and I held him back. It was some time before we could calm him sufficiently to leave him alone. He then went and sat down in the shade at a little distance from his companions, who looked on at him with dull apathy, while he gave way to the feelings which the prickings of his awakened conscience had produced. How he and the mate had got possessed of the pistols we could not guess, till we found the chest of one of the emigrants, a young man, broken open, and from this they had helped themselves. One of them soon after came for a spade which had been landed, and we saw them hurriedly bury the corpse, as if eager to get the silent witness of their crime out of sight. For the remainder of the day they were perfectly quiet, the mate coming humbly when the provisions were served out to ask for their share; still we could not trust them, as we knew that if they could get at more liquor, they would very quickly again be drunk. In the evening, indeed, they were seen walking along the beach, evidently watching for the chance of another cask being washed on shore. They did not find one, however, and the next morning were excessively sulky, keeping together and evidently plotting mischief. They, with the rest of us, were aroused, however, soon after breakfast by the appearance of a sail in the offing. The more sanguine at once declared that she was standing towards us, and that our fears regarding a prolonged stay on the island were groundless; others thought that she would pass by and leave us to our fate. Every spyglass was in requisition, and numerous were the surmises as to the character and nationality of the stranger.

"What if she is an enemy?" observed William.

"She will not find much plunder, at all events," answered Trundle. "There is nothing like being at the bottom of the hill, so that you cannot be kicked lower."

"Even an enemy would respect our condition," remarked O'Carroll; "we have nothing to fear from one, I should hope."

"No, but an enemy would leave us where we are : a friend would carry us away, or send us assistance," said I.

It was dinner-time, and Jacotot had prepared our messes with his usual skill; but so eager were the people watching the approaching stranger, that the food was scarcely touched, except by the children, who of course little knew how much depended on her character. At length there was no doubt that she was standing for the island, and the exhibitions of joy and satisfaction became general among the unfortunate emigrants. They would now be able to leave the island and reach their land of promise; every countenance beamed brightly except O'Carroll's. After some time I saw his fall. It gained a more and more anxious look. He scarcely withdrew the glass from his eye.

"What do you make her out to be, O'Carroll?" I asked.

"Braithwaite, as I am a living man, she's the *Mignonne*," he answered, in a hoarse voice, his countenance still further showing the agitation of his mind : "if that villain La Roche gets hold of me again, he'll not let me escape with my life. And these poor emigrants to have his lawless crew come among them,—it will be terrible; better rather that they had all gone to the bottom in their ill-fated ship with their drunken captain."

Notwithstanding O'Carroll's opinion, I doubted whether the stranger was the *Mignonne*, for she was still too far off, I thought, for him to be certain on the subject. I therefore tried to tranquillise his mind, wondering that a man so brave, and cool, and collected, as he generally was, should have such a dread of the French captain.

"I tell you yonder vessel is the *Mignonne*, and if you had been treated as I was, and had witnessed the scenes I saw enacted on board, you would not have a less horror of La Roche and his scoundrel crew than I have. My reason does not help me; I cannot think of that man without trembling."

I understood him, for I have myself been affected in the same way with regard to one or two people who have done me some injury, or would, I have had reason to believe, do me one should they have the opportunity.

"The only way to escape the pirates is to remain concealed while they are passing," he observed. "As there is no harbour here, and there are no signs of them having been here, they will, in all probability, go to the other side of the island, and we may escape them."

As I still further examined the stranger I began to fear that O'Carroll was right in his conjectures, and I therefore agreed to assist him in trying to persuade the rest of the people to hide themselves till the privateer was out of sight. The emigrants, frightened out of their wits by the account O'Carroll gave of

the privateer's men, were ready enough to do as he
advised, and began running here and there, not knowing where to hide themselves.   We advised them
simply to pull down the tent, to put out the fire, and
to sit quiet among the rocks and shrubs till the ship
had passed.

We then went on to see the . captain and his men.
As we got in sight of where they were, we saw that
they had already got up a spar, which had been
washed on shore, and were in the act of hoisting a
man's shirt to the top of it in order to attract the
attention of the stranger.   On this O'Carroll shouted
out to them in no very gentle tones, "Fools! idiots!
what are you about? would you bring an enemy on
shore to murder us?"   I then told them the character
of the vessel in sight.   "What's that to us?" answered
one of the men.   "All masters are much the same to
us; they'll use us while they want us, and cast us
adrift when they've done with us.   Whether French
or Spaniards, they'll not harm us.   They'll have liquor
aboard, and that is what we shan't have as long as we
remain here."

It was useless attempting to argue with such men.
I turned to the captain.   He had lost all authority
over his people, who treated him as an equal, or
rather as an inferior.   He shrugged his shoulders and
walked away without speaking.   I saw that it was
time, therefore, to interfere, and William and I, rushing
forward, hauled down the signal, which one of the men
was on the point of hoisting.   "If you are willing to

become slaves, we are not!" I exclaimed, in a determined tone, seizing the halliards and hauling down the signal. The men threatened, but as they had no arms, and we were firm, they did not attempt to prevent us from carrying off the spar.

The ship approached, and as she passed along the coast so that we had a broadside view of her, I had no longer any doubt that she was the *Mignonne.* I observed that even the seamen, notwithstanding their bravado, kept so far among the rocks, that unless the privateer's men had been especially examining the shore there was not much probability of our being discovered. We watched the vessel from the highest point of ground we could reach, and we conjectured that she must have touched at the other side of the island, concealed by an intervening ridge of elevated land. "If we are careful we shall escape all molestation from the privateer's men," I remarked, addressing the emigrants. "They are not likely to come to our part of the island."

It was curious to observe the change which had come over O'Carroll. He was no longer the bold and sagacious seaman, but an anxious, nervous, timid man. At night I frequently heard him crying out in his sleep, thinking that the dreaded La Roche was on him, and was about to carry him on board the privateer. As we could not do without a fire to obtain fresh water, we were compelled to light one, though we thus ran the risk, should any of the privateer's men wander into the country, of being discovered. Still that was a risk which must be run. It was curious, also, to observe the humble way in which, after a few hours, the seamen came to beg for a draught of the pure liquid. I was very glad of this, as I saw that it would enable us to exert an influence over them and to keep them in order. The wretched captain held out for some time, but at last came, with parched lips and bloodshot eyes, entreating even for a few drops of the precious fluid to cool the tip of his tongue. It raised our pity to see how the wretched man suffered, physically and mentally, and all the time without hope. In vain I urged him to seek for mercy as a penitent. "Impossible! impossible!" he exclaimed, with a wild laugh. "You do not know what I have done, what I am doomed to do." And tearing himself away from me, he rushed off, and was hid from sight among the rocks and bushes. Day after day passed by, and we kept anxiously hoping that the privateer would take her departure. It was suggested that if she came to the island to refit, the Frenchman might possibly have a storehouse, with boats, perhaps, or means of building one, and that we might thus be assisted to make our escape. At last, so long a time had elapsed since her arrival, that we began to fancy that she had gone out of harbour during a moonlight night, and reached the offing without our perceiving her. To settle the point, William and Trundle volunteered to reconnoitre, and I, afraid that they might venture too far, resolved to go with them. We fixed on that very afternoon to start, our intention being to get as close to the harbour as we could before dark, and then to rest till the moon rose and afforded us light.

"I hope that you'll have success, but it is a dangerous work you are going on, young gentlemen," observed one of the emigrants, a Mr. Peter Lacy, or Lazy, as he was generally called, for it was most difficult to arouse him to any exertion.

"Never fear, Mr. Lazy, danger is a sweet nut we midshipmen are fond of cracking to get at the kernel— honour. We shall be back all safe before morning, and able to give a satisfactory report."

In good spirits we set off, for a considerable part of the distance keeping along the shore, to avoid the tangled bush and rocks of the interior. As, however, we approached the harbour, or rather the place where we supposed the harbour to be, we left the beach and kept a more inland course, taking advantage of all the cover we could find to conceal ourselves. At last the sun went down and it quickly grew dark, so we called a halt, and ate some of our provisions with a good appetite. We listened attentively, but could hear no sound, so we agreed to push on directly the moon got up. As we did not speak above a whisper, a very soporiferous proceeding, I was not surprised that both Toby and William fell asleep. It was more necessary, therefore, that I should keep my eyes and ears open. At last I saw what looked like the illuminated dome of some vast cathedral slowly emerge from the dark line of the horizon ; up it rose, till it assumed a globe-like form,

and appeared to decrease in size, while it cast a bright
silvery light over the hitherto obscured landscape. I
roused up the two midshipmen, who were sleeping as
soundly as if they had been in their hammocks. We
worked our way onward among tangled underwood,
not without sundry scratches and inconvenient rents
in our clothing, till we reached a hill, up which we
climbed. From the top we looked down, as we had
expected to do, on the harbour. Below us lay the
Mignonne, or a ship very like her; her sails were
loose and bulging out with the land breeze, while from
the sounds which reached us it was evident that her
crew were heaving up the anchor preparatory to
sailing; boats were moving backwards and forwards
over the surface of the calm water of the harbour, on
which the moon shone with a refulgence which enabled
us to see all that was taking place. The anchor was
shipped, the sails were sheeted home, and the privateer
slowly glided out of the harbour on her errand of
mischief; two, if not more, boats returned to the
shore fully manned. Farther up the harbour lay
three large hulks, with their lower masts only standing; they were high out of the water, showing that
they had no cargoes in them. There were also several
smaller craft, but all were dismantled, and looked as if
they had been there for some time. The French, then,
had a settlement on the island. The inhabitants were
sure to be armed, and probably were as numerous as
our party. If so, it would be unwise to attempt
gaining anything by force, though of course we might

surprise them. We waited till the people in the boats had had time to turn in and go to sleep, and then descended to reconnoitre the place more nearly. We crept cautiously on till we reached several scattered cottages, or huts rather, built, without any regularity, as the nature of the ground seemed most suitable. There were also two or three storehouses close to the water; indeed, we saw enough to show us that there was a regular settlement made by the French for the purpose of refitting their ships. The barking of several poodles in the cottages made us afraid of moving about much, lest their inmates should look out and discover us. We therefore retraced our steps to the hill.

"A magnificent idea," exclaimed Trundle, as soon as we called a halt. "We'll surprise and capture the place and hold it for the King of England. You'll be made governor, Braithwaite, to a certainty."

"To be turned out by the first French privateer which enters the harbour—to be thrown into prison and perhaps shot. Thank you," said I, "I would rather not."

"This establishment solves a mystery," observed William. "We have often been puzzled to know what has become of vessels which have disappeared, and which, from the fineness of the weather, and for other reasons, we did not suppose had been lost. We should do good service if we could get away without being discovered, and send some of our cruisers to watch in the neighbourhood."

I agreed with William; at the same time the idea of capturing the place was very attractive. If we should make the attempt and succeed, however, we should find liquor there, and the seamen would certainly get drunk and mutinous. No object would be gained, either, unless we could immediately send a vessel to sea, to give notice at the Mauritius of our success and obtain assistance. Discussions on these points occupied us till daylight, when we recommenced our journey to the tents. The news we brought was so far satisfactory to our companions, that we were not likely to be starved to death, and as peace would come some day or other, we might then hope to make our escape. No one, however, seemed at all desirous of attacking the French settlement; the risk was considerable, the gain problematical. It was finally agreed that we should remain quiet where we were, and only in case of extremity make ourselves known to our foreign neighbours. The more energetic of the party became, as may be supposed, very impatient of the inactive life we were compelled to lead. We could do little else than fish all day, and make expeditions in search of water. In this we were at last successful; the spring was more than a mile away, and it became a question whether we should move our camp there, the objection to our so doing being that it was so much nearer the French settlement. The next morning, on going near the spot where the captain and his companions had erected their tent, I saw no one moving. I called to them. There was no reply. I went to the tent. It was empty! It was supposed that they had gone to the newly-discovered spring, but those who had gone to bring water from it told us that they were not there. While we were wondering what had become of the men, as William happened to be sweeping the horizon with his telescope, he cried out that he saw a sail in the offing. In a short time afterwards another was descried, her topsails gradually rising out of the water. She was pronounced to be larger than the first which had appeared.

"It is that scoundrel La Roche again!" exclaimed O'Carroll, after eyeing the nearest stranger for some time. "I knew that it would not be long before he would be back again, and there he comes with a big prize, depend on it."

"But suppose, instead of the big ship being his prize, he has been captured by one of our cruisers, and has been sent in first to show the way?" I suggested.

"No, no, the headmost craft is the *Mignonne*, and the big one is an Indiaman, her prize, depend on that," said O'Carroll.

There seemed every probability that he was right, but this did not increase our satisfaction. The only thing that could be said was that we should now have companions in our misfortune. As may be supposed, however, we watched the approach of the two ships with the greatest interest, feeling assured that in some way or other they would have a considerable influence on our fate.

CHAPTER X.

OUR anxiety to ascertain the fate of those on board
the ship which the *Mignonne* had brought in as
a prize induced me, with my brother William and
Trundle, to make another expedition to the French
settlement. We ventured much nearer during daylight than we had done the first time, as we were
certain that the people would be watching the arrival
of the privateer and her prize. We were able, indeed,
to reach a spot overlooking the harbour, where, among
some thick bushes, we concealed ourselves before the
ships came to an anchor. William had brought his
telescope, and we could almost see the countenances of
the people on the decks of the ships. The large one
was, we saw at once, an Indiaman outward bound.
We knew that by the number of young men and the
young ladies on board, and their clear ruddy com-
plexions. Had she been homeward bound, there would
be old yellow-faced generals and judges, black nurses,
sickly ladies, and little children.

We anxiously watched the proceedings of those on
board. The passengers were walking up and down
in a very disconsolate mood : the crew were clustered

forward. By their looks and gestures as they cast their eyes towards the privateer, we thought that even then they were about to attack the Frenchman, and attempt to regain their liberty.

"I hope they will. I should like to help them," exclaimed William and Trundle, starting up simultaneously.

I drew them back. "Nonsense! we could not help them, and they will not make the attempt," I said. "See, the Frenchmen are going on board armed. They know what they are about."

Two large boats with armed men were pulling from the privateer to the Indiaman to strengthen her prize crew, while Captain La Roche was going on board her in his gig. He was soon up her side, and began bowing and scraping away most politely to the passengers, especially to the ladies. We could almost fancy that we heard him apologising to them for the inconvenience and disappointment he was causing them, with a spice of mockery in his tone, suggesting that it was the fortune of war, and that another day their turn might come uppermost. The crew of the Indiaman were then sent down the side, and rowed off to one of the hulks, while the passengers were conveyed to another.

"Then those hulks are prison ships after all," observed William, when the operation was concluded. "We may get on board them and let out the prisoners some day."

In this I partly agreed with him, though I could not help seeing the difficulties in the way. Even this

hope was likely to be frustrated, for as we watched
the Frenchmen who came on shore, we saw that they
were joined by several men whom we had little
difficulty in recognising as the crew of the wrecked
ship, the very people who had lately deserted us. The
mate was with them, but we did not see the captain.
Perhaps, drunkard as he was, he was ashamed to go
over to the enemy. All the party now entered a
drinking-house together, being evidently on the most
friendly terms.

We had therefore no longer any doubt that our
existence would be made known to the privateer's
men, and that the difficulty of surprising them would
consequently be much greater than we had calculated
on. We found that it was time to retrace our steps,
all we had gained from our expedition being the
knowledge that many of our countrymen and country-
women were in even a worse condition than we were.
Our report when we got back to the tents put our
companions very much out of spirits. What were we
to do? was the question. Some proposed that we
should go at once and deliver ourselves up to the
French, petitioning for their clemency. O'Carroll
strongly opposed this.

"We are at liberty now, boys: if we once get into
the hands of these French they will be our masters,
and make us do what they like," he observed; and his
influence, supported as he was by us, carried the point.

We wondered that Jacotot did not betake himself
to his countrymen; but he laughed and said that he

was now an English subject, that he should then be only one among many, that he was with us not only the principal cook, but the only man worthy to be called a cook; indeed, that he was perfectly content to continue to share our fortunes.

As several days passed and we received no visit from the Frenchmen, we began to hope that the seamen had not betrayed us. So far that was satisfactory, but had they remained faithful, I think that there is little doubt that we should have attempted the rescue of the prisoners. At last once more we saw the *Mignonne* put to sea; and immediately on this, with O'Carroll and Sam Kelson in company, after watching for some time without seeing anything of the English sailors, we therefore conjectured that either they had quarrelled with the French and been put in prison, or had gone on board the privateer—too probably the latter. After a consultation, we agreed that we would, at all events, pay a visit to the passengers of the Indiaman. The French could scarcely think it necessary to keep guards constantly watching them, and we might therefore easily accomplish the undertaking. We accordingly set off to move round the harbour, intending to conceal ourselves in some spot near the Indiaman, that we might watch our opportunity for getting on board. We had gone on for some distance, and were approaching the spot, concealing ourselves carefully as we advanced, when sounds of laughter reached our ears—honest English laughter. We stole on, very much inclined to join in it, considering that we had not had a good laugh for some time, when from some rocks up which we climbed we saw below us a large party of ladies and gentlemen engaged in discussing a dinner in picnic fashion on the grass. They all seemed remarkably merry and happy. The younger gentlemen were running about helping the ladies, and doing the polite in the most approved fashion.

Trundle smacked his lips so loudly at the sight that some of the party turned a hasty glance in the direction where we lay hidden, supposing probably that the noise was made by some bird in the foliage above their heads. In a short time one of the young gentlemen was called on for a song. He without hesitation complied. I forget the strain. It was a right merry one. Another followed him, and then another.

"I say, Braithwaite," whispered Toby Trundle, "just let me go down and introduce myself, and then you know I can introduce you all, and I'm sure that they will be glad to make your acquaintance."

I nodded to Toby, and in an instant he slid down the rock, and was in the very midst of the party before any one observed where he had come from. Their looks of astonishment at finding an English midshipman among them were amusing.

"Why, where have you dropped from, youngster?" exclaimed a civilian, a judge returning from—what was more unusual in those days than at present—a visit to England. "The clouds?"

"Not exactly; 'tis but from up there, where I have a number of friends who would be glad to make your acquaintance," answered Toby promptly. "May I introduce them ? "

"By all means—very happy to see them," answered the nabob, as all civil servants of the Company were called in those days if they were well up the tree, and had made money. "Bring them down at once."

" I have not a gun, sir, or I might do it; but I'll hail them, which will answer the purpose," answered Master Toby, with a twinkle in his eye.

We scarcely waited for his call, but tumbling down one after the other, we stood before the assembled company, to whom Toby, looking as grave as a judge, introduced us formally by name, finishing off with "Sam Kelson, boatswain's mate of his Britannic Majesty's frigate *Phœbe*."

" The very ship we spoke the day before we were captured," observed our friend the judge. "She was on the look-out for Captain La Roche and his merry men, and if she falls in with them, they will have a hard matter to escape ; but sit down, gentlemen, we are very glad to make your acquaintance. We are companions in misfortune, though in some respects you have the advantage over us, by being at liberty."

We found that the passengers were allowed to live as before on board the Indiaman, and were under no sort of restraint, they having given their word not to attempt to escape from the island while the French had possession of it. We were treated in the most friendly manner by all the party, Sam Kelson finding a companion in a corporal, the servant of a military officer going out to rejoin his regiment. Trundle soon let out to our new friends the intention we had entertained of trying to release them. They thanked us, but said that the attempt would have been useless, as the mouth of the harbour was strongly guarded. There were a good many other people on board the ships, while the officers and seamen remained strictly guarded, and were not allowed to visit the shore, except when the *Mignonne* or some other privateer ship of war was in the harbour. Their only fear was that they might run short of provisions before they were released, or that at all events they should have to live on very coarse and scanty food. They advised us to keep out of the Frenchmen's sight, lest we should be pounced on and treated as seamen and belligerents; this we very readily promised to do. Altogether we had a very pleasant and merry meeting, and were sorry when our friends told us that the hour for their return on board had arrived. It was arranged that they should have another picnic party in the same spot in three days, and they kindly invited us to join them. On our way back we had, as may be supposed, plenty of subjects for conversation.

"That Miss Mary Mason," said Toby, "is a sweetly pretty girl. I would go through fire and water to serve her."

"And Julia Arundel is one of the most lively, animated girls I have met for a long time," remarked William, with a sigh. I had observed O'Carroll in conversation with a lady who seemed to be a former acquaintance. He told me that he had known her in her younger and happier days, that she had married an officer in India, had come home with three children, who had all died, and that she was now on her way to rejoin her husband.

" Her case is a very hard one," he remarked.

" So I suspect we shall find are the cases of many," I answered. "Sad indeed are the effects of war ! The non-combatants suffer more even than the combatants. That is to say, a far greater number of people suffer who have nothing to do with the fighting than those who actually carry on the murderous work. Oh, when will war cease throughout the world ? "

"Not until the depraved heart of man is changed, and Satan himself is chained, unable further to hurt the human race," answered O'Carroll. "What has always struck me, besides the wickedness of war, is its utter folly. Who ever heard of a war in which both sides did not come off losers ? The gain in a war can never make amends for the losses, the men slain, the physical suffering, the grief : the victorious side feel that only in a less degree than the losers."

I cordially agreed with him. Yet how many hundreds were daily falling at that time in warfare —how many thousands and tens of thousands were yet to fall, to gratify the insane ambition of a single man, permitted to be the fearful scourge that he was to the human race ? We said as little about our expedition as we could, for the emigrants, as soon as

they heard of so many of their countrymen being in
the neighbourhood, were eager to set out to see them.
We, however, persuaded them to remain where they
were, for a visit of so large a party would not fail to
be discovered by the French, and greatly increase
the annoyances of our position. We, however, paid
our second visit to the passengers of the Indiaman,
and found them on shore at the place where we had
first met them. Their spirits, however, had already
begun to flag; their guards had been less courteous
than at first, sickness had attacked two or three,
gloomy apprehensions were troubling the minds of
many. Still we had a pleasant dinner, and the song
and the jest went round as before. The two midshipmen were the merriest of the party, and paid,
as may be supposed, the most devoted attention to
the two young ladies whom they thought fit to admire.
Their happiness was, however, disagreeably inter-
rupted by the appearance in our midst of half-a-dozen
armed Frenchmen. They nodded familiarly at us.
"Bien, messieurs; you have saved us the trouble of
going to fetch you," said one of them, in a sarcastic
tone. "You will not leave this, but as you are
seamen, you will accompany us to the prison ship."

We soon found that they had been made acquainted
by the seamen of the *Kangaroo* of our being on the
island, and had only waited for leisure to go and
bring us to the settlement. Another party had already been dispatched to bring in the emigrants, and
from the rough unmannerly way in which these

treated our new friends, we could not but feel the gravest apprehensions as to the indignities to which they might be subjected. Our own existence in the hands of lawless ruffians would be very different from what it had hitherto been. The appearance of these unwelcome visitors completely broke up the picnic party, and while our friends returned to their ship, we were marched off towards one of the hulks. We soon had evidence of the bad disposition of our captors towards us, for Toby Trundle, who was very indignant at being thus caught, beginning to saunter along as if he had no intention of hurrying himself to please them, one of them threatened to give him a prog with his bayonet. As we were walking along as slowly as Trundle could contrive to go, the sound of a shot reached our ears. It came from the sea. Our guards started and talked rapidly to each other. Several other shots followed in succession, some close together.

"There are two at it, of that I am sure," exclaimed O'Carroll.

The Frenchmen continued their gesticulations with increased animation. They were evidently eager to get to the mouth of the harbour, whence they could look seaward.

"They think that there is something in the wind, depend on that," observed Trundle.

Presently the firing became more and more rapid, seeming to our ears to come nearer and nearer. The Frenchmen could no longer restrain their eagerness to learn the cause of the firing, and totally disregarding, probably indeed forgetting us, off they set running towards the shore as fast as their legs could carry them. We waited for a few minutes to let them have a fair start, and then followed in their wake for some distance, turning off, however, after a time, to the right, so that, should they come back to look for us, we might not so easily be found. We in a short time reached a high rocky mound, whence we got a view of the sea spread out before us. Within a mile and a half of the land were two ships, both with top-gallant sails set, standing in close-hauled towards the harbour. The wind was somewhat off the land, but yet, if it continued steady, it was possible that they might fetch the harbour-mouth. Such, it appeared evident, was the object of the one, while to prevent her so doing was the aim of the other, which was the larger and nearer to us. As soon as the two midshipmen set eyes on the latter, they clapped their hands like children with delight, exclaiming at the top of their voices, "The *Phœbe*! the *Phœbe*! hurrah! hurrah!" O'Carroll took a more steady glance at the other ship, and then shouted, with no less delight, "And that's the *Mignonne*, and La Roche's day has come at last."

"I should hope so, indeed," cried Trundle ; "depend on it the *Phœbe* won't have done with him till she has made him eat a big dish of humble pie."

The frigate kept firing rapidly her foremost guns at the Frenchman, who replied to them in a spirited manner with his aftermost ones, as they could be brought to bear. He was all the time luffing up, trying to eat into the wind, as it were; but as that was scant, it gave the *Phœbe*, which was well to windward, a great advantage, and she was now rapidly coming up with him. As she did so, she every now and then luffed up for an instant, and let fly her whole broadside, doing considerable execution. We eagerly watched the effect of the shot. The Frenchman's sails were soon riddled, and several of his spars seemed to be wounded, many of his ropes, too, hanging in festoons. At last, directly after another broadside, down came his spanker gaff, shot away in the jaws, while the mizen topsail braces shared the same fate. In vain the crew ran aloft to repair the damage; the ship rapidly fell off, and all prospect of her fetching up to the harbour was lost, unless by a miracle the wind should suddenly shift round. The instant the sail came down, the midshipmen gave vent to their feelings of exultation in a loud "Hip, hip, hurrah!" in which we could not help joining them, and the crew of the *Phœbe*, whom we could fancy at the moment doing the same thing.

"Don't be too sure that the *Mignonne* is taken, however," cried O'Carroll. "I never saw a faster craft, and see, she is keeping away, and going to try what her heels can do for her, dead before the wind."

The *Mignonne*, however, could not keep away without being raked by the *Phœbe*, whose shot, now delivered low, must have told with fearful effect along her decks. This done, the *Phœbe* instantly bore up

in chase, and not having lost a spar, though her sails
had several shot-holes through them, rapidly gained
on her. The Frenchmen, to give themselves every
chance of escape, were now busily employed in getting
out studden-sail booms, in spite of the shot which
went whizzing after them. In a marvellously short
space of time a wide spread of canvas was exhibited
on either side, showing that, though many of her
men had fallen, she had a numerous and well-trained
crew.

"They are smart fellows, indeed," I remarked.
"Many of them fight with halters round their necks."

"That makes fellows smart in more senses than
one," answered O'Carroll.

The *Phœbe*, of course, had to set her studden-sails,
and away the two ships glided before the freshening
breeze. We watched them with breathless interest.
Their speed at first seemed so equal that the chased
had still, it seemed, a chance of escaping.

"Trust to our captain, he'll stick to her till he has
made her strike, or he will chase her round the
world," said the two midshipmen, in the same breath.

The *Mignonne* was firing away all the time with
her stern chasers, while the frigate was replying from
those at her bows. They were both firing at each
other's spars, the one hoping, by crippling her opponent, to escape, the other to prevent her doing so.
What had become of our guards all this time we had
not for a moment thought, while we hoped that they
had equally forgotten us. The chase, indeed, probably

absorbed their attention as it did ours. Few of us doubted that the English frigate would ultimately capture the Frenchman; but should she do so would she of necessity come back with her prize to our island, or would she sail away, and, perhaps ignorant of our existence, leave us to our fate? One thing was evident, that we ought to guard ourselves against the insolence of the French garrison. The men were evidently the scum of society, and should they find themselves without restraint, it was impossible to say what atrocities they might not commit. Anxious as we were to know the result of the chase, we agreed at once to go back to our friends to give them warning, and to consult with them what steps to adopt. Before leaving our look-out place we took one more anxious glance at the two ships. Both O'Carroll and the midshipmen declared that the *Phœbe* was positively overhauling the *Mignonne,* and that in a short time we should see the latter haul down her flag. I doubted it.

CHAPTER XI.

OUR friends on board the Indiaman were thrown into high spirits on hearing of the prospect of being released. They advised us, however, to get on shore again as fast as we could, and hide ourselves, lest the soldiers, hoping to be ultimately successful, should ill-treat us for having run away from them. We told them that our intention had been to release all the English prisoners, and to overpower the Frenchmen.

"Blood will be shed if you do, to no purpose," observed the judge; "should the frigate be successful and come back here, as I have no doubt she will, we shall be released; if the *Mignonne* escapes and returns, her crew would quickly again overpower us and obtain what they wish, a good excuse for ill-treating us, of which they will not fail to avail themselves."

The judge's opinion carried the day, and we hurried on shore, and returned by a circuitous route to the spot whence we had witnessed the engagement between the two vessels. William eagerly swept the dark well-defined line of the horizon with his telescope.

"Hurrah! there is one—yes, there are two sails!

Here, O'Carroll, see what you can make out of them,"
he exclaimed, handing him the glass.

It was some time before O'Carroll would pronounce
an opinion. He then declared positively that there were
two ships, and that they were approaching the land.
There was a strong breeze. We sat down on the
ground, watching anxiously. They came nearer and
nearer. We had no longer any doubt that the *Phœbe*
had captured the privateer. The midshipmen declared positively that the largest was their ship.

"We ought to know her, though, to be sure, it is
more of the inside than the out we see of her," observed
Toby.

All our doubts were set at rest at length, when the
British ensign was seen flying proudly over that of
the French.

Three cheers burst almost involuntarily from our
throats, which could hardly have failed to have shown
our whereabouts to the French soldiers; but if they
guessed the cause, they thought it prudent to take no
notice of our proceedings, but, as we supposed, hurried
back to their abodes, to conceal any property of value
which they might possess. William and Trundle
meantime were unable to resist the temptation of
going on board the Indiaman, to give our new friends
the joyful news. They said that they should be back
in plenty of time to see the ships enter the harbour.
O'Carroll and I preferred waiting to watch proceedings.
At length the frigate and privateer got close in with
the land, when both hove to. What was now to

happen ? Boats were seen passing between the two
vessels, and then the *Mignonne's* head came slowly
round towards the mouth of the harbour, and on she
glided towards it. The flags remained as they were,
and men, we saw, were stationed at the guns. Some
opposition was probably expected. There was a fort
at the entrance of the harbour—not a very formidable-
looking affair—with five ship's guns mounted in it.
Round them we saw the greater part of the mongrel
garrison clustering as if they were going to show fight,
but if so, they thought better of it, for, after a short
consultation, they sneaked away, leaving the fort to
take care of itself. The *Mignonne* came gliding on,
bearing evident traces in her masts and rigging of the
punishment she had received, and of the obstinacy—
or what would have been valour in a better cause—
with which she had been defended. We met the midshipmen running down towards the landing-place, and
jumping into the first boat we could find, we got
alongside her directly she dropped anchor.

"Why, Braithwaite, Trundle ! where have you come
from ?" exclaimed several voices, as the midshipmen
clambered up the side.

They soon gave an account of themselves, and I need
scarcely say that we were heartily welcomed by the
officers of the *Phœbe* in charge of the prize, who were
in high spirits at having captured a vessel which had
proved one of the greatest pests to British commerce
in the Eastern seas. The Frenchmen had not yielded
till more than a third of their number lay dead or

desperately wounded on her decks. Among them were several of the seamen of the unfortunate *Kangaroo*, including her wretched captain and mate. The survivors of the Englishmen declared that they had been forced on board and compelled to fight. We declined to express any opinion on the subject. All we could say was that we had missed them from the encampment, and had every reason to suppose that they had fallen into the hands of the French. They thus escaped hanging, which I certainly believe they deserved. The chief offenders had already paid the penalty of their crimes. I need scarcely describe the delight of the passengers of the Indiaman on finding that they could now proceed on their voyage, or of the prisoners who were released from the different hulks. They were the officers and seamen taken in different prizes by the *Mignonne*. The excuse the Frenchmen gave for treating them thus barbarously was that the French taken by English cruisers were shut up on board hulks in English harbours without good food or any exercise. They pretended not to understand that, in one instance, the prisoners would inevitably have escaped had they been left at liberty, while in the present they had had no opportunity of escaping. The mouth of the harbour having been surveyed, the frigate came in the next day, that her crew might assist in repairing the *Mignonne* and getting the Indiaman and the other vessels ready for sea. I was curious to ascertain what O'Carroll would say to finding La Roche at length a prisoner. I asked him

if he would go on board the frigate with me to see
the French captain.

"I would not do so to triumph over a fallen foe, but
perhaps if I was to set eyes on him again for a few
times I might get over the intense dislike—even more,
the dread, I feel for him," he answered. "I have reason
to feel dislike. He ruined my prospects, he killed my
companions, and he treated me with every indignity
and cruelty he could devise while I remained on board
his ship. He made me serve him as a menial—wait
behind his chair, clean his shoes, arrange his cabin,
and if I displeased him he ordered his men to flog
me. Ay! I never told you that before, I was ashamed
to do so. He well-nigh broke my spirit. Had I remained much longer with him he would have done so,
or I should have gone mad and jumped overboard.
Still I will see him."

We went on board the frigate and enquired for the
privateer captain. Having already, it appeared,
broken his parole in England when he had once
before been taken, Captain Young had refused to
receive it, and he was therefore confined below in
a cabin, with a sentry placed over him. It was naturally supposed that he would otherwise take some
opportunity of getting on shore, and, knowing the
locality, might remain concealed till he could escape
from the island altogether. Accompanied by the
master-at-arms, we entered the cabin. La Roche
was seated in an easy-chair reading a book when
the door opened. He did not rise, but, looking up,

nodded to O'Carroll, whom he seemed instantly to recognise.

"Ah, mon ami! it's the fortune of war, you see. Once I had you in my power, now your countrymen have me," he said, in a cool, unconcerned manner. "It is pleasant, is it not?—pleasanter for you than for me. However, my turn may come next, and then——"

"I hope not. I hope while I live that I may never again be in your hands!" exclaimed O'Carroll, interrupting him. "You remember how you treated me?"

"Oh, well! and it is in your power to inform the captain of this frigate, and probably he will treat me in the same way."

"No, indeed! Englishmen never treat their prisoners as you treated me," answered O'Carroll; "Monsieur knows that well enough. I did not come here to insult you; I did not come to triumph over you. You had inspired me with a horror I could not get over. I came here to be cured. I am so, thoroughly. You have done much injury to the commerce of my country, and the only ill I wish you is that you may be kept a close prisoner till the termination of the war, and never again be able to do an injury to Englishmen."

La Roche shrugged his shoulders at this address, and smiled. "Well, you Irishmen are indeed curious. I should have thought that you would have liked to see me hung up to the yard-arm," he observed, in the same cool tone as before. "However, your

11

moderate wishes may be gratified, or I may make my escape; and if I do, and ever capture you again, I promise you that I will remember your moderation, and treat you to the best of everything I have on board."

We soon after this brought our interview with the famous privateer captain to an end, and O'Carroll assured me that all his unpleasant monomaniacal feelings with regard to him had been, as he hoped, completely dissipated. As we were about to leave the ship Captain Young politely invited us to remain and dine with him. He showed much interest in O'Carroll's account of his misfortunes, and finally arranged that he should take the command of one of the vessels in the harbour to convey the emigrants to New South Wales. I, of course, received no direct communication from Captain Hassall, but from the information Captain Young gave me I had great hopes that the *Barbara*, instead of sailing immediately for the east, had gone to the coast of Madagascar, in which direction the *Phœbe* herself was bound. Captain Young offered me a passage should I wish to rejoin my ship. The Indiaman being refitted for sea by the united exertions of all the crews, we all sailed out of the harbour in succession, the *Phœbe* leading. The *Mignonne*, with her prize crew and some of the prisoners on board, was bound for the Mauritius, to give information of the capture of the island; the emigrant ship was bound for New South Wales, the Indiaman for Calcutta, we for Madagascar. I went on board the

Argo, the ship commanded by O'Carroll. I found him well satisfied with his change of circumstances. There was only one thing about which he was concerned. La Roche, though still a captive, was alive, and might soon regain his liberty.

" If he does I'm sure that he will cause me trouble again," he observed. " I don't know what causes it, but I even now cannot think of the venomous little man without a feeling of dread—a creeping sensation, Braithwaite. Do you know what it is ? "

" Not exactly," said I. " But the remedy I suggest is not to think of him. Whenever his image appears banish him with a kick. Or, let me be serious, O'Carroll. Is it not our own fault if we go on living in fear of death all our life long ? Put your trust in God, and fear not what man can do to you."

" You are right ! you are right ! " exclaimed O'Carroll, warmly; " it is just the want of doing that has made me—no coward, as you know—constantly tremble at unseen dangers. Henceforward I will try to follow your advice. "

"Do," said I ; "and depend on it your dread of the little Frenchman will completely and for ever vanish."

I parted from O'Carroll—as honest a man as ever broke a biscuit—with the sincere hope that we should meet again. The crews of our respective ships gave three hearty cheers as we separated on our respective courses. We accompanied the *Mignonne* for some distance towards the Mauritius, when several sails were reported in sight from the masthead.

"I hope that they are enemies!" I heard Trundle
thoughtlessly exclaim. "Glorious fun to have a fight,
We, too, should soon give a good account of them."

Both ships were speedily got ready for action, for
in those days it was difficult to sail far without meeting an enemy. It might be one to be captured—
snapped up in an instant; it might be one of equal or
not of vastly superior size, to be fought bravely, and
taken in the end; or, mayhap, one so much larger that
it would be necessary to make all sail and run away,
a proceeding not very often practised in those days by
British naval commanders. It was rather doubtful,
however, from the number and size of the ships in
sight, whether we should not find it necessary to have
recourse to the last expedient. We continued, however, steering as before, and rapidly nearing the
strangers, when, to the relief of the less pugnaciously
disposed, first one and then the others made their
number, and we discovered, as we got sufficiently near
to exchange telegraph signals, that they were three
frigates—the *Galatea, Racehorse,* and *Astrea*—on their
way to the coast of Madagascar to look after a French
squadron, which, having been driven away from the
Mauritius, had gone in that direction. We should
now be a fair match for the Frenchmen whenever we
should meet them. Having put most of our prisoners
well guarded on board the *Mignonne,* we parted from
her, she to continue her passage to the Mauritius, we
to accompany our consorts in search of the enemy.

A bright look-out was now kept for the enemy, and

from sunrise to its setting the mastheads were adorned with eager watchers, each wishing to be the first one to espy the Frenchmen. However, the lofty mountain ridges of Madagascar hove in sight before any of them were seen. I had become very anxious about the fate of the *Barbara*. Had she prosecuted her voyage to this coast, and fallen in with the enemy ? If so, she must have been captured, and too probably sent away to one of the settlements. In spite of my advice to O'Carroll, this idea took complete possession of my mind, and I felt convinced that the voyage from which so much had been expected would come to nought.

Night closed in on us, and the usual answer was given to the watch below by those who had come off deck, "Not a sign of a sail in sight." The next morning the sun arose out of his ocean bed brighter even than is his wont in that bright clime, first lighting up the topmost heights of the mountains with a roseate tinge, while a purple hue still lay spread over the calm ocean. As usual, officers and men were going aloft, with telescopes over their shoulders, to take a look round for the enemy, when, as the sun rose higher, a shout of satisfaction burst from many a throat, for there lay, well in with the land, their white canvas shining brightly in his beams, the French frigates of which we were in search. The wind came off the land, and we were far to leeward. They thus had greatly the advantage of us. We did our utmost, however, to beat up to them. Every sail that could draw was set, and we continued to tack and tack hour after hour, hoping to reach them, and that some fortunate shift of wind would give us the weather-gauge and enable us to choose our own time for action. As I went along the decks I was struck by the bold and determined appearance of the men as they stood at their quarters, stripped to the waist, and mostly with handkerchiefs of many colours tied round their heads. The costume was appropriate, for the heat was excessive, besides which, sailors know well that the suffering is much less, should they be wounded, if no pieces of cloth are carried into the body with the shot. They were chatting and laughing, and many of them were cutting all sorts of jokes. I had volunteered to serve as the captain's aide-de-camp, to carry messages for him to any part of the ship, or to assist the surgeons in the cockpit.

"You would do good service on deck, and I respect your feeling in offering to be there," he answered; "but you are a noncombatant. You have nothing to gain by exposing your life. You will therefore oblige me by performing the far more painful task of assisting the surgeons."

I bowed with a feeling of disappointment at my heart, which I probably exhibited.

He smiled and said, "It is possible, after all, that there may be very little employment for your talents."

There was a shout on the upper deck, taken speedily up by the men on the main deck. The enemy

were seen bearing down on us. On they came, nearer
and nearer. Where we lay it had fallen a perfect calm,
and our sails kept flapping against the masts. Still
the breeze favoured them. I felt very queer, I confess.
I had no intention of going below till I was wanted,
and it did not occur to me that I might be turned into
a patient myself. The delight of the sailors at seeing
the French thus boldly approaching was excessive, nor
did they fail to praise them for their courage.

"Bravo! Johnny Crapaud. That's more than I
thought of you. Come along! Don't leave us again.
We won't hurt ye more than we can help. You are
brave fellows, that you are; we always thought so.
Now you show it. Bear a hand, though."

I heard such and similar expressions from most of
the men as I passed along the decks. Suddenly there
was a gloom from one end of the ship to the other.
The breeze which had been bringing the Frenchmen
along suddenly dropped. It had served, them, however, well enough to bring them pretty close up to us.

"Now," I thought to myself, "I shall see what a
regular stand-up sea fight is like."

Still I could not help feeling all the time that my
vocation was one of peace, and that I had no business
to be where I was. That is not a pleasant sensation.
The great thing for a man to feel in time of danger is
that he is at his post and doing his duty. As I was
in for it, I determined to do my best to be of use, and
to trust to the God of mercy for protection. The
enemy soon showed us that they had no intention of

being idle. A shot came whistling over our heads, and fell a considerable distance on the other side of us. This showed them that we were within gunshot range of each other, and immediately they opened fire in earnest. Some of the shot flew over our heads, others on one side or the other, but hitherto none had struck us. I had a hope that, after all, there would be no bloodshed. We meantime had commenced firing, but either the Frenchmen's powder was better or their guns longer, for our shot mostly appeared to fall short, greatly to the vexation of our crew. The enemy also having had the last of the wind, while we were becalmed, were able to take up a better position than we had, and continued warmly engaging us, we often being scarcely able to return a shot.

As I had nothing to do below, I remained on deck. More than once, however, I could not help ducking my head as a shot whistled above it. Possibly it might have been too high to have struck me. However, I soon got accustomed to that, and as no one had as yet been hurt, I began to fancy that after all a sea-fight was not so terrible an affair as I had supposed, and that possibly we and the Frenchmen might part without doing much harm to each other. I had been standing near a fine young fellow, Jem Martin by name, captain of a gun, who had for some time past been cutting, with more than ordinary humour, numbers of jokes on the enemy. I was struck by his bold attitude and thoroughly sailor-like look. His bright blue eye beamed with life and animation. I had turned my head away from him when a shot whistled by, and I heard a piercing shriek, such as a strong man utters but once, wrung from his bosom by mortal agony. I looked round, and on the deck lay the shattered body of a human being. There were a few spasmodic movements of the limbs, and all that remained of Jem Martin was the mangled corpse at my feet. I shuddered, for I could not help feeling that such as he was I might now have been.

The event seemed to affect his shipmates but little ; another seaman took his place, and the gun was loaded, run out, and fired. The fact was that they had no time just then for thought or the indulgence of feeling. The enemy's shot now came thicker and thicker ; many went through the sails, others wounded the masts and spars and cut away the rigging, and several more of our men were hit. As soon as they were carried below, I followed, to assist the surgeon in attending to their wounds. I had long before this forgotten all about the danger to which I was myself exposed, but I could not forget that I had a young brother on board who might any moment be numbered among the killed or wounded. It seemed to me, in-deed, that we were getting so much the worst of it, that I began to dread that the flag of England might have to strike to that of France. The idea was not a pleasant one ; it was not, however, shared in by others on board.

After we had received a pretty severe battering for the space of two hours, the breeze got up, and the

Frenchmen hauled off to repair damages. On seeing
this the rage of our men became very great, and they
cried out to the officers that they might be allowed to
go after them. As the enemy were to windward this
was not easily to be done, and we had to wait patiently
in the hope that the enemy would choose to renew
the fight, while in the meantime our top-men were
knotting and splicing rigging, and the carpenter's
crew were strengthening the wounded yards and
stopping shot-holes. At length the breeze reached us,
and as it filled our sails the crew cheered in anticipa-
tion of being able soon to get to. closer quarters with
the enemy. After making numerous tacks, two of our
squadron got up to two of the French ships, which
seemed in no way disposed to refuse battle. While
our gallant commodore closed with the *Renommé* we
engaged the *Clorinde*. The fight soon gave work for
our surgeons, and I went below, as I had undertaken
to do, to help them. As I left the deck I cast a glance
at my young brother, who had charge of a division of
the guns, and was standing on the deck cheering on
the men, full of life and animation. The shots were
thickly flying about his head; any moment one
might lay him low. I could but offer up a prayer
for his safety.

The surgeon and his mates were already at work.
I hung up my coat and tucked up my sleeves, prepared
to assist them. I will not describe the scene of suffering I witnessed. Most of the poor fellows bore their
agony with wonderful fortitude. Two officers had

been brought below wounded. I kept looking up anxiously every time I saw the feet of men descending the ladder, dreading that they might be bringing down my young brother. Still I kept praying for his safety while I followed the surgeons' directions. A young seaman had been brought down fearfully wounded. I had remarked him on several occasions among the most active and zealous of the crew. The surgeon examined him. He did not groan—indeed, he did not appear to suffer much pain.

The surgeon shook his head. " I can do nothing for him," he whispered to me. " You may be able, perhaps, to speak a word of comfort, and there is nothing just now for you to do."

I was rather surprised at the surgeon saying even thus much. Perhaps the light of the lantern, which at that moment fell on my countenance, revealed my thoughts, for he added, " I was asked to look after the lad, whose mother is a widow, and, God help me ! I have done little for him, and now it is too late."

The young seaman was placed on a hammock opened out on the deck of the cockpit. I knelt down by his side, and, after repeating such passages out of the Word of life as occurred to me, I engaged in prayer. He followed me in a low voice. Suddenly he was silent. I looked toward him ; the immortal spirit had taken its flight from his frail body. Still the battle raged ; more of our poor fellows were brought down, and I once more was called on to assist the surgeons in their painful task.

CHAPTER XII.

A GLORIOUS VICTORY.

I BEGAN seriously to fear that we were getting the worst of it. Shot after shot came crashing on board, and several more men were brought down. I expressed my fears aloud to the surgeon. A poor fellow already on the table about to undergo amputation overheard me. "Don't think of that, sir," he exclaimed; "they are tough ones, those mounseers, but we'll go down with our colours flying sooner than strike them."

At that instant our ears were saluted by loud cheers, which burst from the crew on deck. Still the firing was kept up, and it was evident that our ship continued in action. At last, another wounded man being brought down, we heard that the *Renommé*, the French commodore's frigate, had struck.

In a few minutes another cheer was heard, the firing ceased, and we had the satisfaction of finding that the *Clorinde* had also struck her colours to us. My heart felt intense relief when I found that the action was over, and that my young brother had escaped without a wound. Then I recollected that those who had been killed had not been brought below. I wondered that he had not come below to relieve my anxiety. Those of whom I inquired could not tell me what officers had been killed. The instant, therefore, I could leave the poor suffering fellows I had undertaken to assist, I hurried on deck. When I went below the frigate had presented a trim and orderly appearance. Now her sails were torn and full of shot-holes, her running rigging hung in loose festoons, with blocks swaying here and there, her bulwarks were shattered, her lately clean deck ploughed up with round shot covered with blood and gore, and blackened by powder. The thickening shades of evening threw a peculiar gloom over the whole·scene. I looked anxiously round for William. I could not see him. My heart sank within me. Could he be among the slain? A midshipman hurried past me.

" Where is Braithwaite, my brother ? " I asked, in a trembling voice.

" There; don't you see him on the forecastle ? "

I looked in the direction to which he pointed. My heart bounded up again as I saw him directing the men engaged in bending a fresh foresail, which had before concealed him from my sight. My voice trembled with emotion as I ran forward, and, shaking him by the hand, congratulated him on our victory and his safety. He seemed scarcely to understand my agitation.

" Yes, I am thankful to say we have thrashed the enemy, and I wish there were a few more to treat in the same way. There is one fellow making off, and I am afraid the *Astrea* will not be able to work up to bring her to action."

I looked out as he spoke. One of our frigates, to which he pointed, was a long way to leeward, while a French frigate was standing under all sail to the north-west. Our two antagonists appeared fearfully shattered, both the French commodore's ship and the *Clorinde*, which was even in a worse condition than we were. All our boats had been so injured by shot that we were unable to send one to take possession of our prize, and as the night was now rapidly coming on, we could not hope to do much to repair damages till the morning. As long, however, as the men could work, the carpenter's crew continued putting the ship to rights. The rest of the already overworked crew were then piped below, that they might be able to renew their labours on the morrow. I had plenty to do in assisting the surgeons in attending on the wounded, till at last, well wearied out, I turned into my hammock, thankful that my dear brother and I had escaped the perils of the fight, and sincerely hoping that, as it was my first battle, so it might be the last in which I should be engaged. Before going below I took a look towards our prize, whose light I saw burning brightly at no great distance from us. I had now time to think of my own affairs, and of course was not a little anxious about the fate of the *Barbara*, for it was too probable that she had fallen into the hands of the Frenchmen. If so, they would probably have sent her to France, as she was well provisioned for a long voyage, or to one of their settlements, where she could be disposed of to advantage. My sleep was sadly disturbed with these thoughts and with the scenes of pain and suffering I had witnessed. I awoke soon after it was light, and dressing quickly went on deck. It was to find everybody there in a state of no small anger and vexation.

"She is off, gone clean out of sight," I heard people saying.

I inquired what was the matter.

"Why, it is enough to vex a man, Mr. Braithwaite," observed the first lieutenant. "As we could not send on board last night to take possession of our prize, she has managed to slip away during the darkness. She left a light burning astern on a cask to deceive us. If we ever come up with her we'll make her pay dearly. The other fellow, too, has got clear away; however, we will find him out, wherever he has hid himself."

Soon after this the commodore signalled to us to send our boats to assist in removing the prisoners from the *Renommé*. Thanks to the exertions of the carpenter and his crew, three were already made capable of floating. I asked to take an oar, as I wished to go on board the prize. No sooner did I step on board than I regretted having come. Terrible was the scene of slaughter I witnessed. The frigate had been crowded with troops, nearly one-half of whom had been cut down by the *Galatea's* shot, which she had poured into the Frenchman's hull. The crew were only now beginning to throw the dead bodies of their shipmates overboard. The French commodore, a gallant officer, and many others, were killed. But the wounded nearly doubled the killed, and they chiefly excited our sympathy. Their own surgeons were already almost worn out with attending to them, and of course we could not spare any of ours to render them assistance. The more of the effects of war I saw, even on this small scale, the more I longed for the time when wars are to cease and nations to live at peace with each other. It was not, however, the fashion to speak on that subject in those days, nor do the nations of the world, alas! appear more inclined now than then to bring about that happy state of things!

When taking some of the prisoners on board the *Galatea*, I found she had also suffered severely, though not at all in proportion to the *Renommé*. Captain Schomberg ordered us, as soon as our damages were repaired, to make sail for the port of Tamatave, on the east coast of Madagascar, where he suspected the other French frigate had taken refuge, her captain supposing probably that we should return at once with our prizes to the Mauritius. The *Astrea* coming up, her crew went on board the *Renommé*, to put her to rights, and this being done, all four frigates made sail together for Tamatave. It is merely a reef-formed harbour, and by no means a secure or good one. The English had sent a force of about fifty men there after the reduction of the Mauritius, and they had, we understood, built a fort, or taken possession of an old one. It was a question whether they had been able to hold it against the French, or had been compelled to surrender. As we approached the coast, all our glasses were in requisition, to ascertain whether any ships were at anchor off the place. There were two, certainly, one larger than the other. The wind was light, but we at length got in close enough to see that the French flag flew at their mastheads, as also over the fort, and that there were several smaller vessels. I thought that there would be more fighting, but instead of proceeding to that extremity, the commodore sent in a boat with a flag of truce, pointing out the overpowering force he had under him, and demanding the instant surrender of the ships and fort.

We anxiously watched for the return of the boat, for if the demand were not acceded to we should have, it was understood, to go in and cut out the ships with our boats. Many liked the thought of such an exploit, in spite of its dangerous character. It was very possible that the French captain might hope, with the support of the fort, to be able to beat off the boats, and to hold out until the squadron should be driven off by a storm. At last the boat was seen returning. The frigate was the one which had escaped from us. Her captain wisely agreed to yield to the fortune of war, and to give her up with all her prizes, and the fort into the bargain.

"And what is the name of the other ship?" I asked.

12

"The *Barbara* merchantman," answered the lieutenant. "She was on the point of sailing with a
French crew when we appeared, so that her owners
have had a narrow chance of losing their property."

This was, indeed, satisfactory news. I was, of
course, very eager to go on board and hear from
Captain Hassall what he intended doing. The account brought off as to the state of the English
garrison was melancholy. The fort was built in an
especially unhealthy spot, with marshy undrained
land close round it. The consequence was, that of
the fifty men who had been sent there, when the
French appeared not a dozen were alive, and that
sad remainder were scarcely able to lift their muskets.
They had therefore at once yielded to the enemy.
Several others had since died, but the sickly season
being now over, it was hoped that the remainder would
live on till the next year, when in all probability
during the same season they would share the fate
of their comrades. I got a passage in one of the next
boats which pulled in. Captain Hassall had been
allowed by the French to return to his ship, and he
was taking a turn on deck when I went alongside.
He looked at me curiously two or three times when I
stepped on deck, and, raising his hat, inquired what I
wanted. Suddenly he stopped when he got close up
to me, exclaiming, "What! James Braithwaite, my
dear boy, is it really you? I am delighted to see
you, for to say the truth, I had given you up as lost.
I never supposed that cockleshell of a boat in which

you left the ship would have survived the hurricane which came on directly afterwards."

There was one question above all others I wished to ask him, "Have you written home to tell my friends of my loss ? "

" No," he answered; " I have so often found people turn up whom I thought had been lost, that I am very unwilling to send home bad news till it is absolutely necessary, and as I did not require your signature, I was able to avoid mentioning that you were not on board."

This answer greatly relieved my mind, and I was in a short time able to talk over our arrangements for the future. The capture of the *Barbara* would, of course, be a heavy expense to the owners; but if the voyage should prove as successful as we still hoped it would, a handsome profit might yet be realised. To that object we had now to bend all our energies. We were therefore anxious as soon as we could to proceed on our voyage. I had heard from the captain of the *Phœbe* that an expedition was fitting out in India for the capture of Batavia, the chief town in Java, of which the French now held possession; and we had great hopes, if we could reach it soon after the English had gained the place, which of course we expected they would do, that we should sell a large portion of our cargo to great advantage. Before sailing, however, we determined to see what trade could be carried on with the natives. Fortunately, the French had not touched our cargo for that purpose. Though they had made frequent attempts to form settlements in Madagascar, they had never succeeded in gaining the confidence and good-will of the natives. Had the plans of the Count Benyowsky been carried out when he offered his services to France, they might possibly have obtained a powerful influence in the affairs of the country, if not entire possession of it. His plans were, however, completely defeated by the governor of the Mauritius, who, looking on Madagascar as a dependency of that island, was jealous of his—the Count's—proceedings, and finally drove him to make common cause with the natives against the French Government. I heard some details of the life of that extraordinary adventurer. The Count Benyowsky was a Polish nobleman, who for some political reason was banished by the Russian Government to one of its settlements in the extreme eastern part of Siberia, whence it seemed impossible for him ever to find his way back to Europe. The governor of the town in which the Count was compelled to reside had a daughter, young and lovely, who had conceived a warm affection for him, which appears to have been fully returned. Through the means of this young lady he was able to gain information as to everything which was taking place. He heard, among other things, that two large Russian ships were expected at the neighbouring port. He had long been looking out for the means of making his escape from Siberia.

Here was an opportunity. None but a man of

great boldness and energy would, however, have considered it one. He was a prisoner in a fortified town; it contained a considerable number of his countrymen, but they were prisoners strictly watched. Still he was determined to make the attempt. He set to work and gained over a hundred men to assist in his dangerous undertaking. By some means they were able to provide themselves with arms. The governor's fair daughter undertook to obtain the keys of the fortress, provided her father's life was spared. The adventurers found it impossible to make their escape without first mastering the garrison. The conspirators were mustered, and were ready for the enterprise. The young lady brought her lover the keys. Her last words were, "Do not injure my father."

"Of course not, if he makes no resistance," was the Count's answer.

The gates were opened; the conspirators rushed in. The old governor was, however, not a man to yield without a struggle. Putting himself at the head of some of his men, he endeavoured to keep back the assailants. Again and again he charged them, calling on the troops to rally round him. It was evident to the Count and his companions that if he were allowed to live their undertaking would fail. He therefore, pressed on by numbers, was killed, with all who stood by him.

The adventurers, now putting all who opposed them to the sword, became complete masters of the place, and without difficulty obtained possession also of the two ships which had just arrived. A sufficient number of officers and seamen were found to navigate the ships, and, having provisioned them for a long voyage, the Count, taking the daughter of the governor with him, went on board them, with a hundred companions, and made sail to the southward. The Count had taken precautions against pursuit; indeed, there were probably no Russian men-of-war in those waters at the time, and thus he made good his escape. He touched at a variety of places. He reached Canton in safety. Here he wisely sold his ships, as, had he fallen in with any Russian men-of-war, his destruction would have been certain. At Canton he and his companions embarked on board two French vessels, in which they proceeded to the Isle of France. Here he announced his intention of forming a colony in Madagascar, or perhaps of conquering the country for France.

His plans, as I have said, excited the jealousy of the governor of the Mauritius, and of other people of authority in that island, who determined to oppose him. Notwithstanding, he proceeded to France, where he so completely gained the good opinion of the French minister that he was appointed to take command of an expedition to found the proposed settlement, with the title of governor-general. He had married the daughter of the Russian governor, and she accompanied him in all his travels, but what was her ultimate fate I do not remember having heard.

After returning to the Isle of France, where the governor still kept up his hostility, and opposed him by every means in his power, he set sail with about three hundred men for Madagascar. He landed at Antongil Bay, where he was well received by the chiefs, but he at first was subject to a good deal of opposition from the natives generally. He did his best to conciliate them, but as he had often to employ force, and to keep up a strict military rule at the same time, it must have been difficult to persuade them that his intentions were pacific and philanthropic. He seems to have met with heroic courage all the innumerable difficulties by which he was beset. He lost many of his officers and men by sickness, as the position where he attempted to found his first settlement, from being surrounded by marshes, was very unhealthy. Among others, his only boy lost his life by fever. He was left without the necessary supplies he expected from the Isle of France, the governor purposely neglecting to send them. The natives also were incited by emissaries of the governor to oppose him, while, of the officers sent to him, some were incapable, and others came with the express purpose of betraying him. Notwithstanding all these difficulties, by the middle of 1775 the settlers had built a fort in a more healthy situation, which was called Fort Louis, had constructed all the necessary buildings for the town of Louisbourg, and had formed a road twenty-one miles in length and twenty-four feet in breadth. The Count had also done something towards civilising the people, and among other important measures had persuaded the women to give up their practice of infanticide, which had been terribly prevalent. They, however, refused to ratify the engagement without the presence of the Count's wife, who was residing at the Isle of France. She was accordingly sent for, and on her arrival the women of the different provinces, assembling before her, bound themselves by an oath never to sacrifice any of their children. They agreed that any who should break this oath should be made slaves, while they were to send all deformed children to an institution which had been founded by the Count in the settlement for that purpose.

He had by this time formed alliances with many of the surrounding chiefs, who ever afterwards remained faithful to him. In other parts of the island combinations were formed against him. He accordingly mustered his forces, and marching against his enemies, who had brought forty thousand men into the field, put them to flight. Those who fell into his hands he treated with so much leniency and kindness that he ultimately attached them to his cause. A curious superstition of the natives was the cause of his being at length raised to the dignity of the principal chief of the island. It appears that the hereditary successor to the title was missing, when some of the natives took it into their heads that the Count Benyowsky was the lost heir. The idea gained ground at the very time that the affairs of the Count were in a very precarious condition. His own health was failing, the more faithful among his European officers were dead, his enemies in the Mauritius had succeeded in prejudicing the minds of the members of the French Government against him, and two, if not more, vessels bringing out supplies had been lost. Under these circumstances it is not surprising that he should have accepted the proffered dignity, which shortly led to his being recognised as the principal chief and supreme ruler of the whole island.

Commissioners had been sent out from France to investigate the affairs of the settlement. While they were there he took the opportunity of giving up the command of the setttlement to another officer, and entirely dissolved his connection with it and with France, though he at the same time, with the other chiefs, expressed his desire to live on friendly terms with the inhabitants, and to support the settlement to the best of his ability. He employed some time after this in consolidating his power and in improving the condition of the people. He also drew up a constitution, which for those days was of the most liberal character. Having done all he could to civilise the people, he resolved to go to Europe to establish mercantile relations with different countries for the improvement of the commerce of his adopted country.

In France, though he had some friends who welcomed him cordially, he was coldly received by those in power, though his course was supported by the celebrated Dr. Franklin, who was at that time in Paris. At length, quitting the country, he went to England; but though he offered to place the country under the protection of the English Government, no encouragement was afforded him. All his hopes in Europe having failed, he set sail for the United States, in the vessel he chartered with a cargo of goods suited to the markets of Madagascar. After remaining for some time in the United States and obtaining another ship and cargo, he reached Antongil Bay in July 1785. He was here cordially welcomed by the chiefs, but instead of going into the interior and assuming the reins of government, he remained on the coast for the purpose of establishing trading-posts where his goods might be disposed of. He had captured one port from the French, and was engaged in repairing a fort built by them, when a body of troops landing from a French frigate attacked him. He retired with some few Europeans and natives into the fort, where he attempted to defend himself. The French advanced, he was shot through the body, and being ignominiously dragged out, directly afterwards expired. Poor Count Benyowsky! I could not help feeling sorrow when I heard of his sad fate.

The climate of the low lands near the seashore was, from what we heard, very unhealthy, but in the hill country of the interior it is as healthy as any part of the world. We heard a good deal of the English and French pirates, who had formed, a century before, some flourishing settlements on the northern coasts.

The name of a bay we visited (Antongil) was derived from one of the most celebrated, Anthony Gill. Several other places also obtained their names from members of the fraternity of freebooters. While the pirates continued their depredations on the ocean, they in general behaved well to the natives, but when being hotly pressed by the men-of-war of the people they had been accustomed to rob, they entered upon the most nefarious of all traffics, that of slaves, and to obtain them instigated the people of one tribe to make war on those of another. This traffic has ever since been carried on, greatly contributing to retard the progress of civilization.

CHAPTER XIII

I WAS very sorry to have to part from my brother William, and not a little so from that merriest of merry midshipmen, Toby Trundle.

"We shall meet again one of these days, Trundle," I said, as I warmly shook hands with him. "I hope it will be in smooth water, too; we have had enough of the rough together."

I did my best to express to the captain and officers of the *Phœbe* my sense of the kindness with which they had treated me from the first moment I had stepped on board their frigate to the last. We all sailed together, the men-of-war and their prize, to proceed to the Mauritius, then to refit and get ready for the expedition to Java. We also were bound for Java, but intended first to visit Antongil Bay for the purpose of trading with the natives. I was pleased to find myself among my old shipmates again. They had had no sickness on board, and not a man had been lost. The officers were the same in character, while their individual peculiarities seemed to stand out more prominently than before.

We found the natives at Antongil Bay very honour-

able in their dealings. Many of the chiefs spoke French
perfectly well, and looked like Frenchmen. They
were, we found, indeed, descendants of some of the
Count Benyowsky's followers, who had married native
women. The children of such marriages were generally
highly esteemed by the natives, who had raised them
to the rank of chiefs. From what I saw of all classes
of the natives of Madagascar, but especially of the
upper ranks, I should say that they were capable of
a high state of civilization, and I see no reason why
they should not some day take their place among the
civilized nations of the east. When that time will
come it is impossible to say. Neither adventurers,
like the brave and talented Benyowsky, nor French
settlements, will bring it about. One thing, indeed,
only can produce it—that is, the spread and the firm
establishment of true Christianity among the people.

Some days after our departure we had a distant
view of the island of Rodriguez. In about a fortnight
afterwards we were glad to put on warm clothing instead of the light dress suitable to the tropics; yet we
were only in the same parallel of latitude as Madeira.
It showed us how much keener is the air of the southern
hemisphere than that of the northern. We soon after
fell in with the monsoon, or trade wind, which sent
us flying along at a good rate; till early in August,
on a bright morning, the look-out at the masthead
shouted at the top of his voice, "Land ho! Land
ahead!" It was the north-west cape of New Holland,
or Australia, a region then, as even to the present day,

almost a *terra incognita* to Europeans. As we neared
it, we curiously looked out with our glasses for some
signs of the habitations of men, but nothing could be
seen to lead us to suppose that human beings were to
be found there. The shore was low, sandy, and deso-
late, without the least intermixture of trees or verdure.
A chain of rocks, over which the sea broke furiously,
lined the coast. We continued in sight of this most
inhospitable-looking land till the next morning. I
could not help thinking of the vast extent of country
which intervened between the shore at which we were
gazing and the British settlement at Port Jackson, of
which we had lately heard such flattering accounts.
Was it a region flowing with milk and honey ? one of
lakes and streams, or of lofty mountains? did it contain
one vast inland sea, or was it a sandy desert of burning
sands, impassable for man ?

This was a problem some of my emigrant friends
had been discussing, and which I longed to see solved.
After losing sight of the coast of New Holland, we
had to keep a bright look-out, as we were in the supposed neighbourhood of certain islands which some
navigators, it was reported, had seen, but no land appeared. One clear night we found ourselves suddenly,
it seemed, floating in an ocean of milk, or more properly,
perhaps, a thick solution of chalk in water. The surface was quite unruffled, nor was there the slightest
mixture of that phosphoric appearance often seen on a
dark night when the sea is agitated. The air was still,
though it was not quite a calm, and the sky was per-

fectly clear. It took us some hours to slip through it.
We drew up some in buckets, and found it to contain
a small, scarcely perceptible, portion of a fine filamen-
tuous substance, quite transparent, such as I have
occasionally seen where seaweed is abundant. Whether
this was the cause of the milky appearance of the sea
or not we could not determine. We were now sailing
almost due north, for the Straits of Bally, as the passage is called between that small island and the east
end of the magnificent island of Java. About the
middle of August, early in the morning, again land
was seen from the masthead, and in a few hours we
entered the Straits I have just mentioned. We could
see the shores on both sides, that of Bally somewhat
abrupt, while the Java shore, agreeably diversified by
clumps of cocoa-nut trees and hills clothed with verdure, looked green and smiling, contrasting agreeably
with that of New Holland, which we had so lately left.
A large number of small boats or canoes were moving
about in all directions, those under sail going at great
speed. They were painted white, had one sail, and
were fitted with outriggers. We had to keep a bright
look-out lest we should run suddenly into the jaws
of any French or Dutch man-of-war, which, escaping
from our cruisers, might be pleased to snap up a richly-
laden merchantman like the *Barbara.* We could not
tell at the time whether the proposed expedition had
arrived, or, if it had, whether it had been successful.

As we were coasting along, a hill appeared in sight,
early in the morning, the summit thickly surrounded

by clouds. As this nightcap of vapours cleared away, a remarkable cone was exposed to view, the base covered with the richest vegetation. Soon after this we got so entangled among clusters of rocky islands and coral reefs that we were very much afraid we should be unable to extricate ourselves, and that our ship would get on shore. Though there was not much risk of our losing our lives, the dread of having our ship and cargo destroyed was enough to make us anxious. Fortunately the wind fell, and by keeping look-outs at each fore-yardarm and at the masthead, we were able to perceive the dangers with which we were surrounded before we ran on any of them. At length we got into seemingly more clear water, but there being still several reefs and islands outside of us, Captain Hassall thought it prudent to anchor for the night. The shore off which we lay was lined with cocoa-nut and other palm-trees, rivulets were seen flowing down the sides of the hills, which were clothed with spice-bearing and other shrubs, the whole landscape presenting a scene of great tropical beauty.

"If I ever had to cast anchor anywhere on shore, that's the sort of country I should choose, now," observed Benjie Stubbs, our second officer, who had been examining the coast for some time through his glass.

"I wouldn't change one half-acre of any part of our principality for a thousand of its richest acres," said David Gwynne, our surgeon, to whom he spoke. "Poets talk of the spicy gales of these islands; in most cases they come laden with miasma-bearing fevers and agues on their wings; while if a fellow has to live on shore he gets roasted by day, with a good chance of a sunstroke, and he is stewed at night, and bitten by mosquitoes and other winged and crawling things, and wakes to find a cobra de capella or green snake gliding over his face."

"Oh, a man would soon get accustomed to those trifling inconveniences, as the natives must do; and money goes a long way in these regions for all the necessaries of life," answered Stubbs.

I must confess that, lovely as I had heard are many parts of those eastern isles, I was inclined to agree with the surgeon.

It was discovered this evening that in consequence of the heat, or from careless coopering, our water-casks had let out their contents, and that we had scarcely any fresh water in the ship. At Batavia it was very bad, and it might be some days before we should get there, or we could not tell when, should the expedition not have succeeded. It was therefore necessary to get water without delay, and as a river was marked on the chart near to where we lay, we agreed the next morning to go up, and, should we see no fort, to run in and obtain water and any fresh provisions we might require. Accordingly we weighed by sunrise, and, standing in, ran along the coast till we arrived off the mouth of the river we hoped to find. Some native houses were seen, but no fortifications and no buildings of an European character We therefore thought that we should be perfectly safe in

13

going ashore. On dropping our anchor, several canoes came off laden with turtles, ducks, fowls, cockatoos, monkeys, and other small animals and birds; besides sweet potatoes, yams, and other vegetables, grown by the natives for the supply of the ships passing along the coast. They found plenty of customers among our men, and the ship was soon turned into a perfect menagerie. We without difficulty made the people in the canoes understand that we wanted to replenish our water-casks, and we understood them to say that they would gladly help us. Two boats were therefore lowered and filled with casks; Stubbs took charge of one of them, and I went in the other, accompanied by little Jack Nobs, intending to exchange a few articles which I took with me suitable to the taste of the natives for some of the productions of their country.

As we pulled up the river we saw the low shores on either side lined with houses built on high piles, by which they were raised a considerable distance above the ground, some, I should think, fully twenty feet. The only means of entering them was by a ladder, which we found it was the custom of the inhabitants to lift up at night to prevent the intrusion of strangers, but more especially, I should think, of wild beasts. The chief object, however, of their being built in this way is to raise them above the miasma of the marshy ground, which often rises only two or three feet. They were all on one floor, but had numerous partitions or rooms. The roofs, which were covered with palm leaves, projected some distance beyond the walls, so as to form a wide balcony all round. The ground beneath was also in many instances railed in, and thus served for the habitation of ducks, poultry, and cattle.

At the landing-place some way up a number of natives were collected, who received us in a very friendly way. We saw no Dutchmen nor other Europeans. As we could not make ourselves understood by the natives, we were unable to ascertain what had occurred at the other end of the island. The men in the canoes had for clothing only a cloth round their waists, but the people who now received us were habited in a much more complete fashion. They wore the *sarung*, a piece of coloured cloth about eight feet long and four wide, part of which was thrown over the shoulder like a Highlander's plaid, the rest bound round the waist serving as a kilt. They all had on drawers secured by a sash, and several wore a short frock coat with buttons in front, called a *baju*. All had daggers, and several, who were evidently people of some consequence, had two in copper or silver sheaths. The latter had their teeth blackened, which was evidently looked on as a mark of gentility. They also wore turbans, while the lower orders only had little caps on their heads. The watering-place was some little way up the river, and while the mates proceeded there with the boats, I landed at the village or town. I had not proceeded far when I was given to understand that a chief or some person of consequence wished to see me, for the purpose, I supposed, of trading. His habitation was pointed out to me on the summit of some high ground at a distance from the river. It appeared to be far larger than the houses of the village. Without hesitation I set off, followed by Jack, and accompanied by several of my first acquaintance, towards it. I now more than ever regretted having lost O'Carroll, for understanding as he did the languages of the people of the Archipelago, he would greatly have facilitated our proceedings.

The house or palace of the great man was surrounded, as are all the island habitations of every degree which I saw in Java, with gardens. We entered on the north side into a large square court, on either side of which were rows of Indian fig-trees, with two large fig-trees nearly in the centre. Passing through this we found ourselves in a smaller court, surrounded by pillars, and covered in by a light roof. Here most of my companions remained, but I was conducted up a flight of steps to a handsome terrace in front of a building of considerable size, in the centre of which was a spacious hall, the roof richly painted with red and gold. This hall of audience was on the top of the hill; steps from it led down to other houses which composed the dwelling of the chief and his family.

As I looked down from the terrace, I could see the tops of the houses of the poorer class of people, which surrounded the palace of the chief. They were all in the midst of gardens, and had walls round them. I found, indeed, that I was in the centre of a town, or

large village, though in coming along I had scarcely
seen any habitations, so completely shut in were they
by trees and shrubs. I had thus an example of the
fertility of Java, and of the industry of its inhabitants.
With regard to the habitations of the barbarians whose
lands I visited, I must observe that, though there
were exceptions to the rule, they were generally far
superior in respect to the wants of the occupants than
are the dwellings of a large number of the poorer
classes in Scotland, and especially in Ireland, and in
some districts even in England. They are in good
condition, clean, sufficiently furnished, and well venti-
lated. Granted that the materials of which they are
built are cheap, that from the fertility of the land a
man by labouring three days in the week can supply
all his wants for the remaining four, and has time
to repair his house and furniture, and that he has
no rates and taxes to pay, still I cannot help believing that there is something wrong somewhere,
that God never intended it to be so, and that it is a
matter it behoves us to look to more than we have
done. Though distance seemed to increase my love
for Old England, it did not blind me to her faults, and
I often blushed when I found myself among heathen
savages, and saw the superiority of some of their
ways to ours. These or similar thoughts occupied me
while I stood on the terrace gazing on the fine prospect around, and waiting for the appearance of the
chief.

After some time the chief appeared at the entrance

of the hall of audience, with a gay coloured umbrella
borne over his head, a slave carrying the indispensable
betel-box by his side, a handsome turban on his head,
and his sash stuck full of jewel-hilted daggers with
golden scabbards, while all his attendants stood round
with their bodies bent forward and their eyes cast to
the ground, as a sign of reverence. I thus knew that
I was in the presence of a very important person.
I was rather puzzled to discover who he took me for,
that he treated me with so much state. How we were
to understand each other, and I was to ascertain the
truth, I could not tell. I think I mentioned that
I learned a little Dutch, which I had practised occasionally with Peter Kloops, my old cousin's butler.

I tried the chief with some complimentary phrases in
that language, but he shook his head ; I then tried him
with French. He shook his head still more vehemently, and, from the signs he made, I thought that
he was annoyed that I had not brought an interpreter with me. After a time, however, finding that he
could get nothing out of me, he said something to one
of his attendants, who, raising his hands with his palms
closed till his thumbs touched his nose in rather a
curious fashion, uttered a few words in reply, and then
hurried off by the way I had come. I was after this
conducted into the hall, where on a raised platform
the chief took his seat, making signs to me to sit near
him, his attendants having done the same. Slaves
then brought in some basins of water, in one of which
the chief washed his hands, I following his example.

Trays were then brought in, with meat and rice and fish, and certain vegetables cut up into small fragments. There were no knives, or forks, or spoons. The chief set an example, which I was obliged to follow, of dipping his fingers into the mess before him, and, as it were, clawing up a mouthful and transferring it to his mouth. Had his hands not first been washed, I certainly should not have liked the proceeding, but as I was by this time very hungry, and the dishes were pleasant tasted and well cooked, I did ample justice to the repast.

The chief and his attendants having eaten as much as they well could, my young attendant Jack, who sat somewhat behind me, having done the same, water was again brought in, that everybody might wash their hands.

I heard Jack Nobs in a low tone give rough colloquial expressions of his satisfaction.

"They don't seem much given to talking, though," he added to himself. "I wonder whether it is that they think we don't understand their lingo, or that they don't understand ours; I'll just try them, though."

Whereon in a half whisper he addressed the person sitting next to him, who bowed and salaamed very politely in return, but made no reply.

"What I axes you, mounseer, is, whether you feels comfortable after your dinner," continued Jack, in a loud whisper. "And, I say, will you tell us who the gentleman in the fine clothes is, for I can't make out nohow? Does he know that my master here is a

great merchant, and that if he wishes to do a bit of
trade, he is the man to do it with him?"

The same dumb show on the part of the Javanese
went on as before. Jack's attempt at opening up a
conversation was put a stop to by the return of the
servant with dishes containing a variety of vegetables
and fruits, which were as welcome, probably, to him
as to me. One dish contained a sweet potato cooked.
It must have weighed from twelve to fifteen pounds.
I have heard of one weighing thirty pounds. The
natives appeared very fond of it. We had peas and
artichokes and a dish of sago, the mode of obtaining
which I afterwards saw, and will describe presently.
I heard Jack cry out when he saw one of the dishes
of fruit. It was, I found, the *durian*, a fruit of which
the natives are very fond, and which I got to like,
though its peculiarly offensive odour at first gave me a
dislike to it. It is nearly of the size of a man's head,
and is of a spherical form. It consists of five cells,
each containing from one to four large seeds enveloped
in a rich white pulp, itself covered with a thin pellicle,
which prevents the seed from adhering to it. This
pulp is the edible portion of the fruit. However, a
dish of *mangostins* was more to my taste. It is one
of the most exquisite of Indian fruits. It is mildly
acid, and has an extreme delicacy of flavour without
being luscious or cloying. In external appearance it
resembles a ripe pomegranate, but is smaller and more
completely globular. A rather tough rind, brown
without, and of a deep crimson within, encloses three

or four black seeds surrounded by a soft, semi-transparent, snow-white pulp, having occasionally a very slight crimson plush. The pulp is eaten. We had also the well-known Jack-fruit, a great favourite with the natives ; and the *champaduk,* a much smaller fruit, of more slender form and more oblong shape. It has a slightly farinaceous consistency, and has a very delicate and sweet flavour. I remember several other fruits ; indeed, the chief seemed anxious to show to me, a stranger, the various productions of his country. There were mangoes, shaddocks, and pine-apples in profusion, and several other small fruits, some too luscious for my palate, but others having an agreeable sub-acid taste.

We sat and sat on, waiting for the return of the messenger. I observed that whereas a calabash of water stood near the guests, from which they drank sparingly, a jug was placed close to the chief, and that as he continued to sip from it his eyes began to roll and his head to turn from side to side in a curious manner. Suddenly, as if seized with a generous impulse, or rather having overcome a selfish one, he passed the jug with a sigh over to me, and made signs that if I was so inclined I was to drink from it. I did so without hesitation, but my breath was almost taken away. It was the strongest arrack. I could not ascertain how the chief, who was a Mohammedan, could allow himself to do what is so contrary to the law of the prophet. I observed that his attendants looked away when he drank, as they did when I put

the cup to my lips; so I conclude that they knew
well enough that it was not quite the right thing
to do. All the inhabitants of Java are nominally
Mohammedans, but, in the interior especially, a
number of gross and idolatrous practices are mixed
up with the performance of its ceremonies, while the
upper orders especially are very lax in their principles.
Most of them, in spite of the law of their prophet pro-
hibiting the use of wine and spirits, drink them whenever they can be procured. The rich have as many
wives as they can support, but the poor are obliged to
content themselves with one. I should say that my
host, when I returned him the jar of arrack, deprived
of very little of its contents, gave a grunt of satisfaction,
from which I inferred that his supply had run short,
and that he was thankful that I had not taken more.
I kept anxiously waiting all the time for the arrival
of an interpreter, for whom I was convinced the
chief had sent. After we lost Captain O'Carroll we
returned to our original intention of procuring one at
Batavia. This must account for my being at present
without one. I had come on shore in the hope that
I might make myself sufficiently understood to carry
on a trade by means of signs, as I knew was often
done. As, however, my new friends would not make
the attempt to talk by signs or in any other way, I
had to wait patiently till somebody should arrive to
help us out of our dilemma.

CHAPTER XIV.

A PRISONER OF WAR.

I AT length lost all patience at the non-arrival of the expected interpreter, and, rising, made a profound salaam to the chief, which was, I saw, accurately imitated by Jack, who was at my side with a comical expression of countenance not indicative of much respect for the great man. The chief said something which I understood to mean that he hoped I would remain longer, but as I really was anxious to return on board, I only bowed again lower than before, and pointed towards the harbour, continuing to move in the direction of the entrance. He did not attempt to stop me, and the people who had come with me were, I saw, prepared to accompany me back.

I had just reached the outside, when I saw approaching an individual dressed in the native shirt and *sarung*, or kilt, whom I naturally took to be a Javanese.

He stopped and looked at me attentively, saying in Dutch, "I was sent for by the chief to come and interpret for a French gentleman who has arrived here on some diplomatic business of importance. I shall be happy to do my best, but you are aware that some of the troops of your countrymen will be here soon, and that then there will be no lack of people better able to interpret for you than I am. You of course know that the English attempted to make a landing, but have been defeated, and it is thought probable that they will make another attempt in this direction." He appeared to say this in a very significant manner. The information he gave might or might not be correct, but there was a friendliness in his look and tone which led me to suppose that he knew I was English, and that he wished to warn me of my danger. I was doubtful what to say in return, but quickly resolved to hurry down to the watering party to advise them to return on board and to warn Captain Hassall, that he might be ready immediately to get under way. I turned to the seeming native, whom I now discovered to be a Dutchman, and thanked him for what he had told me, remarking that our business was of no consequence, and that as it was possible the wind might change, I proposed returning on board at once. He smiled, and said he thought it was the best thing I could do. This convinced me of his good feeling, and that he knew I was English. Just at that moment a guard of soldiers emerged from the palace, and their officer, addressing the Dutchman, made signs to me that I was forthwith to return.

"I am sorry," observed the Dutchman to me in English; "we must attend the summons, but your boy need not, and you may send him to let your companions know."

I took the advice and ordered Jack to find his way down to the boats, and to tell the mates to hurry on board with or without water, and to advise Captain Hassall to get under way immediately. I added, "Tell him to stand off and on for a couple of hours. If I am at liberty I will put off in a native boat, but if I am detained, tell him to save the ship and cargo, and that I hope before long to make my escape."

Jack fully understood my message, but I must say, to his credit, that he seemed very unwilling to leave me to my fate.

" I am in no danger," I remarked ; " I may possibly be detained a few days, but I am not likely to suffer any other inconvenience. Now, quick, my lad, or the ship and all hands may be caught in a trap."

Jack gave me a nod, and was off like a shot. I scarcely expected, however, that he would be allowed to go free ; but no one, I suppose, had received orders to stop him, and so he pursued his way unmolested. The officers of the guard had, in the meantime, been speaking to the Dutchman, who told me that I must return forthwith, as the chief was waiting to receive me. I of course could do nothing else than face about, and with my new friend accompany the guard. The men were armed with formidable long spears and daggers, but the officer carried a musket, which looked more like an ensign of authority than a weapon to be used. As I returned through the courtyard I considered what I should say to the chief. " Tell the truth and be not afraid," said conscience. I determined to do so.

When I re-entered the hall of audience, the chief
was seated on his divan, and evidently intended to
receive me in greater state. Some of the assemblage
sat down cross-legged on cushions in front of the
divan, while others stood with their bodies bent forward on either side, the guards who remained turning
their backs on the great man. The Dutchman and I
took our seats on cushions directly below the divan.
I found afterwards that among the Javanese a sitting
posture is considered more respectful than an upright
one. The chief, through the Dutch interpreter, now
asked me a number of questions, which, according to
my previous determination, I answered correctly.
The great man, I thought, looked somewhat surprised
at finding that I was not so important a person as he
had at first supposed.

Occasionally my Dutch friend remarked that I had
better not reply to some of the questions put to me,
but I answered that I was perfectly ready to stand
by the consequences of anything I might say. Such
has been my practice through life—I might say, more
modestly, my endeavour—to do right on all occasions,
to avow whatever I have done, and to take the consequences, whatever they may be. I do not say that
such a mode of proceeding may not occasionally get a
man seemingly into trouble, but I do say that it is the
only right course, and that he is equally certain to get
out of it again ; whereas an opposite course must lead
him into difficulties, and involve him more and more
as he tries to extricate himself by prevarication, sub-

terfuge, or falsehood. I therefore told the chief that I had come on shore hoping to open up a trade with him, under the belief that the country was no longer either in possession of the Dutch or French, but that it was now under the rule of England. If I was mistaken I was ready to undergo the penalty, and must run the risk of being treated as a prisoner of war should I fall into the hands of the French, but that as the English were the friends of the rulers and people of Java, I expected to be treated by him as a friend.

This answer, which I had reason to believe the Dutchman faithfully interpreted, seemed to please the chief. However, he made no direct reply to me, but spoke for some time aside to his companions, whom I took to be officially counsellors or advisers. One made a remark, then another, and at last one said something at which I thought my friend the Dutchman looked rather blank. A good deal of discussion took place, when I heard the chief issue some orders to the officers of the guards. Immediately on this two of the counsellors got up, and with the officer and several other persons, and part of the guard, left the hall.

The movement seemed to give great satisfaction to the counsellors, especially to the gentleman who had made the suggestion, as I fancied, which led to it, while a pleased smile played over the countenance of the chief. All the time the honest Dutchman looked very much annoyed. At length I asked him what it was all about.

"I suppose that I shall not be found fault with for telling you," he answered. "And I assure you that I would much rather not have to give you such unpleasant information. Do not look surprised or annoyed, and no harm can come of it. The fact is that the chief here, the governor of this district, Mulock Ben Azel, is not a bright genius, and though he had made up his mind to detain you, it had not occurred to him to detain your vessel. The idea, however, was suggested to him just now by one of these cunning gentlemen, and he has sent a party to stop her. The Javanese are rather daring fellows, so that the captain must be smart if he would get away from them."

This was indeed a disagreeable announcement. I congratulated myself, however, at having sent off Jack to warn Captain Hassall, and I had great hopes that he would have followed my advice and got the *Barbara* under way before the Javanese could reach her. I thanked the Dutchman for his sympathy and kindness.

"I have a warm regard for the English," he answered: "I have received much kindness at the hands of your countrymen, and am glad of an opportunity of proving my gratitude. As far as you are concerned I may be of service, but if these gentry get hold of your vessel, I am afraid that they will not let her go till they have cleaned out her hold."

I, of course, on hearing all this became very impatient to go and see whether the *Barbara* was leaving the harbour, but as far as I could I concealed my feelings, and desired my Dutch friend to inquire of Mulock Ben Azel whether he desired my presence any longer; and if not, I begged leave to go forth into the open air that I might gaze on the beautiful scenery amidst which he had the happiness of dwelling and I had the happiness of finding myself. I fancy that the interpreter gave my request a more oriental turn. The chief was at all events pleased to comply with it, and directed some of his attendants and my Dutch friend to accompany me. I made a profound salaam, as if I was highly pleased at all that had occurred. The act was somewhat hypocritical, I must confess, but, at all events, I was heartily glad to get over the audience, which was becoming very tedious.

As soon as I got out on the terrace I have before described as affording a magnificent view of the surrounding country, I eagerly looked seaward in search of the *Barbara*. I almost gave a shout of satisfaction as I saw her with a strong breeze off shore, standing away under all the canvas she could carry. She had good reason to make the best use of her heels, for a whole fleet of boats, some of considerable size and full of men, were in hot chase after her. I stood with my companions eagerly watching the chase, though the objects of our interest were very different. I was anxious that the *Barbara* should escape, they that she should be caught. I knew for one, though, that if good seamanship would enable him to get away, Captain Hassall would give his pursuers the slip.

14

I knew too that he would not be taken, even if the boats should catch him up, without a fight. My earnest hope was therefore that the breeze might continue. In that climate, however, the land wind often falls towards the evening, and if it should do so, it would give the Javanese a great advantage. I found my new friend by my side, and I glanced at him.

"Your vessel sails well, and I am glad of it," he observed. "The orders were to bring her in at all risks; at the same time, if her captain shows a bold front I do not think the natives will dare to attack him at a distance from the land."

My hopes and fears alternately rose and fell as I watched the chase. Sometimes the boats seemed to be gaining on her. At other times she appeared to be obtaining the advantage. She continued to increase her canvas till every stitch she could carry was set on her, studding sails on either side, royals, and even still lighter sails above them, which we used to call skyscrapers. I now observed that although there were several large boats engaged in the chase, they were but slow sailers, and that the small ones were drawing ahead of them. These of course would be more easily dealt with by the *Barbara's* crew than the larger craft.

The latter were vessels of about forty tons, carrying fifty or sixty persons. The hulls of those I had seen on landing were neatly built, with round heads and sterns; and over the hulls were light small houses, composed of bamboos, and divided into three or four cabins. The sides were formed of split bamboos about four feet high, with windows in them to open and shut at pleasure; the roofs were almost flat, and thatched with palm leaves. The oars are worked by the crew standing at the fore and after part of the vessel. I thought that probably the boats now in chase of the *Barbara* were modifications of this sort of craft, and more adapted to warlike purposes than they were. The natives became at length even more excited than I was as the breeze occasionally fell and gave their boats an advantage. They knew also that the land breeze would soon set in, which I did not. They probably fancied that when it did the vessel would be caught in a trap, not knowing that she could haul her wind and still keep ahead of them.

I stood watching the various circumstances of the chase, till at length, greatly to my relief, I saw the boats, as if by signal, begin to return together towards the shore, while the *Barbara* continued standing off shore till she met the sea breeze, when she hauled her wind and stood away to the northward. My Dutch friend congratulated me on her escape.

"And as it appears that you are not to be detained as a prisoner, the sooner you get out of this place the better," he observed. "I will gladly welcome you to my abode, where you can remain till we gain further information as to the result of the British expedition against Batavia. If it is ultimately successful, your ship will put in at that place, and you can rejoin her."

I gladly accepted his offer. As we passed through the large entrance court he pointed out two large Indian-fig-trees, and told me that under them was the place where criminals were executed. On each side of the court was a row of the same description of tree. We descended the hill towards the harbour. On approaching it I heard the shrill voice of a boy crying out loudly amid the shouts and chattering of a number of natives. I soon recognised the voice of Jack Nobs, who had, I had hoped, made his escape in the boats. The people, seeing me accompanied by guards, made way for Jack, who ran towards me, crying out,—

"Oh, save me, Mr. Braithwaite! save me, sir! These savinges are a-going to cut off my head, or to hang me up and cook and eat me. They eat people in these parts, and they look as if they would make nothing of devouring me."

In vain I tried to pacify him. He seemed to fear that the natives were going to treat me in the same way he thought that they were about to treat him.

"But what made you come back, Jack?" I asked. "I thought that you had gone off to the ship."

"What, leave you all alone among the savinges!" he answered, looking up reproachfully at me. "No, no, sir. After you have been so kind to me, and always took me with you wherever you've been, and we was nearly all drowned together! No, no, if harm is to come of it, I says to myself, I'll go shares with Mr. Braithwaite, whatever happens; so, when the boats

shoved off, I scud away, and when the men called me
to come along with them, and not to mind you, for
that I could do you no good, I wouldn't go back, but
kept beckoning them to be off; so away they went,
and I ran up in shore and hid myself. The savinges,
howsomdever, found me out at last, and as long as
they thought that they should get hold of the ship
they treated me civil enough, as they might a pet
monkey; but when they found that they could not
catch her, they turned their rage on me, and what
they're going to do with us I'm sure I don't know.
Oh dear! oh dear!"

Jack's fears were very natural, for the dark-skinned,
half-naked Javanese, with their glittering kreeses or
daggers in their hands, which they flourished about
while they vociferated loudly, were very ferocious-
looking fellows.

"They are disappointed," said the Dutchman, "at
the escape of your ship, and they accuse the boy of
being the cause of the boats going off and giving her
warning. Let him, however, keep close to me, and I
will do my best to protect him."

My new friend, who, by-the-bye, told me his name
was Peter Van Deck, now addressed the people and
told them that the boy was not to blame; whatever
he had done was in consequence of the orders he
had received, and that he had no intention of offending
them. I had slipped a few small pieces of coin, which
I had fortunately in my pocket, into his hand, and on
his distributing these among the most influential of

the assemblage, public opinion was turned completely
in our favour, and we were allowed to proceed without further molestation. A small sum bestowed on
the officer of the guard had a like beneficial effect, and
after receiving an assurance from Mynheer Van Deck
that we would not run away, and would be found at
his house if wanted, he and his men, very much to my
relief, took their departure, while the Dutchman, Jack,
and I set off in an opposite direction.

The island of Java, it must be remembered, runs
about due east and west. Our course was towards
the west, or in the direction of Batavia. There was,
however, not far off—about twenty miles I understood
—a town and fort, garrisoned by French troops, called
Cheribon. The scenery was very fine, heightened by
the luxuriance of tropical vegetation. On our left rose
a succession of heights, beyond which appeared the summits of the ridge of lofty mountains which runs down
the centre of the island, dividing it longitudinally
into two parts, of which, however, the northern is the
largest, most fertile, and best known. My Dutch
friend was very communicative respecting the productions of the country, and the manners and customs
of the inhabitants. I noted down, therefore, the information I received from him, which I give in as
concise a form as I can.

The climate is certainly hot, as might be expected
from being so near the equator, but it is much more
endurable than I had expected to find it, and on the
sides of the mountains it is often quite cool, so that thick

clothing is necessary. As also the nights are nearly the same length as the days, there is time for the air to cool while the sun is below the horizon. The bad or unhealthy monsoon blows from the west, from the end of November to the beginning of March. This is the rainy season. After it the easterly winds blow for some time. The breaking up of the monsoon is the most unhealthy season of all. There are no navigable rivers, but numerous streams descend from the mountains and irrigate the land. One of the chief productions of this country is pepper. It is produced from a plant of the vine kind, *Piper nigrum*, which twines its tendrils round poles or trees, like ivy or hops. The pepper-corns grow in bunches close to each other. They are first green, but afterwards turn black. When dried they are separated from the dust and partly from the outward membranous coat by means of a kind of winnow, and are then laid up in warehouses. The white pepper is the same production as the black. It undergoes a process to change its colour, being laid in lime, which takes off the outer black coat and leaves it white.

Rice is also produced in large quantities. It grows chiefly in low fenny ground. After it has been sown, and has shot up about half a foot from the ground, it is transplanted by little bundles of one or more plants in rows; then, by damming up the many rivulets which abound in this country, the rice is inundated in the rainy season, and kept under water till the stalks have attained sufficient strength, when the land is drained by opening the dams, and it is soon dried by the great heat of the sun. At the time of the rice harvest the fields have much the same appearance as our wheat and barley fields, and indeed are uniformly covered with a still more brilliantly golden hue. The sickle is not used in reaping the rice, but instead of it a small knife, with which the stalk is cut about a foot under the ear; this is done one by one, and the ears are then bound in sheaves, the tenth of which is the pay of the mower. The *paddee*, which is the name given to the rice while in the husk, does not grow, like wheat and barley, in compact ears, but, like oats, in loose spikes. It is not threshed to separate it from the husks, but pounded in large wooden blocks hollowed out, and the more it is pounded the whiter it becomes when boiled. Rice, with fish or a little meat chopped up, constitute the chief food of the inhabitants. Sugar, coffee, and indigo are also largely produced.

For the purposes of agriculture buffaloes are used instead of horses. They are very large animals, bigger and heavier than our largest oxen, furnished with great ears, and horns which project straight forward and bend inwards. A hole is bored through the cartilage of the nose, and these huge animals are guided by a cord which is passed through it. They have little eyes, and their colour is generally ashy grey. They are so accustomed to be led three times a day into the water to cool themselves, that they cannot without doing so be brought to work. The

people themselves, by-the-bye, are great bathers, both
men and women, the children, who seldom wear
clothes till they are seven or eight, being constantly
in the water. That said custom must be a great
saving of expense to the parents of a large family.
The people are generally of a light brown colour,
of the middle height, and well proportioned, with a
broad forehead and a flattish nose, which has a slight
curve downward at the tip. Their hair is black, and
is always kept smooth and shining with cocoa-nut oil.
The dress of the women consists of a piece of cotton
cloth wrapped round the body and covering the
bosom, under which it is secured; it then hangs down
to the knees, and sometimes to the ankles, while the
shoulders and part of the back remain uncovered.
The hair of their head, which they wear very long,
is turned up and twisted round like a fillet, fastened
with long bodkins of different sorts of wood, tortoise-
shell, silver, or gold, according to the rank of the lady.
It is often adorned with a variety of flowers. The
Javanese are nominally Mohammedans, but in the
interior especially a number of idolatrous practices are
still kept up.

Pleasantly conversing we at length reached the
residence of Mynheer Van Deck. It was built in
the best style of native architecture, that is to say,
on a raised platform of stone or brick; the outer
walls were of brick, with a verandah of bamboo, all
round which the partitions, as was most of the
furniture, were of bamboo, which had a very cool

appearance, and was sufficient for a hot climate. My host was a bachelor, not from choice, he assured me, but from necessity, on account of the scarcity of European ladies in the island.

"Those who are born here are so ill-educated, and so indolent, that a man is better without their society," he remarked.

In spite of this drawback he received me very hospitably and kindly, and though I was vexed at having again been separated from my ship, I confessed to myself that I had very little cause to complain of my lot. I was leaning back on an easy bamboo chair and gazing out through a vista of palm-trees on the deep blue sea, when the clatter of horses' feet coming along the road caught our ears. As they drew near the clank of sabres was heard at the same time. The voice of an officer crying "Halt" was next heard, and soon afterwards we saw him approaching the house. My host, with a look of considerable annoyance, rose to receive him. He was a young and pleasant-looking man.

"Ah, Mynheer Van Deck, bon jour," he said. "You have in your house, I am given to understand, a foreigner, supposed to be an English spy. I am come to demand him from you."

"I am the person to whom you allude, monsieur," I said, rising from my seat and going forward "You are, however, wrongly informed. I am an Englishman, but not a spy. I landed, not knowing that this part of the island was in possession of the French,

and had I not been detained I should have returned
to my ship."

"I am not here to dispute the point, monsieur,"
he said, bowing politely. "I must perform my duty,
and that is to convey you with me to Cheribon,
where my superior officers will investigate the matter.
You have supped, I conclude; we will therefore take
advantage of the cool of the evening, and make good
as much of our journey as the waning day will allow
us to perform."

My Dutch friend shrugged his shoulders. There
was not much time for consideration. I saw that
I had no resource but to obey, though I must own
that 1 did so with a very bad grace.

CHAPTER XV

PIRATES.

MY host, in spite of his annoyance, did not forget the duties of hospitality, and warmly pressed our unwelcome visitor to take some refreshment. The young officer, however, declined, on the plea that the day was already far spent, and that he had no time to spare. On going round to the front of the house, I found two led horses under the charge of a soldier. They were absurdly small for cavalry, and would have been quickly ridden over by any one of our heavy regiments.

I was about to bid Mynheer Van Deck farewell.

"No, not yet, my friend," he answered. "I purpose accompanying you to Cheribon, that I may render you any service in my power. I have a horse, and will follow immediately."

The officer made a sign of impatience, so I mounted one of the steeds, and Jack sprang on the back of the other, where he sat very much as a big monkey would have done, fully resolved, it seemed, to enjoy any fun which might be forthcoming. As the French soldiers treated him kindly, and spoke in a good-natured tone to him, though he could not understand what they

said, his fears quickly vanished, and he was speedily
" hail fellow well met " with them all.

The officer I found a very gentlemanly young man.
He rode up alongside me after we had proceeded a
little way, and seemed eager enough to talk about
La Belle France and Paris; but when I endeavoured
to draw any information from him respecting the
proceedings at the west end of the island, he closed
his mouth, or gave only vague answers. From this
I argued that affairs had not gone with the French
in quite as satisfactory a manner as they wished. I
asked him at last whether he thought that I should
be detained or be otherwise inconvenienced by the
commandant at Cheribon.

"We shoot spies," he answered laconically, at the
same time shrugging his shoulders as a Frenchman
only can do. "C'est la fortune de la guerre."

" But, my dear sir, I am no spy," I answered. "The
governor, or native chief, purposed to seize my vessel,
and I was left on shore while she made her escape.
I am but a supercargo anxious to sell the goods entrusted to me."

The young officer gave a smile of incredulity, yet
with an air of so much politeness that I really could
not be angry with him; indeed it would have done
me no good if I were. We were in a short time
joined by Mynheer Van Deck, who came galloping
up on a much finer horse than any possessed by the
French soldiers. I found from my captor that the
journey would be far longer than I had expected, as

we had to make a considerable *détour* to visit a native chief, or prince, to whom he had a message. My belief was that he was beating up for native recruits to oppose the British force, which, if not arrived, must have been hourly expected. We had several natives with us, armed with long spears and daggers, a few only having firelocks. Van Deck told me that we should soon have to pass a river, rather a dangerous spot, on account of the number of tigers which came there to drink, and which had already carried off several natives.

"But surely they would not venture to attack so large a body of men as this," I remarked.

"Not if we could keep together, unless they happen to be very hungry," he answered. "Unfortunately, however, the path in some places is so narrow that we have to proceed in single file, and as there are fallen trees and other impediments in the way, travellers are apt to get separated, when, of course, they are more liable to be picked off. I always keep my pistol cocked in my hand, that I may have a chance of shooting my assailant."

"But I came on shore unarmed, and have no pistols," I answered.

"Then keep ahead of me, and if I see a tiger spring at you I will fire at him, and do my best to save you."

"But the poor boy who is with me—he has a poor chance, I am afraid," I observed, after I had thanked my friend for his offer.

"Oh, he is safe enough if he keeps close to the

soldiers; the clatter of their arms frightens the beasts."

While the Dutchman was speaking we came in sight of the river. It was fordable, though rather deep, and as the leading men on their small horses plunged in the water was up to their saddle-girths. I naturally looked out on either side for our expected enemies. Three or four large animals sprang off just as the leading horses reached the opposite bank. I thought they were tigers.

"Oh, no, they are only wild cats," said Van Deck. "Rather unpleasant to be caught by one of them asleep, but they are easily frightened."

I thought to myself, If those creatures are Java wild cats, what must Java tigers be like? We all passed across the stream without any accident, a small body of half-clad natives bringing up the rear. They were climbing up the somewhat steep bank, when a fearful shriek, followed by loud shouts and cries, made me turn my head, and I caught sight of a monster bounding along the bank, with the writhing, struggling body of a human being between his huge jaws. The poor wretch's *sarung*, or plaid, had become loose, and dragged after him. Already several natives were setting off in chase, while others were discharging their firearms at the animal, though at the risk of killing the man. The French officer called out to them to desist, and seizing a lance from one of the people, gallantly dashed after the tiger. I naturally wished to join in the chase, but Van

Deck entreated me to stop, telling me that I should very likely, if I went, be picked off by another tiger on my return. As it would have been folly to disregard his advice, we pushed on as fast as we could to get out of the narrow defile. We could for several minutes hear the shouts of the natives still in pursuit of the tiger. After some time they rejoined us, but they had not saved the poor man, and had, moreover, lost another of their number, who had been carried off by a tiger just as the first leaped over a cliff fifty feet above the valley, with the man still in its mouth. It was followed triumphantly by its companion.

"This is not the country I should choose to travel in, still less to live in," I said.

"It cannot be helped," observed the Dutchman. "I am well off here, a great man among small people. I should be a beggar elsewhere. This is not, however, the country in which a man of education and mind would choose to pitch his tent."

Torches were lit for the latter part of our journey. It will be remembered that so nearly under the equator as we were the days and nights are of equal length all the year round; we therefore did not enjoy the delightful twilight of a northern clime.

Notice had been given of our proposed visit to the chief, or prince, who was, I was told, of Malay descent. Preparations were therefore made for our reception, and very handsome they were. Though a prisoner, I was treated like the rest of the guests. The house was much in the style of those I have before described. But I was not prepared to find a table elegantly set out and spread with fine linen and beautiful silver plate. It was lighted by four large wax flambeaux in massive silver candlesticks. The provisions were dressed in the Malay fashion, many of the dishes being very palatable, and toasts were drunk with three times three, the Malays of inferior rank, who sat round the room on the ground against the walls to the number of thirty, joining in the huzzas. It was altogether a curious scene of barbaric splendour. The prince escorted us to our rooms, where we found capital beds, beautiful linen, and very fine mosquito-nets, ornamented with fringe. The Malay servants slept under the beds on mats, or in the corners of the rooms, to be in readiness if required. Breakfast was prepared at daybreak, that we might continue our journey in the cool of the morning.

We rested under the shade of some trees during the day, the soldiers keeping up a fearful din to scare away any wild beast who might chance to be prowling about in search of a dinner. The young officer had fortunately a French cook among his men, who very soon contrived to place before us a capital dinner, though of what it was composed I could not discover. I rather think that hashed monkey formed one of the dishes. As, towards night, we approached Cheribon, my kind Dutch friend did his best to keep up my spirits, assuring me that he would spare no pains to prove that I was not a spy. He was not quite sure that the accounts received of

the defeat of the English were correct ; and the French
commandant would scarcely venture to hang me
without very strong proofs of my guilt, and with
the possibility of being made a prisoner himself by my
countrymen ere long, should they have been victorious.
Still it was with no very pleasant feelings that I was
formally conducted into the fort as a prisoner.

The forts of Cheribon had been allowed to fall into
decay by the Dutch, but since the French occupation
of the island had been repaired and considerably
strengthened. I was told that the commandant
boasted that he could hold out against any force
likely to be sent against him, even should my
countrymen gain the day. I was taken at once before
him and examined, but though he had no evidence to
prove me guilty, as I was accused of being a spy he
would not take my parole. I was by his orders
accordingly locked up in a cell with iron bars to the
windows, a three-legged stool, and a heap of straw
in a corner for a bed. Mr. Van Deck had not entered
the fort. In a little time Jack was thrust into the
cell with very little ceremony. He brought me a
message from my Dutch friend, saying that there had
been a battle, and he suspected that the French had
been defeated. I heartily hoped that he was correct.
I had reason to believe that my prison, bad as it was, was
the best in the fort, for Jack told me that he had seen
guards going round with messes of food which they
had put into wretched dark holes, and in one, as he
was led along, he saw a miserable gaunt man, with

long matted hair, put out a lean yellow hand to take
the food. This information made me hope more than
ever than Van Deck was right in his suspicions, for
I had no fancy to be shut up in a dark cell for months
in such a climate, with the possibility of being taken
out and shot as a spy. Had I been a naval or military man I should not have been thus treated.
Several very unpleasant days and nights passed by,
a scanty allowance of coarse food only being brought
to me and my young companion.

At length, one day the sergeant threw open my
prison door, and Van Deck appearing, took me by
the hand and led me out of my noisome dungeon,
followed by Jack, who gave a shout of joy as he
found himself in the open air.

"I sent to Batavia, where your ship has arrived,
and where your statement was fully corroborated, and
the commandant had therefore no further excuse for
keeping you a prisoner," said my friend. "But there
is another reason why he would not venture to do
so much longer. Look there!"

He pointed seaward, where several large ships were
seen approaching the land. He handed me a glass.
I examined them eagerly; they were frigates, with
the flag of Old England flying at their peaks. Jack,
when he heard this, gave a loud huzza, and threw up
his cap with delight, jumping and clapping his hands,
and committing other extravagances, till I ordered
him to be quiet lest the French soldiers should put
a sudden stop to the exhibition of his feelings.

The frigates approached till they had got just within long gunshot range of the fort, when after some time a boat put off from one of them and approached the fort, bearing a flag of truce. That was, at all events, pleasant. There was a chance of a battle being avoided, yet the commandant had so loudly sworn that nothing should make him yield to the English that I was afraid he might be obstinate and insist on holding out. We were on the point of hurrying down to meet the boat, when a sergeant with a guard stopped us and told us politely enough that we must stay where we were, or that Jack and I must go back to prison.

" We must obey orders," observed Van Deck. "The fact is, that the commandant is aware that you are acquainted with the weak points of the fort, that the gun-carriages are rotten, and many of the guns are themselves honeycombed or dismounted."

We were conducted out of the way when the officer with the flag of truce entered the fort. Looking from the ramparts, however, we could see the boat and the people in her through Van Deck's glass, and a young middy was amusing himself, so it appeared to me, by daring some little Dutch, or rather native boys to come off and fight him, which they seemed in no way disposed to do, for whenever he held up his fists they ran off at a great rate. Of one thing I was very sure, that if the French commandant did not yield with a good grace he would be very soon compelled to do so. That squadron of frigates had not come merely to give a civil message and to sail away again. We walked up and down, impatiently waiting to hear what was to be done.

At length, after an hour's delay, the officer who had brought the message—Captain Warren, of the *President*—issued from the commandant's house with his coxswain bearing a flag under his arm. Down came the tricolour of France, and up went the glorious flag of England. Jack was beside himself on seeing this, and I could scarcely refrain from joining in his "Hurra! hurra!" as I hurried forward to meet the English captain, whose acquaintance I had made at the Mauritius. The French commandant intimated, on this, that I was at liberty; but as I felt it would be ungrateful to leave my friend Van Dock abruptly, I resolved to remain on shore for the present with him.

In a very short time the marines came on shore to secure the thus easily acquired possession, but scarcely had they formed on the beach than it was ascertained that a large body of the enemy had entered the town. The order was given to charge through them, and, taken by surprise, the French and Dutchmen threw down their arms, and several officers and others were taken prisoners. Among them was General Jumel, second in command to General Janssen, and Colonel Knotzer, aide-de-camp to the latter, who with others were at once carried off to the ships.

Cheribon I found to be a much larger place than I at first supposed; the streets are narrow but numerous, and in the outskirts especially the houses of the

natives are so completely surrounded by trees and
bushes that it is impossible to calculate their number.
I heard that the *Phœbe* was one of the squadron, and
soon had the satisfaction of shaking hands with my
brother William, Toby Trundle, and other officers
belonging to her. From them I heard a full account
of the engagement which had given the greater part
of the magnificent island of Java to the English. I
was the more interested as my military brother had
taken part in it, and distinguished himself. I hoped
to meet him when I got to Batavia.

The army which was commanded by Sir Samuel
Auchmuty, consisting of 11,000 men, half being
Europeans, disembarked on the evening of the 5th of
August at the village of Chillingchin, twelve miles
north of Batavia. Colonel Gillespie advanced on the
city of Batavia, of which he took possession, and beat
off the enemy, who attempted to retake it. A general
engagement took place on the 10th at Welteureden,
when the French were defeated and compelled to
retire to the strongly entrenched camp of Cornelis.
It was supposed to contain 250 pieces of cannon.
Here General Janssen commanded in person, with
General Jumel, a Frenchman, under him, with an
army of 13,000 men. Notwithstanding this, the
forts were stormed and taken, and the greater number
of the officers captured. The commander-in-chief,
with General Jumel, escaped—the latter, as I have
mentioned, to fall very soon afterwards into our
hands.

An expedition, consisting of marines and blue-jackets, was now organised to meet a body of the fugitive army said to be marching from Cornelis. As William was of the party, I got leave to accompany it. That we might move the faster, horses had been obtained, and both marines and blue-jackets were mounted—that is to say, they had horses given them to ride, but as the animals, though small, were frisky and untrained, they were sent very frequently sprawling into the dust, and were much oftener on their feet than in their saddles. Our force, as we advanced, certainly presented a very unmilitary appearance, though we made clatter enough for a dozen regiments of dragoons. We were in search of the military chest said to be with the fugitives. We fell in with a large party, who, however, having had fighting enough, sent forward a flag of truce and capitulated. We got possession, however, of some waggon-loads of ingots, but they were ingots of copper, and were said to be of so little value in the country as to have been fired as grape-shot from Cornelis. The moon shone brightly forth for the first part of the march, but no sooner did it become obscured than a considerable number of the marines were seized with a temporary defective vision very common within the tropics, called, " Nyctalopia," or night blindness. The attack was sudden; the vision seldom became totally obscured, but so indistinct that the shape of objects could not be distinguished. While in this state the sufferers had to be led by their comrades. With some it lasted more than an hour, with others not more than twenty minutes, and on the approach of day all traces of it had disappeared.

On our march, during the heat of the day, we passed through a wood, every tree in which seemed to have been blasted by lightning. Not a branch nor leaf remained to afford us shelter from the scorching rays of the sun. Had I not known that the story of the noxious effects produced by the upas-tree was a fiction, I might have supposed that the destruction had been caused by a blast passing amid the boughs of one of those so-called death-dealing trees in the neighbourhood. Probably the forest had been destroyed partly by lightning and partly by the conflagration it had caused.

On returning to Cheribon, I found that my friend Van Deck was anxious to proceed to Batavia, and I was fortunate in being able to procure him a passage on board the *Phœbe*, which was going there at once.

" Well, Braithwaite, I shall never despair of your turning up safe ! " exclaimed Captain Hassall, shaking my hand warmly as I stepped on the deck of the *Barbara*. " You saved the ship and cargo by your promptness, for had I not got your message by young Jack there I should have been captured to a certainty. Garrard, Janrin and Co. have reason to be grateful to you, and I have no doubt that they will be so."

Everybody knows that Batavia is a large Dutch town built in the tropics—that is to say, it has broad streets, with rows of trees in them, and canals in the centre of stagnant water, full of filth, and surrounded

BATAVIA FROM THE SEA.—*Page 257.*

by miasma-exuding marshes. But the neighbourhood is healthy, and the merchants and officials mostly only come into the town in the daytime, and return to their country houses at night. Some seasons are worse than others, nobody knows why. Captain Cook was there on his first voyage round the world during a very bad one, and, in spite of all his care, lost a number of people. We were more fortunate, but did not escape without some sickness.

Captain Hassall had disposed of most of that portion of our cargo suited for the Batavian market, so that I soon got rid of the rest. I then made arrangements for the purchase of sugar, tea, coffee, spices, and several other commodities which I believed would sell well at Sydney, to which place we proposed to proceed, touching at a few other points perhaps on our way.

The articles had, however, first to be collected, as the army had consumed the greater portion in store at Batavia. Part of the purchase I made from a brother of my friend Van Deck. He was on the point of sailing in a brig he owned along the coast to collect produce, and invited me to accompany him. I gladly accepted his offer, as the *Barbara* could not sail till his return.

In those days, as well, indeed, as from the memory of man, these seas swarmed with pirates, many of whom had their headquarters on the coast of Borneo. Among them was a chief, or rajah, named Raga, notorious for the boldness and success of his undertakings. We, however, believed that with so many British men-of-

war about he would seek some more distant field for
his operations. The harbour was full of native craft of
all sorts. Of the native prahus alone there are many
varieties, some built after European models, and carrying sails similar to those of our English luggers.
Others are of native construction, with lateen sails ;
and many, built with high stems and sterns, have the
square mat-sail, such as impels the Batavian fishing
prahus. Of course, among so many craft a pirate chief
could easily find spies ready to give him information
of all that was going forward. However, we troubled
our heads very little about the pirates.

By-the-bye, I have not said anything about the
alligators of Java, which are, I believe, larger than in
any other part of the world. The Government will not
allow those in the harbour of Batavia to be disturbed,
as they act the part of scavengers by eating up the
garbage which floats on the water, and might otherwise produce a pestilence. I often passed them floating on the surface, and snapping at the morsels which
came in their way, quite indifferent to the boats going
to and fro close to them. Captain Beaver, of the
Nisus frigate, described to me one he saw in another
part of the island when on an exploring expedition.
It was first discovered basking on a mud-bank, and
neither he nor the officers with him would believe that
it was an animal, but thought at first that it was the
huge trunk of a tree. At the lowest computation it
was forty feet in length. The circumference of the
thickest part of the body seemed nearly that of a

bullock, and this continued for about double the length. The extent of the jaws was calculated to be at least eight feet. The eyes glistened like two large emeralds, but with a lustre which nothing inanimate could express. The officers examined it through their glasses, and came to the conclusion that it was asleep, but the native guides assured them that it was not. To prove this, one of them fearlessly leaped on shore and approached the creature, when it glided into the water, creating a commotion like that produced by the launch of a small vessel.

I bade farewell to William and my friends of the *Phœbe*, not without some sadness at my heart. In those time of active warfare it might be we should never meet again. Of my soldier brother I got but a hurried glimpse before he embarked on an expedition which was sent to capture Sourabaya, at the other end of the island. A few words of greeting, and inquiries and remarks, a warm long grasp of hands, and we parted. Directly I stepped on board Van Deck's brig the *Theodora*, the anchor was weighed, and we stood out of the harbour with a strong land breeze. The easterly monsoon which prevailed was in our teeth, so that we were only able to progress by taking advantage of the land and sea breezes. The land breeze commenced about midnight, and as it blew directly from the shore, we were able to steer our course the greater part of the night; but after sunrise the wind always drew round to the eastward, and we were consequently forced off the shore. The anchor was then dropped till towards noon, when the sea breeze set in. Again we weighed, and stood towards the shore, as near as possible to which we anchored, and waited for the land breeze at night.

We had thus slowly proceeded for three or four days, having called off two estates for cargo, when, as we lay at anchor, a fleet of five or six prahus was seen standing towards us with the sea breeze, which had not yet filled our sails. Van Deck, after examining them through his glass, said that he did not at all like their appearance, and that he feared they intended us no good. On they came, still directly for us. We got up all the arms on deck and distributed them to the crew, who, to the number of thirty, promised to fight to the last. Then we weighed anchor and made sail, ready for the breeze. It came at last, but not till the prahus were close up to us. Under sail we were more likely to beat them off than at anchor. They soon swarmed round us, but their courage was damped by the sight of our muskets and guns. Of their character, however, we had not a shadow of doubt. After a short time of most painful suspense to us they lowered their sails and allowed us to sail on towards the shore. Here we anchored, as usual, to wait for the land breeze. Had there been a harbour, we would gladly have taken shelter within it, for the merchant, the elder Van Deck, said that he knew the pirates too well, and that they might still be waiting for an opportunity to attack us. There was, however, no harbour, and so we had to wait in our exposed situation, in the full belief that

PURSUED BY PIRATICAL JUNKS.—*Page 263.*

'the pirates were still in the offing, and might any moment pounce down upon us. The Van Decks agreed that we might beat them off, but that if they should gain the upper hand they would murder every one on board the vessel. " We might abandon the vessel and so escape any risk," observed the merchant—not in a tone as if he intended to do so. " You, at all events, Mr. Braithwaite, can be landed, and you can easily get back to Batavia." Against this proposal of course my manhood rebelled, though I had a presentiment, if I may use the expression, that we should be attacked. " No, no ! I will stay by you and share your fate, whatever that may be," I replied. Night came on, and darkness hid all distant objects from view.

We were in the handsome, well-fitted-up cabin, enjoying our evening meal, when the mate, a Javanese, put his head down the skylight and said some words in his native tongue, which made the Dutchmen start from their seats, and, seizing their pistols and swords, rush on deck. I had no difficulty, when I followed them, in interpreting what had been said. The pirate prahus were close upon us.

CHAPTER XVI.

MUTINY ON BOARD THE "BARBARA."

WE have learned from the sad experience of centuries that nominal Christianity, which men call religion, is utterly powerless to stop warfare; it may, in a few instances, have lessened some of its horrors, but only a few. The annals of the wars which have taken place for the last three hundred years since the world has improved in civilization, show that nations rush into war as eagerly as ever, and that cruelties and abominations of all sorts, such as the fiercest savages cannot surpass, are committed by men who profess to be Christians. Read the accounts of the wars of the Duke of Alva and his successors in the Netherlands, the civil wars of France, the foreign wars of Napoleon, the deeds of horror done at the storming and capture of towns during the war in the Peninsula, not only by Frenchmen and Spaniards, but by the British soldiers, and indeed the accounts of all the wars in the pages of history, and we shall learn what a fearful and dreadful thing war is, and strive to assist the spread of the true principles of the Gospel as the only means of putting a stop to it.

Such thoughts as these had been occupying my

mind on board the brig, on the morning of that eventful day of which I have just been speaking. Here was I, a peace-loving man, engaged in a peaceable occupation, and yet finding myself continually in the midst of fighting, and now there was every probability of my having to engage in a desperate battle, the termination of which it was impossible to foretell. As I reached the deck I could see a number of dark phantom-looking objects gliding slowly over the water towards us almost noiselessly, the only sound heard being that produced by their oars as they dipped into the water. The pirates, for such we were still certain they must be, expected, perhaps, to find us asleep. The guns were loaded and run out as before. The men stood with their muskets in their hands, and pikes and cutlasses ready for use. The strangers drew closer and closer. They still hoped, we concluded, to catch us unprepared. We, however, did not wish to begin the combat unless they gave us indubitable signs of their intentions.

The elder Van Deck, who had, I found, been a naval man, took the command, and everybody on board looked up to him. We were not left long in doubt that the strangers were pirates, and purposed to destroy us. Not, however, till they were close to us with the evident intention of boarding did our chief give the order to fire. The effect was to make them sheer off, but only for a moment. Directly afterwards they arranged themselves on our starboard bow and quarter, and commenced a fire with gingalls, matchlocks, and guns of various sorts, sending missiles of all shapes and sizes on board us. Our men kept firing away bravely, but in a short time, so rapid was the fire kept up on us, that three or four were killed and several wounded. I was standing near the brave Dutchman when a dart shot from a gun struck him, and he fell to the deck. I ran to raise him up, but he had ceased to breathe. His death soon becoming known among the crew, their fire visibly slackened. The pirates probably perceived this, and with fearful cries came dashing alongside. The Javanese are brave fellows, and though they knew that death awaited them, they drew their swords and daggers and met the enemy as they sprang upon our deck. On came the pirates in overwhelming numbers, their sharp kreeses making fearful havoc among our poor fellows.

I saw that all was lost. I was still unwounded. Rather than fall alive into the hands of the pirates, as with the survivors of the crew I was driven across the deck, I determined to leap overboard, and endeavour to swim to land. That was not a moment for considering the distance or the dangers to be encountered. Death was certain if I remained in the ship. Unnoticed by the enemy, I threw myself overboard, and struck out in the direction, as I believed, of the shore. I was a good swimmer, but light as were my clothes, I was not aware of the impediment they would prove to me. Already I was beginning to grow tired, and to feel that I could not reach the shore. Yet life was sweet, very sweet, in prospect.

I prayed for strength, and resolved to struggle on as long as I could move an arm. I threw myself on my back to float. I could see the brig, at no great distance, surrounded by the prahus. All sounds of strife had ceased. Only the confused murmurs of many tongues moving at once reached my ears. Now that I had ceased for a few minutes to exert myself, two fearful ideas occurred to me: one, that I might be swimming from the land, the other, that at any moment a shark might seize me and carry me to the depths below. Had I allowed my mind to dwell on these ideas, I should speedily have lost courage, but instead I had recourse to the only means by which, under similar trials and dangers, a man can hope to be supported. I turned my thoughts upwards, and prayed earnestly for protection and deliverance.

I was striking out gently with my feet to keep myself moving through the water when my head struck something floating on the surface. I turned round, and found that it was one of the long bamboo buoys employed by the native fishermen on the coast to mark where their nets, or fish traps, are placed. They are very long and buoyant, and capable of supporting more than one man with ease. I threw my arms over the one I had found, and was grateful that I had thus found an object by means of which my life might possibly be preserved.

I looked round me; the prahus and brig were still to be seen, but after watching them for some time, they appeared to be drifting away with the faint land breeze from the spot where I lay. Thus was the danger of being seen by them at daylight lessened. Hitherto I had feared, among other things, should I be unable to swim on shore, that when the pirates discovered me in the morning they would send a boat and give me a quieting knock on the head. Still my position was a very dreadful one. Any moment a passing shark might seize hold of me; that I escaped was owing, I think, humanly speaking, to my having on dark clothes, and my having kept constantly splashing with my legs. I was afraid of resting, also, lest I should lose consciousness, and, letting go my hold of the bamboo, be swept away by the tide.

At length, when my legs became weary of moving about, I thought that I would try the effect of my voice in keeping the sharks at a distance. I first ascertained that the pirate prahus had drifted to such a distance that I was not likely to be heard by them, then I began shouting away at the top of my voice.

What was my surprise, as soon as I stopped, to hear an answer! For a moment I fancied that it must be some mockery of my imagination; then again I heard the voice say, "What, Braithwaite! is that you?"

It must be, I knew, my friend Van Deck who spoke, yet the voice sounded hollow and strange, very unlike his.

I can scarcely describe the relief I felt at discovering, in the first place that my friend had escaped, and then on finding that a civilized human being was near me. I could not tell whether he knew that his brother was killed. I did not allude to the subject. We did our best to encourage each other. We would gladly have got nearer together to talk with more ease, but were afraid of letting go our hold of the support, frail though it seemed, to which we clung. Van Deck encouraged me by the assurance that it would soon be daylight, and that at early dawn the fishermen would come off to examine the nets.

"They bear the Dutch, I am sorry to say, no good will," he observed. "We are accused too justly of laying the produce of their industry under tribute; but they will respect you as an Englishman, and for your sake save the lives of both of us. Till I found that you had escaped I was very anxious on that score."

As I have said, we talked continually, for silence was painful, as I could not tell when my companion's voice was silent whether he had been drawn down suddenly by a shark, or had sunk overcome by fatigue. Even with conversation kept up in this way the time passed very slowly by. How much worse off I should have been alone! At length Van Deck exclaimed that he saw the dawn breaking in the sky. Rapidly after this objects became more and more distinct; the tall bamboo buoys, with their tufts of dry grass at the top, floating on the glassy water; then I could distinguish my companion's head and shoulders just above the surface; and the land about two miles off, on which, however, a surf broke which would have made landing difficult, if not dangerous. The tall trees and the mountains, range above range, seemed to rise directly out of it.

Soon the fishermen's voices, as they pulled out, singing in chorus, towards their buoys, greeted our ears. Two boats came close to us. The fishermen exhibited much surprise at finding us, but instead of at once coming up and taking us on board, they lay on their oars, and appeared to be consulting what they should do with the strangers. How the discussion might have terminated seemed doubtful, had not Van Deck told them that I was an Englishman, whose countrymen had just conquered the island; that he was my friend; and that if any harm happened to us my people would come and cut off all the people in the district, whereas if we were well treated they would be munificently rewarded. This address, which, taken in its oriental meaning, was literally true, had the desired effect; one of the boats approached me. Immediately that I was in the boat I fainted, and I believe that my friend was much in the same condition. He, however, quickly recovered, and by the promise of an increased reward induced the fishermen to return at once to the shore. I did not return to consciousness till I found myself being lifted out of the boat and placed on a litter of wicker-work. Van Deck was carried in the same way, as he was too weak to walk. We were thus conveyed to the house of a chief, who resided not far from the shore, built on the summit of a rising ground overlooking the sea.

The chief, who was every inch a gentleman, received

us with the greatest hospitality, and, seeing what we
most required, had us both put into clean, comfortable
beds in a large airy room, where, after we had taken a
few cups of hot coffee, we fell asleep, and did not awake
again till the evening. Our host had then a sump-
tuous repast ready for us, of which by that time we
were pretty well capable of partaking. Poor Van
Deck was naturally very much out of spirits at the
loss of his brother, but the necessity of interpreting
for me kept him from dwelling on his own grief.

At the time of which I have hitherto been speaking,
when I was in the east, the spot on which Singapore,
with its streets of stone palaces, its superb public
edifices and rich warehouses, now stands, was a sandy
flat, with a few straggling huts inhabited by fishermen
or pirates. I am about to give a piece of history
posterior to my voyage as a supercargo. After the
peace of 1814, when Java and its dependencies were
given up to the Dutch, their first act was to impose
restrictions on British commerce in the Archipelago.
They were enabled to effect this object from the
position of their settlements, those in the Straits of
Malacca and Sunda commanding all the western en-
trances to the China and Java seas, and it therefore
became evident that, without some effort to destroy
their monopolies, the sale of British manufactures in
the eastern islands would soon cease. Sir Stamford
Raffles, who was at that time Governor of Bencoolen,
represented the case so strongly to the Supreme
Government at Bengal that the governor-general gave

him the permission he asked to make a settlement
near the north-east entrance of the Straits of Malacca.
He accordingly, in the year 1819, fixed on Singapore,
which stands on the south side of an island, about
sixty miles in circumference, separated by a narrow
strait from the Malay peninsula. Of course the establishment was opposed by the Dutch, who so strenu-
ously remonstrated with the British Government that
the latter declined having anything to do with it, and
threw the whole responsibility on Sir Stamford Raffles.
It was not until it had been established for three
years—in the last of which the trade was already
estimated at several millions of dollars—that Singapore was recognised by Great Britain.

After a rest of a couple of days, poor Van Deck and
I were sufficiently recovered to commence our journey
back to Batavia. He was anxious to be there that he
might take charge of his late brother's affairs—I, that
I might report the loss of the brig, and make fresh
arrangements for securing a cargo for Sydney. We
met with no adventures worthy of note on our
journey.

On our return to Batavia much sympathy was excited for my friend Van Deck among the merchants at
the loss of his brother, and the naval commander-in-
chief, returning soon after from Sourabaya, dispatched
two frigates and a brig of war in search of the pirates.
They were supposed to belong to some place on the
coast of Borneo, which has for many years abounded
with nests of these desperadoes. The fleet in question

was supposed to belong to a famous chief, the very ·
idol of his followers on account of the success of his
expeditions. His title was the Rajah Raga, and he
was brother to the Sultan Coti, a potentate of Borneo.
The Raja Raga had subsequently some wonderful
escapes, for he probably got due notice that an English
squadron was looking after him, and took good care
to keep out of their way. He was afterwards cruising
with three large prahus, when he fell in with an
English sloop-of-war, which he was compelled to engage. Two of his prahus, by placing themselves between him and the enemy, held her in check a sufficient
time to enable him to escape, and were themselves
then sent to the bottom ; indeed, they must have
expected no other fate.

On another occasion the rajah remained on shore,
but sent his own prahu, which carried upwards of a
hundred and fifty men and several large guns, on a
cruise, under the command of his favourite panglima,
or captain. Falling in after some time with a brig
merchantman, as he supposed, and wishing to distinguish himself by her capture, he fired into her, and
made preparations to board. Great was his dismay
when he saw a line of ports open in the side of his
expected prize, and he found himself under the guns
of a` British man-of-war. The panglima hailed, and
with many apologies tried to make it appear that he
had acted under a misapprehension, but his subterfuge
was of no avail; a broadside from the man-of-war sent
his vessel at once to the bottom, and he and all his

crew perished, with the exception of two or three who, clinging to a piece of the wreck, were picked up by a native craft, and carried an account of the disaster to their chief.

Piracy had been the bane of these seas for years.

We were fortunate in obtaining the full amount of the goods we required without having to wait much longer at Batavia. There is an old proverb, " It is an ill wind that blows no one good." The vessel for which they were intended had lost her master and both mates by sickness, and the merchant therefore sold them to me. We had not altogether escaped, and several of our men who were perfectly healthy when we entered the harbour fell victims to the fever engendered by the pestiferous climate. We were compelled to fill up their places with others, who afterwards gave us much trouble.

It was with sincere regret I parted from my friend Van Deck. I was glad, however, to find that he was likely to obtain employment suited to his talents under the English Government. The most direct course for New South Wales would have been through Torres Straits, but the east trade wind still blowing, compelled us to take the longer route round the south of New Holland, and through Bass's Straits, not many years before discovered, between that vast island and the smaller one of Van Diemen's Land. A northerly breeze at length coming on, enabled us to sight the south-west point of New Holland, and thence we sailed along the coast, occasionally seeing tall columns of smoke ascending from the wood, showing the presence of natives.

On approaching Bass's Straits, the captain was one day expressing his regret to me that we had not time to anchor off one of the islands in it to catch seals, great numbers of which animals frequented the place in those days. He had known, he remarked, considerable sums made in that way in a very short time. Our conversation, it appeared, was overheard by one of the men we had shipped at Batavia. We had had a good deal of insubordination among the crew since we left that place, and we traced it all to that man, Miles Badham, as he called himself. He was about thirty, very plausible and insinuating in his manner, a regular sea-lawyer, a character very dangerous on board ship, and greatly disliked by most captains. He had managed to gain a considerable influence over the crew, especially the younger portion. His appearance was in his favour, and in spite of the qualities I have mentioned, I would not have supposed him capable of the acts of atrocity which were with good reason laid to his charge. Ben Stubbs, the second mate, had charge of the deck one night, and, unable to sleep, I was taking a turn with him, when Mr. Gwynne, the surgeon, came up to us.

" There is something wrong going on among the people below," he whispered. " I cannot make out what it is exactly, but if we do not look out we may possibly all have our throats cut before morning."

" You must have been dreaming, Gwynne," answered

Stubbs; "there isn't a man in the ship would dare do such a thing."

"I am not certain of that," I observed; "at all events, let us be on the right side. Fore-warned, fore-armed. We will let the captain know, and I trust thatwe may thus defeat the plot, whatever it is."

CHAPTER XVII.

HOME AGAIN!

I WENT down into the captain's cabin, and, awakening him, told him what the surgeon had said.

"Mutiny!" he exclaimed, as he dressed himself with the usual rapidity of a seaman. "We will soon settle that matter." He stuck his pistols into a belt he put on for the purpose, and took a cutlass in his hand. "Here, Braithwaite, arm yourself," he said. "Tell the officers to do so likewise. We will soon see which of the two, that sea-lawyer or I, is to command the *Barbara*."

Telling Gwynne and Toby to guard the arm-chest, and Randolph to rally round him the most trustworthy men on deck, he desired Stubbs and me to follow him forward. Without a word of warning he suddenly appeared among the men, who were supposed to be in their berths asleep. Going directly up to the berth Badham occupied, he seized hold of him and dragged him on deck, with a pistol pointed at his head, exclaiming at the same time, "Shoot any one who offers to interfere!"

The captain was very confident that he had the ringleader, and that the rest would not move without him. "Now!" he exclaimed, when he had got him on the quarterdeck. "Confess who are your accomplices, and what you intended to do! Remember, no falsehood! I shall cross-question the others. If you are obstinate, overboard you go."

Badham, surprised by the sudden seizure, and confused, was completely cowed. In an abject tone he whined out, "Spare my life, sir, and I will tell you all."

"Out with it then!" answered the captain. "We have no time to spare."

"Well, sir, then I will tell you all. We didn't intend to injure any one, that we didn't, believe me, sir; but some of us didn't want to go back to Sydney, so we agreed that we would just wreck the ship, and as there are plenty of seals to be got hereabouts, go sealing on our own account, and sell the oil and skins to the ships passing through the straits, and, when we should get tired of the work, go home in one of them."

"And so, for the sake of gaining a few hundred dollars for yourself, you deliberately planned the destruction of this fine ship, and very likely of all on board. Now, understand, you will be put in irons, and if I find the slightest attempt among the crew to rescue you, up you go to the yard-arm, and the leader of the party will keep you company on the other."

Badham, in his whining tone, acknowledged that he understood clearly what the captain said, and hoped never again to offend. On this he was led by two of the mates to one of the after store-rooms, where he

could be under their sight, when irons were put on
him, and he was left to his meditations, the door being
locked on him. The next morning the crew went
about their work as usual, Badham's dupes or accomplices being easily distinguished by their downcast,
cowed looks, and by the unusual promptness with
which they obeyed all orders. The officers and I
continued to wear our pistols and side-arms as a
precautionary measure, though we might safely
have dispensed with them.

A short time before this, in 1802, a settlement had
been formed in Van Diemen's Land, and lately
Hobart Town, the capital, had been commenced. It
was, however, a convict station, and no ships were
allowed to land cargoes there except those which came
from England direct with stores or were sent from
Sydney,—in consequence of which restriction the
colonists were several times nearly on the point of
starvation.

The heads of Port Jackson at length hove in sight,
and we entered that magnificent harbour, the entrance
of which Cook saw and named. Wanting in his usual
sagacity, he took it for a small boat harbour, and
passed by without further exploring it. Having first
brought up in Neutral Bay, that we might be reported
to the governor, we proceeded some miles up to Sydney
Cove, where we anchored in excellent holding ground
about half-pistol-shot from the shore. Sydney had
already begun to assume the appearance of a town of
some consideration, and contained fully 5,000 inhabit-

ants, though still called the camp by some of the old settlers. It is divided into two parts by a river which runs into the cove, and affords it unrivalled advantages of water communication. Several settlements in the country had already been established, among the chief of which were Paramatta and Hawkesbury. The latter settlement was about six miles long, and about forty miles from Sydney; vessels of two hundred tons could ascend by the river up it a distance of at least forty miles. The town, such as it then was, covered about a mile of ground from one end to the other, and already gave promise of becoming a place of consider- able extent. A wise and active governor, Lieutenant- Colonel Lachlan Macquarie, had ruled the settlement for about a year, during which period it had made rapid progress. The previous governor was the notorious Captain Bligh, whose tyrannical conduct when in command of the *Bounty* produced the dis- astrous mutiny which took place on board that ship. The same style of conduct when governor of New South Wales, especially in his treatment of Mr. John McArthur, the father, as he was called, of the settle- ment, induced the colonists to depose him. The officers and men of the New South Wales corps marched up to the Government House, and, after hunting for him for some time, found him concealed under a bed. His person and property were, however, carefully protected, and he was shortly afterwards put on board the *Porpoise* sloop-of-war, and sent off to England. The settlement, however, quickly recovered from the mismanagement of this unhappy man, and was at the time of my visit in a flourishing condition.

I was fortunate in disposing of the larger part of the cargo under my charge at good prices. Hassall and I agreed, however, that more might be done for our owners, and we proposed, therefore, visiting some of the islands in the Pacific, and either returning home the way we had come, or continuing on round Cape Horn. We had not been long in harbour before O'Carroll made his appearance on board. He had brought the ship of which he had taken charge in safety into harbour, when the emigrants presented him with so handsome a testimonial that he resolved to settle in the colony and lay it out to advantage. The governor had made him a grant of a large extent of farm land, and assigned him some twenty convict servants, land in those days being given away to free settlers, and labour of the nature I have described found them gratis.

"Altogether I am in a fair way of some day becoming a rich man," he observed, "the which I should never have been had I continued ploughing the salt ocean. Besides," he added, with a twinkle in his eye, "how do I know, if I did, that I should not some day fall into the clutches of that fearful little monster La Roche? and if I did, I know that he would not spare me. Do you know that even to this day I cannot altogether get over my old feelings, and often congratulate myself as I ride through the bush that I am far out of his reach."

O'Carroll kept to his resolution, and became a very successful and wealthy settler. I frequently received letters from him after my return home. In one of them he told me that he had had a surprise. The governor asked him one day, as he could speak French, whether he would like to have some French convicts assigned to him. He had no objection, as he thought that he could manage them easily. What was his astonishment, when the party arrived at the farm, to recognize among them, in a little wizened-looking old man, his once dreaded enemy La Roche! He determined to try and melt the man's stony heart by kindness. At first he was almost hopeless in the matter, but he succeeded at last. La Roche confessed that he had placed himself within the power of the British laws in consequence of a visit he paid to England after the war, for the purpose of carrying out a speculation which ended unfortunately. It was satisfactory to hear that he lived to become a changed man, truly repenting of his misspent life, and thankful that he had been spared to repent.

I have not spoken of the would-be mutineer, Badham. It must be remembered that he had committed no overt act of mutiny, and though Captain Hassall was perfectly right in putting him in irons, he could not have been brought to trial on shore. The day before we reached Sydney he pleaded so hard to be forgiven, and so vehemently promised amendment in all respects, that the captain resolved to give him a trial. It must be confessed that he was not altogether disinterested in this, as it would have been impossible to get fresh hands at Sydney, the temptation to settle in the country having by that time become very great, so that it was with difficulty we could keep several of our people who had come from England.

Once more we were at sea. We touched at Norfolk Island, to which convicts from New South Wales were sent. It seemed a pity that so fertile a spot, so perfect a little paradise, should be given up for such a purpose. We obtained here a supply of vegetables and pork, which were not to be got at that time at any price at Sydney. After a rapid voyage from this lovely little island we anchored in Matavai Bay, in the island of Otaheite. It was at an interesting time of the history of the island and its king, Otoo, who since the death of his father had taken the name of Pomarre. For many years the band of zealous missionaries who had come out in the ship *Duff* had laboured on among the people, but though they taught the king, the young prince Otoo, and some of their people, to read and write, they confessed that they had not made one satisfactory convert. In 1808 the greater number of the missionaries retired from Otaheite to the island of Huahine, and the following year all the married ones left that island for New South Wales, in consequence of the wars in which the king was constantly engaged, the destruction of all their property, the risk they ran of losing their lives, and the seeming hopelessness of introducing Christianity among such a people. After an absence

17

of between two and three years, several of them, having wished to make a fresh attempt to carry out the work, sailed from Sydney for Tahiti, but stopped at the neighbouring island of Eimeo, where the king was residing, as Tahiti was still in a state of rebellion. They taught the people as before, and now some began to listen to them gladly. They still seemed to have considered the king as a hopeless heathen; but misfortune had humbled him, he felt his own nothingness and sinfulness, and the utter inability of the faith of his fathers to give him relief. After the missionaries had lived in the island about a year, the king came to them and offered himself as a candidate for baptism, declaring that it was his fixed determination to worship Jehovah, the true God, and expressing his desire to be further instructed in the principles of religion. The king proved his sincerity, and ever after remained a true and earnest Christian. He still resided at Eimeo, but a considerable number of people in Tahiti had by this time been converted, and the old heathen gods were falling into disrepute.

So devastating had been the character of the late wars in Tahiti, that we found it impossible to obtain supplies, and we therefore sailed for Ulitea, the largest of the Georgian group, where we were informed that we should probably be more successful. No sooner had we dropped anchor within the coral bed which surrounds the island than the king and queen came off to pay us a visit. They were very polite, but not disinterested, as their object was to collect as many

gifts as we were disposed to bestow.   This island was
the chief seat of the idolatry of the Society Islands.
It was looked upon as a sacred isle by the inhabitants
of the other islands of the group, and more idols existed
and more human sacrifices were offered up there than
in all the others.   We were so completely deceived by
the plausible manners of the king and queen and those
who accompanied them, that the captain and I, the
surgeon, and two of the mates, went on shore to visit
them in return, accompanied by several of the crew,
leaving the ship in charge of Mr. Randolph, the first
mate.   We fortunately carried our arms, though deem-
ing it an unnecessary measure of precaution.   The
king had an entertainment ready for us, and afterwards we were allowed to roam about the island
wherever we pleased.   I observed the people at length
pressing round us, and not liking their looks, advised
Captain Hassall to order our men to keep together,
and to be prepared for an attack.   Whether or not
they saw that we were suspicious of them we could
not tell, but from this time their conduct changed, and
they would only allow us to proceed in the direction
they chose.   At length, however, we got down to the
landing-place.   As we approached the boats we saw
a band of armed natives making for them.   We rushed
down to the beach, and reaching the boats just before
they did, we jumped in and shoved off.   These savages,
though savage as ever, were also more formidable
enemies than formerly, as many of them had firearms,
and all had sharp daggers or swords.

On reaching the ship we found that Badham and his associates had, soon after we left, seized a boat, and, in spite of all Mr. Randolph could say or do, had taken all their clothes and other property with them, and gone on shore. Although by this conduct Badham showed that he could no longer be trusted, and therefore that we were well rid of him, it was important that we should get back the other men, and we agreed to go on shore the next morning to recover them. Accordingly, the chief mate and I went on shore as we proposed, with eight well-armed men, and demanded an interview with the king. He did not come himself, but sent his prime minister, who agreed, for six hatchets and a piece of cloth, to deliver them up. We waited for some hours, but the deserters were not forthcoming, and at last the minister and another chief appeared, and declared that as the men were likely to fight for their liberty, it would be necessary that we should lend them our arms.

"Very likely, indeed, gentlemen," answered Mr. Randolph, at once detecting the palpable trick to get us into their power.

"I say, Braithwaite, what say you to seizing these fellows and carrying them on board as hostages? It could easily be done."

"Cook lost his life in making a similar attempt, and we might lose ours," I answered. "I would rather lose the men than run any such risk."

In vain we endeavoured by diplomacy to recover the men, and at last we returned on board, the minister losing the hatchets and piece of cloth. A feeling of anxiety prevented me from turning in, and I walked the deck for some time with Benjie Stubbs, the officer of the watch. At length I went below and threw myself on my bed, all standing, as sailors say when they keep their clothes on. I had scarcely dropped asleep when I was awoke by hearing Stubbs order the lead to be hove. I was on deck in a moment, followed by the captain and the other officers.

" We are on shore to a certainty," exclaimed Stubbs, in an agitated tone.

"Impossible!" observed the captain, " the anchors are holding."

" We'll haul in on the cables and see, sir," answered Stubbs, calling some of the crew to his assistance. The cables immediately came on board. They had been cut through. Still there was a perceptible motion of the ship towards the shore. Another anchor with an iron stock was immediately cleared away, but some time was lost in stocking it, and before it could be let go we felt the ship strike against a coral reef with considerable force. Happily there was no wind, or she would speedily have gone to pieces. At last we carried the anchors out, and ·hauled her off, but not without unusual difficulty. Suddenly the captain jumped into a boat and pulled round the ship.

" I thought so!" he exclaimed; " the villains have fastened a rope to her rudder, and were towing us on the rocks." He cut the rope as he spoke, and with comparative ease we got the ship out of her perilous position. Still she was so near the high cliffs which almost surrounded us that we might be seriously annoyed, not only by musketry but by stones and darts. It was evident, also, that should a breeze set in from the sea, the single anchor would not hold, and that we must be driven back again on the coral rocks.

We were not left long in doubt as to the intention of the savages and the deserters, their instigators. Suddenly fearful shouts burst from the cliffs above us, and we were assailed by a fire of musketry and by darts and stones hurled on our deck. To return it would have been useless; for we could not see our enemies. Meantime we kept the men under cover as much as possible, and got another anchor stocked and ready to carry out ahead. The savages must have seen the boat, for as soon as she was clear of the ship they opened fire on her, and it was not without difficulty that the anchor was carried out to the required distance, and the crew of the boat hurriedly returned on board.

Owing to Badham's machinations, some of the crew had at first been disaffected, but a common danger now united them, as they saw full well the treatment they might expect should the savages get possession of the ship. Besides the ship's guns we had four swivels, thirty muskets, and several blunderbusses and braces of pistols. These were all loaded and placed ready for use, with a number of boarding-pikes, for we thought that at any moment the savages would come off in their canoes and attempt to board us. The whole night long they kept us on the alert, howling and shrieking in the most fearful manner. Soon after day broke their numbers increased, and as they could now take aim with their firearms our danger became greater. Fortunately they were very bad marksmen, or they would have picked us all off. Strange as it may seem, no one was hit, though our rigging and boats received much damage. After the crew had breakfasted we sent two boats out ahead to tow off the ship, but the bullets and other missiles flew so thickly about them that they returned, the men declaring that the work was too dangerous. However, Benjie Stubbs, jumping into one of the boats, persuaded them to go again, while we opened a fire from the deck of the ship. As soon as the savages saw us ready to fire, they dodged behind the rocks, so that none of them were wounded. Still we hoped that by this means the boats would be allowed to tow ahead without molestation. We were mistaken, for the savages shifted their ground, and once more drove the boats on board. We clearly distinguished Badham and the rest of the deserters among the savages, and several times they were seen to fire at us. Happily they also were wretched shots, and their muskets thoroughly bad also. That they should venture to fire showed that they had no doubt of getting us into their power, for should we escape and inform against them, they would run a great chance of being captured and hanged. Later in the day, Jack and I again made attempts to tow out the ship from her perilous position.

The savages all the day continued howling and shrieking and working themselves into what seemed an ungovernable fury, while they were, however, biding their time, knowing that probably a strong sea-breeze would soon spring up and cast the ship helpless into their power. Thus another night closed on us. Ere long great was our joy to feel a light air blowing off the shore. The pauls of the windlass were muffled, and not a word was spoken. The anchors were lifted, the top-sails were suddenly let drop, and slowly we glided off from the land. The weather becoming very thick and dark, we were compelled again to anchor, lest we might have run on one of the many reefs surrounding the island. Here we remained on our guard till daylight, when we could see the natives dancing and gesticulating with rage at finding that we had escaped them. The favourable breeze continuing, we were soon able to get far out of their reach, I for one deeply thankful that we had not only escaped without loss ourselves, but without killing any of the unhappy savages. The treatment we received was such as at that time might have been expected from the inhabitants of nearly all the islands of the Pacific, including those of New Zealand, and numberless were the instances of ships' companies and boats' crews cut off by them.

A very few years after our visit, this same island

was brought under missionary influence, the idols were overthrown, heathenism and all its abominable practices disappeared, and the inhabitants became a thoroughly well-ordered, God-fearing, and law-obeying Christian community. The same account may be given of the larger number of the islands which stud the wide Pacific, and ships may now sail from north to south, and east to west, without the slightest danger from the inhabitants of by far the greater portion of them.

But it is time that I should bring my narrative to a conclusion. This adventure at Ulitca was amongst my last. Finding that our trading expedition to the Pacific Islands was not likely to prove of advantage to our owners, Captain Hassall and I resolved to proceed home at once round Cape Horn.

We happily accomplished our voyage without accident and without any further occurrence worthy of note. Our path was no longer beset by hostile cruisers, for there was a lull in the affairs of Europe. After the many excitements of the past few months, the days seemed long and tedious as I had never known them before; and it was with a sense of relief, as well as of real pleasure, that I again saw in the early morning light the shores of old England looming clear in the distance. I need not dwell on all the happy circumstances of my return, or on the special satisfaction with which I looked again on one familiar face. Suffice it to say that I had the gratification of receiving the commendation of my kind friend Mr.

Janrin for the way in which I had carried out his instructions and performed my duties as Supercargo; and that this voyage prepared the way for more substantial proofs of his favour.